Sisters of Gavinville

Copyright © 2024 John Warner Smith

Cover art: Felicia Noelle

Cover design: Morgan Bliadd

Willow River Press
Between the Lines Publishing
1769 Lexington Ave North #286
Roseville MN 55113
btwnthelines.com

First Published: December 2024

Willow River Press is an imprint of Between the Lines Publishing. The Willow River Press name and logo are trademarks of Between the Lines Publishing.

ISBN: (paperback) 978-1-965059-18-0

ISBN: (eBook) 978-1-965059-19-7

Library of Congress Control Number: 2024949880

Sisters of Gavinville

John Warner Smith

Sisters of Jacinville

John Warner Smith

Chapter 1

Gladys Hayes was buried on a balmy, sunny afternoon on December 11, 2020, among rows of women who had heard about her but never knew her and men whom she had known but never loved. In the final days, as her breath choked and her voice cracked in the slipknot of respiratory arrest, Gladys spoke words that she hoped would forever close and seal the book of the tumultuous years spent with her husband Willie Frank, who had been dead for fifty years.

"And about my funeral," she whispered in a voice that could barely be heard, "I don't want the word 'Frank' to be written or spoken in my obituary, and I don't want it put on my headstone. Bury me as far from Willie Frank as you can put me."

The Hayes family had already collected two hand fans that year. This one bore the newly proclaimed motto of Johnson Funeral Home: *We'll go a heavenly mile to serve you.* On the flip side of the fan was a print of a hand sketched portrait of Dr. Martin Luther King Jr., his half-moon eyes gleaming against a sky-blue backdrop beneath the white glow of chandeliers. That, too, was one of Gladys' demands—that her body go to Johnson and not Cole Funeral Home.

The rivalry between Johnson and Cole dated back to 1913, the year Dr. Phillip Cole sent his boy Phillip Jr. off to undertaker school to return and start a new mortuary in Gavinville, Louisiana. Until then, Johnson was the only colored undertaker within a hundred miles. Many expressed resentment that Cole had broken with tradition. Others welcomed the competition. Gladys had her own reasons for not wanting to be associated with Cole, one she harbored for over sixty years, others she also voiced before her death.

"Whatever you do, don't let Cole come near my body. I don't want Phillip Cole to touch a hair on my head. It's a damn shame that a man with so much money is so cheap. He should have changed that roof years ago. I don't want rain falling on my flowers. Besides, he's never on time. Leave it to him and I'll be rotten by the time they put me in the ground. Carmen should have known better."

Carmen Hawkins, one of Gladys' five sisters, had long ago insisted, against the advice and objection of her oldest sister, that Cole handle her arrangements. Sure enough, on the night of Carmen's wake six months ago, a terrible storm blew through Gavinville, causing the roof to leak and the wake to be postponed until the next morning and moved to St. Paul Catholic Church, where the funeral service immediately followed. Much to the angst of mourners who had made plans to see the traditional blessing of the boats at the opening of the annual seafood festival, Phillip Cole Jr. pulled up to the church with Carmen's body forty-five minutes late.

Family members close to Gladys knew that her objection to Cole had little to do with burying the dead and more to do with the fling Willie once had with Betty, the Coles' only daughter. Willie had been chasing Betty Cole long before he started dating Gladys. He eventually got his wish—in the carriage of Cole's brand new 1957 Cadillac LaSalle funeral hearse on the afternoon of his and Gladys' second wedding anniversary.

"Shh. Somebody's here," Betty whispered.

"Who?"

"Don't know. Shh. Be still, Willie."

"Thought you said nobody was around."

"Shh. Be still, Willie."

"I think he's gone. Pull your pants up, Willie. Get up."

"Who, why?"

"Phillip Jr."

"Thought you said they had no funeral today. He's going see us through the window."

"How can he see us with the curtains down? Pull your pants up, Willie. Hurry!" Junior must have to pick up a body. Hurry up."

"My zipper stuck."

"What?"

"I'm trying. I'm trying. Mercy me. If I get caught, Gladys will kill me."

"My Daddy's going to kill you first. Hurry, Willie!"

"What are we going to do?"

"Just get your pants on and be quiet. Shh. I think he's coming back."

"If he's got to get a body, he's going to have to move the casket. What are we going to say?"

"Get your pants on, Willie. Hurry."

"I'm hurrying."

"Shh. He's coming back. Sounds like Pookie Abraham's with him. Close the lid. Hurry."

"What?"

"Close the lid, Willie, so they won't see us. Might not be leaving yet. Close the lid and lie down. Hurry."

"It's too small. We don't fit."

"Close the lid, Willie. Hurry."

"We're too big."

"Close the lid and lie down."

"I can't. It won't close. We're too big. Oh no. They're opening the door."

"Willie Frank? Betty? What? What the…what the hell's going on?"

"I . . . I . . . I can explain Junior. It's not what you think."

"I don't need to think. I can see with my two eyes."

"We didn't do nothing, Junior. I swear." said Betty, crawling out of the foot of the casket. "Just a little petting, that's all."

"She . . . she's . . . she's right, Junior," said Willie, backing up out of Junior's reach as quickly as he can. "Betty's telling the truth. That's all we did."

"You're lying, both of you."

"That's the honest, honest truth, Junior. I swear. I . . . I best be going," said Willie, now ten feet away from Junior with his eyes pointing toward the street.

Betty's stomach turned at the thought of Dr. Cole finding out. It hadn't been two months since his heart attack, and the news would do worse than shatter his faith in her as a loyal, hardworking, joint heir to his inheritance, someone who understood the "delicacies of customer relations" that he often talked about. But she knew that her secret was as good as kept with Junior. He was the least of her worries, considering what she knew about his creeping out the back door at Ms. Harvey's Boarding House. Besides, the last thing Junior wanted to do was explain to Mrs. Kelly how her husband A.D.'s casket was christened before she even got a glimpse of it. But Pookie Abraham, Junior's assistant, was another matter.

A short, extremely overweight man in his late fifties—putting him ten years older than his boss—Pookie was generally viewed as Junior's grunt, relegated to any task that kept Junior's hands clean and his suit from wrinkling. Though he plainly understood the damage that the information could cause the funeral business, Pookie's craving for recognition as someone important to Cole wouldn't let him sleep one night with the story under his pillow. By sundown, Willie's unfortunate exposure to daylight was being celebrated as the best knee-slapping, tear-wiping joke ever told at Boozy's Barber Shop, peppered with Pookie's own expletives and punctuations.

"And then Willie jumped out of the hearse buck naked in broad daylight," Pookie said in telling the story the third time. "The po boy was sweatin' like a rat pinned between a trap and a piece a cheese."

"What he did then, Pookie?" Old Sam Foucault asked. "Show us that move again."

"For about three seconds he stood there like this . . . dead as a fly on a hot biscuit, all but one part of him anyway. Then he took off like a jackrabbit high tailin' it down the street."

"No, no, Pookie. Show us how he tippy toed over the water."

"Oh yeah. Oh yeah. When Willie got a little ways down the street, Junior yelled, 'Negro come get these clothes.' Willie stopped and looked back. I guess he thought about it for a second or two before he realized it was too late to turn around and go back. Then he started tippy toein' through the water puddle like he had pants and shoes on." At that point, Pookie raised his arms and walked on his toes like he was crossing a field of land mines. "The boy is a real ballarinie," Pookie said, "a little too big for me though."

Needless to say, Pookie's version spread quickly and found its way to Gladys, cementing a lifetime of animosity between her and the Cole family, not to mention the gulf that had already begun to widen between her and Willie.

That afternoon, Gladys cooked Willie's favorite meal. Greens were simmering while garlic-stuffed duck and sweet potatoes warmed in the oven. Willie savored the smell as he hopped Old Sam Foucault's fence and crept through the back yard later that evening, hoping to get past the back door unnoticed. He had rehearsed his whole lie on the way home, unaware that Gladys had already heard two versions of Pookie's joke, one with Willie's pants down to his knees and another with his pants off. Gladys was standing calmly at the screen door with her hand on the lock when Willie arrived.

"What you want here, Willie James Frank? Ain't you got your belly full already?"

"Sweet baby girl, I . . . I smelled your cooking a half mile away. Open up. Let me in. I . . . I got something special for you."

"Not this evening Willie, not ever. You can turn right around and go get your sweetness where you left it, in the back of Cole's funeral hearse."

"Now Gladys Faye, I . . . I can explain. Betty tricked me into the whole thing. She . . . she tricked me. The whole thing was a mistake. I didn't mean to cause you no hurt."

"Not what I heard. They say you stuttered a lot when Junior threatened to put a whipping on you. You always stutter when you're lying Willie, just like you're doing now. And I see you found your shirt and pants. You can pick up the rest of your clothes in the cesspool out back. Maybe Betty Cole can wash them for you."

"Come on sweetie, open . . . open the door. Let me in."

"I ain't your sweetie, not this evening, not tomorrow, not ever. And if you get any closer to this door handle, that hot pot of grease on the stove will cook you more than that duck you're smelling. You best be going down to your Mama while I'm calm enough to leave that grease where it is, or better yet, go to that little whore you crawled into a casket with. Go on now."

There would be many such arguments between Gladys and Willie, even as Willie grew too old to chase young women. Their confrontations grew increasingly contentious over time, but they usually ended like this one, with Gladys putting Willie outdoors and taking him back after a few days. But those days had been long forgotten by those who might have heard about the disputes and were still living. Any lasting memories of them were completely overshadowed now by the solemn, obligatory ceremony of a very old woman being laid to rest.

Like every Hayes preceding her, Gladys' funeral mass was celebrated at St. Paul, the only Black Catholic Church in town. Father Antoine, a handsome, bearded priest in his mid-thirties whom many went to church just to hear sing, seemed in a hurry. It was 11:00 a.m. on Saturday, and it would not be sacrilegious to think that the alligator-boot wearing priest had a noon lunch date at Café Versailles, where he was often seen, and that he imagined a garnished plate of stuffed redfish with fine white linen flapping across his lap as he stood at the altar polishing the gold chalice.

Father Antoine could have done what the old Baptist preacher had done at Willie's funeral, and slowly, almost to the point of lulling the congregation to sleep, taken them deep into the woods with a tale about an empty hammock tied between two pear trees that sprung up in the middle of a pecan grove. No one really understood the metaphor, but some assumed that the parable about fruit symbolized something good about Willie. Of course, everybody there knew what the preacher had surely known himself, that in Willie's prime he had a reputation for sleeping around anywhere and anytime he found a willing whore, and that he did it often enough and in such unusual places, chances are he did it in a hammock tied to two pear trees.

Father Antoine took a slightly different approach to eulogizing Gladys. He skipped the eulogy entirely and went directly from a Gospel reading in the New Testament to an obviously canned, overused homily on sin, redemption, and immortality—barely saying anything that made anyone know that the person lying in the pall-draped coffin was Gladys Hayes, the oldest person to ever live in Gavinville. But true to his very popular, crowd stirring way of connecting a walk with Jesus to some form of contemporary pop culture, the young priest stepped down toward the casket, and with his arms raised like a candelabra began to do his own version of a sanctified, call and response.

"Sister Hayes didn't live large but she lived long. Like all of us, I'm sure she had a few regrets. But we know there is no condemnation in them that love the Lord. Can the church say Amen?"

"Amen," a few shouted.

"And I don't believe that Sister Hayes was one to cry that song, "My sweet Lord, if I have one more prayer, one more walk, one more dance with you, I'd play a song that would last forever."

Before the keyboard player could catch up, the pastor's silky-smooth alto jumped to another frame. "Yes, Lord. If I could have just one more step, just one final glimpse, just one last dance with you, I'd sing with you in eternity."

"Tell me, church, did Gladys walk with Jesus?"

"Amen."

"Did she see Him?"

"Amen."

"Did she dance?"

"Amen," some shouted louder with a little mix of laughter.

In the midst of the laughter, some heads turned with mouths and eyes wide open in shock and disbelief, not for Father Antoine's improvisational though seemingly awkward and ill-timed rendition of Luther Vandross's hit song, but for the clergyman's apparent lack of respect for both the living and the dead. Whispers bobbled like pin drops on the soft cushioned pews.

"Oh, I know he didn't," said Sharon Granger, an older distant cousin of the family, leaning over and whispering to her sister Margaret.

"I don't believe. Child, you think he knows?" asked Margaret, covering her mouth.

"How could he? No way. That happened decades ago."

"I bet he knows. Maybe Gladys confessed to him."

"Maybe one of the sisters told him."

"I doubt that. But even if he knows, why would he pull Gladys' skeleton out of the closet? How dare him drag the family's dirty laundry out into the open, and at a time like this."

"I don't think he knows. But it might have helped if somebody told him."

Father Antoine, of course, had no idea that in taking the old woman's soul into his hands with a hurried but entertaining hip hop style homily, he had stepped into the darkest shadow of Gladys' past, the one no one dared talk about, especially not now.

With the keyboard chiming softly in the background, the priest started his descent, his voice rising and falling like the sound of a door hinge. Pointing at the congregation, he asked, "My beloved brothers and sisters, will you be the one who waits too late to dance with Jesus? Will you be the one crying for one more look, one more chance, one more walk with the Lord? Don't be late."

Caught up in the spirit and overcome with grief, Nancy Hebert, another of Gladys' older cousins, stood just long enough to scream, "Help me Jesus!" before collapsing to the floor. Before long, half the congregation was crying, and those who were old enough to have heard about Gladys' past life as a strip club dancer were either whispering or laughing. It was one of those strange moments that made you take notice, like the sun beaming through a black cloud in the middle of an April shower.

Seated on the front row unmoved and with blank stares of indifference were Hattie, Rita, and Thelma, the three surviving, widowed daughters of Jesse and Ella Hayes. Because Jesse and Ella married young and lived so long, their six daughters were in their seventies when their parents died. And when all the sisters lived past ninety it became apparent to the residents of Gavinville that, like their parents, the Hayes sisters had a strange issue of blood. But the real talk of the town was not that the sisters were old. What everyone found unusual was that, as aged as they looked on the outside, the sisters just didn't think, talk and act old, bestowing a somewhat comical and at times frightening distinction of their being alien or otherworldly.

To the community at large, the Hayes sisters had come to be known as "the Aunties." It was as much a form of classification as it was a term of endearment, for no one had ever known or encountered a group of women quite like this one. Their relations with relatives and with residents and staff at Hayes Place, where they lived, were generally regarded as collective, as if the Aunties were a small tribe of outsiders who had come to inhabit the village. As individuals, they had unique idiosyncrasies and eccentricities, but rarely were the sisters ever spoken or thought of as individuals. When they were all living, the people in Gavinville regarded them as a group and thought of them mostly in the context of their group identity, speaking in such terms as "Ms. Carmen is the most outspoken of the Aunties, or Ms. Rita is the quietest and most sensible, or Ms. Hattie talks the loudest, or of the Aunties, Ms. Thelma is the most stubborn."

How and why the Aunties lost their individual identities in the minds of strangers and people closest to them is probably best explained by what they had in common. Although they rarely got out and about the town of Gavinville, seldom were they not seen together. They lived together at Hayes Place, an assistant living facility that they personally financed and built. They were the children of Ella and Jesse Hayes. And they were all very old.

Longevity and sound minds had come to be seen as a blessing and a curse on the Hayes family. Ella and Jesse had both lived to be nearly one hundred years old and died three years apart. Gladys, the oldest daughter, lived to be 101. Two others, Carmen and Antoinette, who lived to be 100 and 99, were buried in the last six months. With the exception of Judy, who died in an automobile accident at the age of twenty-three, the Hayes daughters lived as if they would never die. It is this very fact, that death in the Hayes family rarely occurred, that drew so much attention to the recent deaths. The talk around town was that the circle would soon be drawn. Bets at Hayes Place were high that Hattie, 98, Rita, 97, and Thelma, 96, wouldn't live another year, in spite of their sound minds and relatively good health.

Many who sat in the church that day had never met Gladys Hayes. They had gone to pay respect to the Hayes family and to get a final glimpse of "Mama Ella" Hayes' oldest daughter, who bore a remarkably striking resemblance to her mother. Mama Ella was a local legend, the town's first and only traiteuse, a woman faith healer. A former resident, Maurice Placide Montgomery, had been a treater or male faith healer in the late 1800's, but many associated his practice with Haitian voodoo. Ella's potions and chants were rumored to have raised a body from the undertaker's gurney. For over three quarters of a century, people traveled great distances for her to lay hands on them and be cured of every kind of sickness, from common colds to rheumatism and epilepsy. Although the practice wasn't passed on by natural hands, Ella knew she had inherited the gift from her father, who was born to two freed slaves from West Africa. He died of typhoid fever shortly after Ella was born.

Recent deaths in the Hayes family seem to have brought Ella Hayes back to life larger than ever. Several weeks after Antoinette's burial, the local weekly gazette did a feature story about Ella's extraordinary faith and reputation as a healer, interviewing family members, town leaders, and older residents who knew her personally. Much of the story dealt with an event that had occurred in 1939, when Ella was forty-two years old, a story which by now was more myth than legend, but which firmly established Ella Hayes' reputation as a woman with special powers from God.

Chapter 2

Ella and Jesse moved into their three-bedroom rent house on Carver Street in 1917, the year they married. Located across from the cemetery and coulee that separate colored residents from the white section of the Hilcrest Section, Carver Street is mostly dotted with one-bedroom shotgun rent houses. Ella wanted a big house, something a family can grow into, but she hadn't expected the rooms to shrink in so short a time.

This Friday morning, she heard the squeaky, cringing sound of the hinges, then a sudden flap, and she knew she was running late. Big John never knocked when he stopped by in the morning. He assumed that Ella and her daughters had already left for work and school.

"Ella, that you I hear?"

"Still here, John. Be leaving in a minute. Trolley will be there soon."

"How's my buddy?"

"Oh, stubborn and silly as usual. Come on through. He was just asking about you."

Big John's boots knocked loudly against the pine floor of the house. Ella met him halfway as she walked toward the front door.

"Lord, I hate to leave him with that fever," said Ella, shaking her head. "He sweated all night and had nightmares again. Last night, the moon was so empty I couldn't even see it, so I stayed up praying and rubbing him down real good. My mama always said, when the moon is empty the hands of God are full of miracles. Maybe the fever will break."

"Well don't you worry none about Jesse. I'll see Sam this morning. You know Sam. One word about Jesse being sick and you got half the neighborhood on the front porch."

"There's cool water beside Jesse's bed," said Ella, looking back through the porch screen. "And tell Sam there's fresh soup on the stove."

Doctors gave up on Jesse's chances of surviving within weeks of the accident, but Ella took him home and nursed him with her homemade potions and rubbing salves. He gradually improved, enabling Ella to take the job cleaning and ironing for the Stanfords, but Jesse remained an invalid and his condition was always tenuous, prone to bed sores and frequent bouts of pneumonia. He lay on his back most of the day and could only move his head and raise his right arm at the elbow. He spoke in a low slow slur, though his wit was as pointed and sharp as the fingernails he refused to have cut. Neighbors like Big John Williams and Sam Foucault stopped by every morning to turn him on his side, give him water, and lift his spirit with some local gossip. Ella worried about Jesse lately. His fever was rising and his eyes were glassy and yellow. She feared he'd have a massive stroke while she was at the Stanfords. It hurt her to leave him alone.

Before the accident, Jesse stood above most men. At six feet, eight inches, he had a way of tapping you on the shoulder when he told stories about his days growing up in the fields—bottled memories of picking pecans, whacking sugarcane, and shucking corn like peeled bananas. When he married Ella, Big John helped him to get a job on the river, packing ice and doing odd jobs for the fishing boats. Big John always had a fresh tale about the fishermen, like the one he'd tell this Friday morning before going to the icehouse.

"Jerry Gauthreaux came in spittin' fire and cussin' up a storm yesterday because he lost his boat to the bank. You should have heard him, Jesse," Big John said while raising Jesse's head to give him a cup of water. 'What the hell dey gonna do with my goddam boat, sail de high sea looking for some goddamn treasure? A pirate in a blue suit. I'd like to take and ram a fishing pole up that banker's ass and feed him to de gators.' Boy, Jerry was mad."

"If he's talking about that banker on Front Street with his hair parted down the middle, that pole probably ain't long enough," Jesse joked. "I could tell years ago by the way he looked at me when I passed him on the street."

Big John's laughter rolled like thunder. His blue denim overalls and sunset orange undershirt brightened the bare, drabby walls and furnishings of Jesse's room. If you didn't know Big John, you'd look twice to see if he was colored or white. Like Jesse, his skin tone was high-yellow. His straight black hair was pulled completely to the back. "Jerry. Now that's a Cajun if I ever seen one. He talks more stuff without his front teeth than when he had them. But he's a good man, Jesse, treats the coloreds fair."

Big John paused and put his hands around Jesse's torso and legs. "Okay buddy, time to turn you. Things are really bad out there, Jesse.

People can't find work. Crops ain't paying. With all the fish in the water, people are starving to death. I'm lucky to be packing ice, and you're lucky to have a woman like Ella to look after you."

"Yep. The Lord sure knew what a man needed when he made my Souffie. I ever told you how I gave her that name?" Jesse asked in a pitch nearly drowned by the mockingbird outside his window."

"No, but I know you will."

"Well, it was the night we got married. You know, we got married in New Orleans in a little holiness church down in the Lower Bottom. That night, I took Souffie out to get the finest dinner money can buy. I mean, we walked in like we belonged in the place. Nobody knew it was the first time we ever sat down in a restaurant. Well, after we ate, they brought out the sweet stuff."

Jesse paused to catch his breath. "I said, what they call this, Ella? She said, chocolate soufflé, Jesse. You'll like it. Look how fluffy it is. And I said . . . Souffie. And she said, no Jesse . . . soufflé. It's French. My mama used to make em and put chocolate in em just like these. Hurry up and eat it before it flops down."

Jesse slowly raised his right hand and gestured like he was putting something in his mouth. "Boy, I put the whole thing in my mouth with one big swallow. I said, girl, from now on you're going to be my Souffie. Then she said, you can't call me that, Jesse. What will people think? And I said, they're going to think what I think, that you're as sweet as chocolate . . . and fluffy too. That's how she got the name."

Big John laughed until he cried. "Partner, I've heard you tell stories, but that one tops it all."

To Ella, Jesse always said the right words. Even when they sounded simple and silly, they warmed her deepest parts. And though he never stopped flattering her about her looks, his brown, lily-pond eyes always seemed to look right through her as if he weren't seeing her at all. Ella knew that was Jesse's special way of touching her in a place that no other man could, seeing the woman she was on the inside, beneath the face and body.

Big John sighed. "Well, I best be going down to the river big fella. The shrimp boats are going out. There's lots to do. Sam's probably going to stop by later, him and that no hunting hound of his. I'll see you in the morning."

"Well, as always, I appreciate you stopping."

Ella stepped onto the loose, rotted boards of the front porch and slowly made her way toward the trolley, the only one in Gavinville, a small fisheries town in southeast Louisiana. Within minutes she'll stand on the same spot where Jesse was thrown from a horse one Saturday evening three years ago, paralyzing him from the neck down. After a short wait for the 7:30 stop, she'll step aboard the trolley. Her destination is 510 Burbank Avenue, the home of Dr. and Mrs. Edwin Stanford. God only knows what will happen along the way.

Giving birth to seven children in six years took a toll, but you wouldn't know it by the looks of Ella Hayes. It's been fifteen years since her last child, and at forty-two she's still the envy of many women in Gavinville, colored and white. Two things people noticed about her right away: She's black, not brown or Creole tan, but nighttime black, with an ashy dryness that accentuates her high cheek bones, uncommon white teeth, and doll-like, unblemished complexion. She's a tall woman with a regal stature, and to any man other than Jesse her figure makes staring a lonely dream. Jesse jokes that "she makes jelly when she walks," even with the arthritis she has in both feet. When her ankles swelled, as they did this morning, a slight limp caused her broad shoulders to tilt as she gently tugged her purse against her left hip.

Strolling down Carver Street, Ella sensed the small, soft sounds of nature speaking louder than usual. Mindful of dips and potholes in the narrow dirt road that stretched a mile from her front yard to the tiny steeple of Mount Calvary Baptist Church, she stepped gingerly into the leaves rattling down from the maples. She reminisced in the scent of fresh soil turning in Margie Franklin's vegetable garden and the cock-a-doodle-doo of a rooster flapping off the chicken coup.

This was Ella's favorite time, her quiet time with God and questions, when she listened to hear the changes that stirred inside her. Walking east into the blooming chameleon dawn, she remembered that she was a woman, an African woman, and the child of a big God. She never knew her papa, but in those minutes alone she dreamt of the man he must have been to win her mama's heart. She silently retold the stories her mama told her when she was a child, how her papa had a gift of healing that was passed down to him by his grandmother, but he died before his time, and how her papa's grandmother, who lived on the Ivory Coast, could interpret dreams and foretell the future, and lived to be 120 years old. In those moments, Ella knew she was more than a wife and a mother. She cradled the child she once was and saw herself growing up all over again. She looked into the mirror of her mind, imagining herself as the person her papa might have been—until the mirror got hazy and all she saw was Jesse paralyzed and lying in bed.

The road climbed before it fell and meandered to the side and back of the small wooden church, where it became a trail cutting through a thick patch of wild trees. They've started a colored school at Mount Calvary, and all five of the Hawkins boys are already out throwing rocks at stray dogs. Bebo, one of the boys, sneaked up behind Ella while she was deep in thought.

"There's that bird again," Ella said to herself before entering a canopy of tangled sweetbriar and honeysuckle still wet with morning. "Those wings spread like hands of God. Lord, did you send that bird to spy on me and tell you my troubles? But you don't need a bird to spy on me. You made me and that bird and you know everything there is to know. Maybe you're trying to point me a way. Maybe you're calling me home."

The boy, who couldn't be more than six or seven years old, wore a torn striped shirt. He walked barefoot alongside Ella with his thumbs resting on the edge of the back pockets of his khaki shorts. His eyes searched the sky. "What bird you talkin to, Miss Ella? I heard him, too, but I don't see him."

Ella's shoulders shuddered slightly as she turned and looked down in the direction of a voice. "Bebo! Child, you made my heart skip. I was so caught up in another space, I didn't know you were walking beside me. Don't mind me, child. That's just the way I pray sometimes. How's your mama doing?"

"She doin fine."

"How's that leg of hers?"

"I guess she doing okay. She don't move around much."

"You tell her I'm going by there tomorrow to put something on it."

"Yes Ma'am."

Bebo hunched his shoulders and looked toward the ground, his thumbs now gripping the inside of his pockets. "We sorry bout the rock, Miss Ella. I saw you duckin."

"Well, I declare. Your mama raised a mighty fine boy. That's real gentleman of you. I'll be sure to tell Eliza when I see her. You get on over to the church now."

Ella walked, thinking about her friend Eliza, who suffers from diabetes and has gangrene in her left leg. She wonders what would happen to Bebo and his brothers with no daddy and a mama with one leg. "Lord, don't let them take that leg," she prayed as she looked down at her feet, stepping slowly and painfully toward the flat wooden bridge over the coulee. That's where Jesse's horse bucked, at the front of the bridge, throwing him against the rail that broke and caused him to drop fifty feet and land on a giant boulder banking the coulee.

She reassured herself that by now—three years after the accident, a year on the job—crossing the forty-yard bridge isn't so painful. Without realizing it, she held her breath, and her pace and heartbeat quickened. She never looked down, but she couldn't resist looking back. As she crossed over and entered the white section of Hillcrest, she was oblivious to the big green yards and houses that sat far back far from the road. She stared into the moss-bearded oaks that lined Fourth Street as if she were listening for them to speak. Stopping a few feet short of the corner, she stood away from a small circle of white trolley riders and waited.

There's nothing unusual about this Friday morning, no reason to expect today's trolley ride to be any different than others. It's a hot and humid day. Ella wore the loose-fitting white uniform that she had grown accustomed to, at least until recently. Mrs. Stanford insisted that she put the uniforms away when Dr. Stanford retired and built a smaller house, but Ella still wore them on occasion when the wash piled up. No one riding the trolley asked her why she made the switch to skirts, blouses, and bright colored dresses, and it wasn't her practice to discuss the Stanford's business with anyone but Jesse. Still, she knew the change was the topic of small talk on the rear couch. That all ended this week when she wore a uniform four straight days.

Ella didn't plan it to happen, but by Wednesday the trifling talk at the back of the trolley grew so loud that she felt compelled to go the distance, if for no other reason than to show Lucy Daniels that she wouldn't be moved by all the hand fanning nonsense at the back of the trolley. Normally, the fanning didn't start until the trolley was in high gear, but today Clara Batiste and Lucy had started flapping hand fans and stretching their necks like wild geese before the trolley approached the Fourth Street stop.

They're an odd pair, Clara and Lucy. They boarded the trolley at the railroad depot, two stops ahead of Fourth Street. Colored trolley riders knew them as community busybodies who could always be counted on for a twisted and rather humorous account of the latest "society news." But Ella knew that beneath their gossip was a deep-seated resentment toward her that dates back to years when they all competed for Jesse's attention and affection. Being the only colored maid working in the "rich white folk side of town" only fueled the animosity.

The trolley pulled up and Ella stepped aboard. "Morning Ella," said Al, the driver.

"Morning Al."

"How's Jesse?"

"Oh, still stubborn as a mule. Can't get it in his head that one of us got to work. I hate leaving him alone, especially now when his fever is up. Lord I hope it's not pneumonia again." Ella took her usual seat on the first colored row. She didn't bother to wipe the tears swelling in her eyes as she gazed out the open window.

"Umh, guess dem skirts started gittin a little too tight and pretty for her own good," Lucy muttered to Clara. "Dr. Stanford musta took too much notice. Miz Stanford sho waited a long time to git jealous of havin another woman round the house. Lord knows it's too late now."

"Lucy, you oughta be ashame," said Clara, moving her cardboard fan back and forth.

"You know it's true. She prancin' and struttin' round with her tail and head in the sky like she's every man's dream. I wouldn't be surprised if her and Reverend Braxton got a little something going on. She ain't been sittin on the front row at Mount Calvary just to hear the choir."

"Now Lucy, you goin too far. Jesse ain't dead yet."

"He just as well be. All he can do is lay there and look at it."

"I sho wouldn't put it past Perry Braxton," said Clara. Child, he still ain't nuttin but a street hustler. I don't care how reverend he claim to be."

"And dem girls of hers is just as bad, specially dat oldest, sassy one. A man stealer if I ever seen one. I hear three of em done run off to somewhere for the summer . . . nuttin but a trail of broken homes. Dat's all they leave behind."

Before Lucy could say another word, Percy Guillory, a regular who rode on Saturdays, was seen running alongside the trolley barefoot with his shirt completely unbuttoned, waving his arms and yelling at the top of his lungs. "Ella, Ella, Ella! Is Ella on the trolley? She gotta go home. Ella, Ella, you gotta go home!"

"Stop the trolley, stop the trolley!" someone yelled.

Al, a beastly looking, red haired war veteran who wore his medals on the shirt pocket of his uniform, had been driving the trolley since it started rolling five years ago. He's heard a lot of stories and seen a lot of excitement, and he knew more about the regular passengers than they know about each other. Something had to be terribly wrong for speakeasy Percy Guillory to go running down the street screaming for Ella. Al slammed his foot on the break while putting his head out the window. "What's the problem, Percy?"

Half out of breath, Percy shouted, "Don't know. We got a phone call. Said lot of commotion down on Carver Street front of Ella's place. Said the trolley was coming this way. Ella need to go home . . . right away. That's all they said."

"Hold on, Ella, I'll take you. I'm turning around folks," Al said in the growly voice he used when he talked to the rear passengers. "It's just a few blocks, but if anybody wants to get off here they can."

Al turned at the next intersection and started heading back. He'll have to make several more turns to get to Carver Street. Ella had already grabbed her purse and leaped toward the front row. She could only think the worst, that Jesse took his last breath sometime after Big John left. She shook uncontrollably as she stood in the aisle, gripping the handrail as the trolley sped along.

Several colored passengers rushed to her side and said comforting words but Ella couldn't hold back the tears. The eight white passengers sitting in front of the color line were unmoved. Their faces showed indifference, but Al knew they were concerned, if not downright curious about what's causing so much excitement in the colored neighborhood so early in the day. Lucy Daniels and Clara Batiste stopped fanning and looked away from each other. Neither said a word.

The trolley had never rolled down Carver Street, and it was quite a spectacle to see the big green and gold machine making its way down the hill. Ella saw the street crowd in the distance.

"Hurry Al, please hurry. Where is he? Where's Jesse? I don't see the ambulance. Where's Jesse?"

The street grew more crowed as the trolley bounced along. In full view of the house, Ella moved restlessly from side to side looking for a sign, a sound, something that would say what was happening. What she saw baffled her. Neighbors smiled, cheered, and waved as the trolley pushed through. Questions raced through her mind. "What are they happy about? What's going on? Where's Jesse?" Suddenly, she caught a glimpse of a figure, a man standing behind the porch screen, a tall man whose head she couldn't see, a man who would have to bend his back and stoop down to walk through the door. "Jesse, Jesse?" she asked herself. "Jessseee!" she screamed.

Ella's eyes saw nothing but Jesse as she rushed off the trolley, screaming his name and running toward him. She couldn't feel or think. When she reached the porch, the ground sank beneath her. She couldn't run or walk. She was sinking and everything was standing still. The air was too thick and heavy to breathe. Then everything turned cold, silent, and black.

Ella awoke to find herself lying on the porch. It was all a dream, she thought—Jesse kneeling beside her, holding her in his arms. His blood made the sound of a brook bubbling across a bed of stones. The warmth of his body and his face next to hers was like the sun beaming on her morning walk. But as quickly as Jesse was near her, she felt his distance. Suddenly, she was alone inside a bright beaming light. Behind it was the porch screen. Something pulled her toward it. She stood up and stared into the dark gray mesh, its torn seams, and buckled opening. Then she closed her eyes and fell to her knees. She looked again. And there it was—an image of praying hands etched inside the screen.

Feeling Jesse's presence, Ella turned to find him still kneeling beside her. She wanted to embrace him, but couldn't, neither could he. They shivered at the sight of the image in the screen. Ella extended her hand and traced the blackened lines that formed two hands clasped in prayer. The hands opened and Ella pressed a finger against the indentations of scarred flesh and bone. "Oh Jesus. Oh, my Lord, what have you done? Where am I?" Jesse took both of her hands into his. Only then did she realize what had happened. Ella reached up to Jesse and held his face in her hands. "You're healed Jesse. You're healed with the blood of Jesus. He was here in this house. I felt Him, Jesse, and I heard your blood moving. He was in this house."

Jesse stood up and lifted Ella to him. It had been three years since she stood beneath him, wrapped inside the weight of his big arms and hands. She hadn't thought of time in that sense, but at that moment three years seemed like twenty-two, like the day Jesse first held her. Her tears melted in his embrace. They faced the screen to see the image, but it was gone. Not a trace of it was left and it never reappeared.

Ella Hayes emerged from that day in 1939 as a woman endowed with powers from on high. Only she saw the beaming light. Only she and Jesse saw the image. But there was little doubt that a miracle had come to Gavinville, maybe God himself. Within hours, the whole town was parading past the Hayes' front yard or lining up to see Jesse and get a glimpse of the porch screen. For many whites, it was their first time on the colored side of the Hillcrest neighborhood.

There were doubters of course. Two days after the incident, an entourage of the Catholic Diocese, led by none other than Archbishop Harold Scott, came out to see Jesse and take photographs of the screen. He extended his blessings but failed to issue an official statement of the Church.

Doctors at State Hospital could offer no earthly explanation for Jesse's miraculous recovery, but Jesse had his own story. "You see, I was having a dream, and in the dream a big bird came and picked me up out of bed and carried me down a hill to the river. And then it brought me in the woods, and I shot a rabbit, and I went home and kicked my boots at the front door. I had the rabbit in one hand and a string of Gou and catfish in the other hand and I was dripping wet. Then I woke up." To the Town of Gavinville, Jesse's miracle and their newfound healer of pain and sickness brought hope. Soon Ella was laying hands on half the town. The Great Depression of the 1930s had taken a terrible toll on the local economy, and the town's merchants benefitted from the increased patronage of surrounding townspeople who came to Gavinville in search of a cure. Ella never asked for money herself, but her "children," as she called them, always felt obliged to drop something in the tin pot she kept by the front door. Eventually, the donations were regular enough for her to quit the Stanfords. Jesse was strong enough to get around with a walking stick, but not enough to take a job.

As years and decades passed, Mama Ella, as she was later called, was both revered and awed, the former for her healing powers and the latter for her and Jesse's outright refusal to close their eyes and die as every other town resident had done who was there when the spirit appeared on the porch. In fact, Ella and Jesse outlived any and everybody who had cast their eyes on the porch screen, including the surrounding townspeople and youngsters who skipped school or made a date out of the sighting. In time, the Hayes' longevity was associated with everyone else's short life, to the point that people began to relate the sighting to a curse on everyone who had looked at the screen.

Chapter 3

Ella and Jesse raised their girls, Gladys, Judy, Carmen, Antoinette, Hattie, Rita, and Thelma, to always be on good behavior, do well in school, and fear God. By most accounts they succeeded, at least until the girls grew old enough to discover the pleasures and pitfalls of dating. The Hayes girls intimidated most boys. They all had the same coffee-milk complexion, a mix of their jet-black Mama and high-yellow Daddy. Perhaps it was their broad shoulders and above average height or their straight, short-cut hair and high cheek bones that made them look older than most girls their age. Still, the boys came courting, and evenings at the Hayes home were never without drama and surprises, like nights when Ella's bedroom door unexpectedly flung open, and her footsteps rumbled quickly across the loose hardwood floorboards. Some nights, Ella just stood in her bedroom doorway and spoke a thunderous but curious soliloquy of cuss and prayer that suspended a whisper and a sex wish in midair, pushing trouble out the door like flies in the hole of the porch screen. Jesse would waken to the sounds of walls and panes rattling like loose pipes and the backdoor hinge popping.

After graduating from high school, the girls took jobs at Gavinville's clothing factory. Outside of work, they rarely dressed casually and were almost always seen in groups of three or four. They had the aura and appearance of women not poor and colored. Jesse and Ella couldn't afford to send any of their daughters to one of the two Negro colleges in the state, but their children had more than enough of what colored folks called "street sense." They were what the men of Gavinville called "pretty," almost doll-like in their fashionable hats and cut-out, hand-sewn dresses, and they projected the arrogance and confidence that even white women quietly envied and no doubt talked about. None of the daughters were ready to settle down with a husband and children, and Ella was beginning to wonder whether she'd ever be a grandmother.

By her early twenties, Gladys, the oldest, was an accomplished seamstress. But she soon discovered that her looks, coupled with the shapely body she inherited from her Mama, could earn far more money at the local juke joints than any place else in Gavinville. She started waiting tables but eventually became a dancer at the colored strip club next door to the gambling shack across the tracks. Needless to say, Jesse and Ella were terribly upset that their oldest daughter was strip dancing but there was nothing they could say to change Gladys' mind. Three months later, she took the name "Ebony" at Harry's, the only white-owned strip club in town and was a crowd favorite, especially among the wealthy old men who arrived right after sundown on Friday and Saturday evenings. Her most loyal customer was Gerald Stone, the oldest lawyer in Gavinville, owner of the only supermarket, and landlord of nearly every rent house inhabited by colored folks, including the Hayes family.

In addition to the one-dollar bills Stone tossed at Gladys' feet as she spiraled down a pole in the middle of the stage with both legs pointed to the ceiling, and the larger bills he paid for backroom lap dancing, Stone managed to spin a delusion around Gladys' head that she would one day be left a portion of his bequeathed inheritance. Sure enough, to everyone's surprise, when Stone died of a massive heart attack in 1945, his will had given his highly recognizable classic, sky-blue Plymouth convertible to Gladys Hayes. Being a widower with no children, no one contested the old man's gift.

Ella and Jesse voiced their strong objection. "Girl, now everybody in town knows who that car belonged to," said Ella. "It's the only one Stone drove and the only one like it in town. And everybody's going to know why he gave it to you. It's a disgrace. You might as well paint Harry's sign on your forehead."

Jesse, with a finger within inches of Gladys' face, was furious. "You take that car, you best drive as far from Gavinville as it'll take you, cause you'll be the gossip of the town, and you ain't gonna put another foot in my house. I promise."

"Mr. Stone gave the car to me. It's mine. I earned it, and I ain't letting it go. You should be glad. At least we can get around town without having to walk or catch a trolley."

Ella quickly fired back. "You earned it alright, but at what price? Where's your dignity?"

"Dignity? What's so dignified about riding the trolley and white people telling you to go sit at the back? Telling you to stand up and give a seat to some poor white trash ten years younger than you, after you've spent the day cleaning white folks toilets and washing and ironing their clothes. You call that dignity? I call it plain old sorriness, you and Daddy both, and all the other sorry niggers in this town."

Gladys kept the convertible and Jesse kept his promise. She moved out and went to live with Mary Guillory, a much older, distant cousin who was prone to excessive drinking and long nights at the gambling shack. Just as Jesse warned, in a town of only 7,000 people, Gladys and her sky-blue convertible became the talk of it, especially among colored residents. Naturally, Lucy Daniels and Clara Batiste, still riding the trolley, had much to say.

Lucy quickly seized the opportunity to bash Ella. "Child, Ella's little ho done really outdid herself. Can you believe? Ridin around blasting the radio in that car. Wonder what her holier than thou mama got to say about dat, her oldest child selling her soul to the devil and her body to every rich white man in town."

"Everybody still wondering why Ella left Mount Calvary after all dem years to join St. Paul. Make you wonder how far the apple done fell from the tree, or if it fell at all," said Clara.

"Well, ain't no colored man can compete with dat, not even Perry Braxton and the used Cadillac he done bought with po folks money."

"You think he be down at Harry's?"

"Think? I know for a fact!" Lucy snapped. "Probly got a front row seat. When it come down to the devil's work, white folk don't care what color you is. Question is whether he collecting enough quarters from po Negroes to have pockets deep enough to git it de way Gerald Stone had her."

"Lucy, you need to hush."

"I kinda feel sorry for dat girl, though," said Lucy. "Ain't her fault. Funny how the mama can heal everybody's sickness but can't cast out the demons in her own house. Make you wonder whether her God sits high or low, don't it, or if he sits at all when it come to dat mess Jesse done got hisself into."

"Lord help him," said Clara, shaking her head from side to side.

Sitting on the banks of the Atchafalaya River, Gavinville has a history of high water flooding streets, businesses, and homes in low-lying areas near the river, particularly during heavy spring downpours and fall tropical storms. The morning of November 28, 1947 showed signs of severe weather on its way, but to Gladys and Judy, her twenty-three-year-old sister and Carmen's identical twin, it was just another windy, rainy day. By nightfall, the weather had worsened, but not enough to change their Friday night plans for drinks and dancing to celebrate Gladys' twenty-eighth birthday. The other sisters warned them not to go out, but Gladys had made a new dress for the occasion and was determined to show it off. It had been two years since she inherited the Plymouth convertible, and she had done little to maintain it. Most times it barely had oil or gas, as was the case this evening, but Gladys knew exactly how far she could go before the engine died.

When they left the night club around 1:00 o'clock the next morning, wind was knocking down tree limbs, streets were a river of high water, and slashing rain made it nearly impossible for Gladys to see the road. The car sputtered to a near death. With her eyes fixed on the fuel gauge, Gladys unknowingly drove the small vehicle into a flooded underpass beneath a railroad bridge. The car sank instantly.

Gladys awoke in a bed at Gavinville General Hospital later that day surrounded by Jesse, Ella, and her sisters, and had no memory of what had happened earlier that morning. Rescuers had managed to pull her out in time, but they weren't able to reach Judy soon enough. Gladys had been unconscious and suffered a few bruises, but the prognosis for a full recovery was positive. When she opened her eyes, the first face she saw was her mama's.

"You and that damn car killed your sister," Ella said in a voice that conveyed both anger and pain.

"What you talking about, Mama?"

"You drove that damn car into six feet of water and Judy drowned. Didn't you know you were in the middle of a storm?"

"Oh my God," Gladys said, covering her face with both hands. "Oh my God."

"Covering your face won't bring your sister back. We told you that car would be trouble. When it's long gone, you'll have to live with this. God have mercy on you."

Jesse didn't speak. Looking down at Gladys, his silence and watery, bloodshot eyes said enough. He turned and left the room.

Sobbing loudly, Carmen, Antoinette, Hattie, Rita, and Thelma huddled closer to their sister's bed. Sensitive to her brokenness and overcome by their own grief, they couldn't have spoken if they wanted to.

Within a week after leaving the hospital, Gladys went back to Harry's, dancing and doing backroom tricks. She spent most of the daylight hours sleeping and seldom answered knocks on Mary's door. She deeply regretted accepting the gift that Stone had bequeathed her and was even more regretful for driving in the storm. She hated that she had caused her family so much pain and wished that she could turn back the clock. She was drowning in guilt and shame, but she was too proud to admit it to anyone, especially her family. Going back to Harry's was as much to keep her from mentally breaking down and falling apart as it was to earn a living.

Gladys' sisters avoided saying anything to her about the accident before and during Judy's burial and for the days and weeks that followed. After the funeral, the younger sisters, Hattie, Rita, and

Thelma, saw little of Gladys, except for incidental, unexpected encounters in stores around town. Inwardly, they felt resentment toward their oldest sister for Judy's death, but they lacked the courage to tell her. In their unexpected encounters with her they smiled and hugged, but the greetings were mostly peppered with small, unimportant talk about store bargains and other people's business, never the intimacy and affection of sisters who had the same Mama and Daddy and had grown up together in the same house. The resentment became an albatross around their necks that only time and forgiveness would lift.

Maybe because they were closer in age, Carmen and Antoinette felt a stronger bond with Gladys. While they harbored resentment, they knew that she hurt just as much, if not more, than they did. In time, their pent-up anger toward her would boil over, but for now they were willing to embrace her as a sister and not be confrontational or show bitterness toward her for the accident. From time to time, they stopped by Mary's to visit their oldest sister, still avoiding any mention of the accident and Judy's death.

"How's Mama and Daddy?"

"Oh, they're fine," said Carmen, holding her breath to the thought of any of them mentioning Judy's death. "Mama's got strangers coming and going all hours of the day and night, wanting her to lay hands on them. Some days there's a line stretching out to the street."

"And Daddy?"

"Walking better and doing a little fixing up work with Big John on Saturdays. Doing a little fishing, too, but still not strong enough to go hunting rabbits with Mr. Sam."

"How you doing, Sis?" Antoinette asked.

"Can't complain about much. Just work and trying to keep Mary out of trouble. She lost her rent money at the gambling shack the other night, but she swears she'll win it back."

"That guy at the supermarket asked about you again. I think he wants to ask you out," Carmen said smiling.

"Willie Frank? Girl, no way."

"Why not? He's got a steady job. Been at the market a few years now."

"Cause he's too short for one thing. And I ain't going to be another one of his one-night girlfriends. Besides, I got my hands full with those fools down at Harry's. Ain't got time to be getting serious and tied down with some boy trying to prove his manhood."

"Well, we best be going. I hate to make the visit short but we've got some grocery shopping to do for Mama."

"Nice of y'all to stop by. Give me a hug. And tell my little sisters I said hello."

As Maple leaves turned brown and the cool, fall weather set in, Gladys reminisced about nights when she and her sisters bundled up beneath the bed covers, and those Saturday afternoons when they strolled down Front Street wearing tight-fitting dresses and wool scarves that couldn't be bought in stores, making every man's head turn and look their way. Thanksgiving was around the corner, and she remembered the smell and taste of her Mama's gumbo, garlic-stuffed turkey, baked ham, greens, and casseroles, and the fun she and her sisters had baking sweet potato pies.

Thanksgiving was more than a holiday to the Hayes family. Ella and Jesse spent the three days before Thanksgiving fasting and praying, and they encouraged their children to do the same. The girls did their own version of the sacrifice, mixed with a little nighttime fun and indulgence, but they generally honored their parents' ritual. Gladys hadn't set foot in her parents' home in over two years, not since the day she moved out and sped into a sunset with the top down on her convertible. No one expected her to show up on this holiday, but she did, uninvited, and with Mary at her side.

It was a quarter past 8:00 on Thanksgiving morning. Jesse had gone to Stone's Grocery to pick up more seasoning to chop for the dressing mix. Having been up way past midnight baking pies, the Hayes daughters were still asleep. Ella had just pulled the ham out of the oven and slid the turkey onto the rack when she heard a knock at the back door. Gladys always went to the backdoor, mainly out of her habit of sneaking in before the sun came up to avoid waking anybody. When she moved out, Jesse started locking the door before bedtime.

"Gladys, everything okay?"

"Hi Mama. Surprise! Guess I couldn't take another day without tasting your cooking." Hope there's enough for two more mouths, pointing to Mary with her eyes."

"You know there's always more than enough. Give your Mama a hug."

"Mornin, Mama Ella. Happy Thanksgiving."

"Mary! Girl it's been a while. Happy Thanksgiving to you. Ya'll come on in. I'm doing the usual," said Ella, turning to go back into the kitchen. "Got the turkey on and about to start the dressing. Your Daddy went down to Stone's for more celery and parsley."

"Got it smelling real good in here, Mama. That's sweet potato I'm smelling?"

"Yes, indeed. Your sisters sat up half the night baking as usual. Don't think they'll be waking up soon. Go on in there."

Ella sat still as a rock at the kitchen table. She knew it would be the last moment she'd have alone to feel and think to herself before Jesse returned and all hell broke loose. She didn't quite know how to react to Gladys being home. She missed her oldest child and was hoping they'd patch things up, but she was still grieving the loss of Judy. In her heart, she wasn't sure whether she had forgiven Gladys. How would Jesse react? What would he say or do? Of all the days, why did Gladys choose this one to come home? Why did she come at all? "Lord," she whispered, "give us peace." Then she heard the front porch screen door.

"Thought I'd never get out of that place," Jesse said, resting his walking cane against a chair while giving the bag of groceries to Ella. "Everybody doing last minute buying and Stone's planning to close at noon. Soon as I wash-up, I'll start chopping the seasoning."

"Jesse, Gladys is here. She's in the back."

"What? You invited her?"

"No, she just showed up, and she brought Mary with her."

"She must be in trouble. What she need, money? I hear Mary been on a long losing streak down at the gambling shack. Neither of them is welcome in this house."

"Jesse, I think it's time we all made peace. She's still our child, and I know you love her as much as she loves you."

"If she's got any feelings about anybody but herself, she would stop disgracing this family and come out of the streets, especially that whore house."

"Jesse, calm down. It's Thanksgiving. Lord knows we've been blessed and have a lot to be thankful for. I think it's time you let it go. The Lord wants you to."

"I'm thankful. You know I am, but Gladys doesn't give a damn about our blessings. She doesn't care about the sacrifices we made to provide for her. There was nothing she needed that we didn't give her, even if it took the last dollar in my pocket. The only thank you we get from her is a kick in the ass. I told her not to ever set foot in this house again."

Jesse went to the bathroom to wash up while Ella stood at the sink humming one of her favorite spirituals while rinsing parsley and celery. She hadn't heard her daughters leave the bedrooms and slip quietly into the dining room, three at a time, first Thelma, Antoinette, and Hattie, then Rita, Carmen, and Gladys. Mary had decided to lie down and nap, probably needing to sober up from the night before. The dining room adjourns the kitchen and is separated by a wall with a narrow, door-less, arched walkway. The daughters were seated at the large, mahogany dining table, set with Ella's best plates and silverware. The matching buffet, usually adorned with old photographs, is now covered with sweet potato pies and cakes. Unseen, the daughters heard most of what their Daddy said. They hadn't planned to be quiet and unnoticed, but Jesse's words had seeped through the walls. Like Ella's prayerful moment of reflection before Jesse returned from the store, they needed time and silence to feel and think about the words their father had spoken.

The reaction was mixed. Rita, Hattie, and Thelma had no intention of speaking. They were close to Judy and grieved the loss of her, but not nearly as much as Carmen and Antoinette, who like Gladys, had known Judy and their parents in a different way. As a twin of Carmen, Judy was one of the "big sisters" to the younger ones. Being closer in age to Gladys, Carmen and Antoinette had seen more of the dark shadow that their oldest sister cast on the Hayes family. They never confronted or criticized her for the life she lived, at least not in the presence of their parents, but quietly they resented her for it. Carmen let her feelings be known.

"Gladys, Daddy's right. If you care about us, you wouldn't be dancing at Harry's and you wouldn't have taken that car. In respect to Judy, you shouldn't have gone back to Harry's after the accident. I love you but I hate the life you live."

"Who are you to throw a stone, Carmen? You're no saint. None of ya'll is. None of ya'll is perfect. At least I ain't pretending to be somebody I'm not."

"But who are you, Gladys?" Antoinette asked. "You're my big sister, but not the sister I look up to, not the sister I want to follow as much as I used to. You've changed, and I don't like the change."

"I made a mistake. Don't we all make mistakes?"

"We do," said Carmen, "and we all have regrets, but I agree with Daddy. I don't think you care or think about how your mistakes affect us. You just go on doing the things you want to do. You don't think about how you're hurting the people who love you. It's all about you and nobody else."

By then, Jesse and Ella were standing near the doorway but still in the kitchen, instinct telling them to keep a distance in the shock of hearing Carmen and Antoinette openly confront Gladys about her street life for the first time.

"Well, this isn't a happy Thanksgiving after all, and it won't be as long as I'm here. I'll just leave. Ya'll can do whatever you want to do with Mary," Gladys said, rising from her chair.

"Gladys, don't leave," Ella stepped forward and pleaded. "At least we're talking."

"No, ya'll are talking, and it's all about me and how I'm a disgrace to this family. I'm sorry that I make everybody so unhappy."

Gladys left hurriedly through the front door, not bothering to close it. Without a car and the trolley not running on a holiday, she and Mary had taken a taxi, but Gladys left walking, not giving any thought to the five miles she'd have to travel on foot.

When she crossed the railroad tracks about a mile from her parents' house, Gladys heard a car slowing down and glanced over as it pulled up beside her. The driver was Willie Frank, who had made it no secret among Gladys' sisters and friends that he admired her.

"Look like somebody can use a ride."

"Hi Willie. No thank you. I'm fine just walking."

"Come on now. Where are you going? Be glad to take you."

"Going home."

"Home? Look like you're leaving, not going."

"Going to my Cousin Mary on St. Elizabeth."

"That's four or five miles down the road. Why don't you hop in?"

"No thank you, Willie."

"Why are you being so stubborn? Why won't you let me take you?"

"For the third time, Willie, I said no."

"Well, how about a date tomorrow night?"

"Go on, Willie. Stop pestering me. I'm not in the mood for your silliness."

"Who's being silly? I'm trying to be nice."

"Well, I appreciate the offer. Just not interested."

"Suit yourself, but I ain't giving up. I'm going to marry you one day and take real good care of you."

"Have a good day, Willie."

Gladys awoke shortly before noon the next day thinking of food. She had missed Thanksgiving Day dinner and hadn't eaten since the day before. Mary's refrigerator and pantry were nearly empty. She dreaded going down to Stone's Grocery knowing that Willie might see her and harass her again about going on a date. Willie. Gladys looked down on him in more ways than one. He can't be more than five feet, two or three inches tall, is pudgy, and wears eyeglasses with lens so thick that you can barely see his eyes. She wondered how he was able to pass the test to get a driver's license, let alone have a car. In school, he was what all the teachers politely called "slow," and he dropped out after ninth grade. Thirty-two years old and he still lived with his mama and daddy. To Gladys' recollection, the only job Willie ever had was bagging and carrying groceries at Stone's. Although he often bragged about being a lady's man and having what women want, she never knew him to have a steady girlfriend, and the only so-called dates she ever saw him with were women much older than him, some old enough to be his mother. Gladys admired his confidence, quick-wit, and handsome, infectious smile, but that could never be enough for her to give him the time of day.

"Well, well, look who come to see Willie. I knew you'd come around. The pretty ones always do."

"Just bag the groceries, Willie. I'm in a hurry," said Gladys when Willie stopped bagging. "Got no time for your foolishness."

"So why you come here if not to see Willie?"

"Cause I needed some groceries."

"Yeah, sure. Marry me and I'll buy you everything you need. You'll never want for nothing."

"I'm sure you say that to all those old women you're sleeping around with, but I ain't one of them."

"Girl, you know I think the world of you. All I'm asking for is one date. Harry's closed on Sunday nights. Let's say we go out, see a movie. I'll pick you up at seven o'clock, then we'll go dancing at the Oasis. They say that new band from Petersville be rocking the floor. Just want to have a little fun, that's all."

Gladys stopped thinking and for a moment felt that somebody, even if it was Willie Frank, appreciated her for who she was and made her feel wanted. "I don't believe I'm saying this, Willie, but okay, just one date, that's all. And I ain't going to end up at Loretta's Inn, waking up under some filthy sheets that's been slept on all week."

"I wouldn't think of it, not for a queen like you. Soon as I get off work I'm going downtown to buy me a new shirt. And don't be surprised when you see me holding a pretty little box when you open Mary's front door. I'm already feeling like a brand new man."

"See you Sunday evening, Willie."

Gladys couldn't believe what she had done, agreed to go on a date with little Willie Frank. But she felt good. He had said words that made her feel special, made her feel like a woman, not some object of a man's lust. And Willie wasn't judging her for how she made a living.

Gavinville's Opera House Movie Theatre had two entrances and two levels, the main door and ground level for whites, and the side door, stairway, and balcony for coloreds. Willie had bought a carnation corsage and pinned it to Gladys' blouse. Walking up the stairway behind him, she felt five years younger and Willie seemed a foot taller. His constant smile and laughter brought the calm and peace of sunsets that she hadn't felt since she was a little girl. Willie bought popcorn, candy, and sodas, and put an arm around her about halfway through the movie.

The Oasis Lounge was crowded and hot as usual, even in late November, but she and Willie danced on nearly every song. Even the slow ones made Willie look and feel taller than her. True to his word, Willie didn't pressure her about getting a motel room when the club closed. He drove her straight home, kissed her on the cheek, and thanked her for the evening.

"No way, no way," Gladys thought to herself as she lay in bed the next morning. "No way anything can become of Willie Frank and me." He had made her laugh and brought sunshine into her life, but she knew that she could never love him. But in the months that followed, Willie was there, in nearly every free moment Gladys had, always a gentleman full of laughs, and putting her on a pedestal high above the life that even she had grown to hate.

Time created more distance between Gladys and her family. As impossible as it seemed for a town as small as Gavinville, they rarely crossed paths in the months and years following the Thanksgiving Day argument. Much of that had to do with Gladys's nightlife and the time she and Willie were spending together during the day. For Jesse and Ella, both in their early fifties, life had become a daily routine. Ella spent the day healing the sick. Jesse had gone back to the icehouse and was now supervising younger, less experienced workers. The other daughters were still sewing at the garment factory.

Gavinville grew more segregated as colored families left their farms and moved to Dixie Manor, a housing project built for the town's poorest residents by the Eisenhower administration on the east side of town, where there was little else other than the colored school and the town's graveyard. The only road leading to the housing project ran alongside the railroad track and adjourning woods, which completely cut the development off from the rest of town. The housing units were bricked duplexes of three or four bedrooms. Those closest to the tracks were two-story.

Since their shotgun rent house had gotten past the stage of patching holes in the floors, keeping rain from pouring through the roof and blocking winter air from blowing through the doors and windows, Jesse and Ella decided that it was time to move. No one at Dixie Manor had an actual "street" address, although each unit was "numbered." The Hayes' new home became 1416 Dixie Manor.

With Gladys being away, the other Hayes daughters, all in their late twenties and early thirties, still not married, slept in three of the four bedrooms, none of which had enough space for more than one bed and a dresser. Thelma, the youngest, luckily drew the lot to have a room to herself.

In many ways, the Hayes women had long ago outgrown Gavinville. All the college-educated men were married, and most of the few hard-working single-colored men felt too intimidated to ask them out. Those who did were soon brushed off because of too much talk about sex, which none of the daughters seemed to have any interest in, at least not with the men of Gavinville. Besides, every man who came courting knew that he would have to win the heart of the town's most beloved citizen and not one but five of its most beautiful yet strangely bonded women.

Ella hoped that one of her children would have "the gift," but she knew that the cycle had to go back to a male, a man like her papa. She wanted grandchildren, especially boys, so she wasn't saddened when Carmen, Antoinette, Hattie, and Rita decided to pack up and move to Southside Chicago to stay with the Grangers, the neighbors who had occupied the adjacent duplex at Dixie Manor. The big city offered the promise of better paying jobs and an escape from the oppressive, dehumanizing Jim Crow laws of the Deep South. The Grangers, children included, had found work. They managed to buy a rundown boarding house that had plenty of room for the Hayes daughters. Thelma, the youngest, and still very much a daddy's girl, decided to stay home.

Chapter 4

After a two-hour bus ride from Gavinville, the Hayes sisters arrived at New Orleans Union Station on South Rampart Street on January 2, 1950. There, they boarded the Illinois Central Railroad for the three-day trip to Chicago. It was the first time that any of them had traveled more than twenty miles outside of Gavinville. The train took them through Mississippi, up to Memphis, through Southern Kentucky, and across the entire south to north corridor of Illinois. They hardly slept, eating their Mama's baked cookies and pie, and laughing themselves silly in anticipation of the new world ahead. The temperature in Chicago was 24 degrees, 50 degrees colder than the weather they left in Louisiana, for which they had mistakenly dressed.

From Illinois Central they took the Red Line to Federal Street. The L-Train dropped them off two blocks from the Grangers' place, so they didn't have far to walk with their suitcases in hand.

"My Lord, look at all those Negroes. Where are they going in this freezing weather?" Hattie asked.

"I'm freezing, too," said Antoinette, pulling the collar of her blouse up to her neck.

"Hope we ain't got too far to go. The map says just around the corner, but these blocks are awful long," said Carmen. "You think we're going in the right direction?"

"There it is!" Antoinette shouted, pointing at the street sign that read Federal Street.

"But ain't no houses around here," said Rita. "Where do people live? Nothing here but tall buildings. You suppose they're living way up there?"

"Says 1040 Federal Street, but this can't be the place," said Antoinette. "Can't imagine anybody living here. This old building is about a minute from falling down. You think it has lights and water. Maybe we have the wrong address."

As they made their way up the steps, the front door opened. "Welcome to Chicago, ladies. How was the trip? Harry, help them with the bags. It's freezing out here. And I know you're hungry for some good Louisiana cooking. Come on in."

"Hi Miss Granger," they all spoke in unison.

"Now before you start thinking, I know the place needs some fixing up, but it ain't as bad as it looks. We've got good plumbing and electricity, a lot more than most folks around here, and the installment is low. We were lucky to get it. Whites don't sell to coloreds around here, but a Jew fellow down at the Country Club where Margaret cooks took a liking to us and gave us a real good deal. And you have your own bathroom right down the hall, all to yourselves. We plan to fix the place up and rent the rest of the rooms."

"And guess what? Harry's already got jobs for each of you down at the clothing factory. Harry's at the steel plant but he met a white lady at the market who needs some help at the clothing factory. It's called Hart. When he told her about your jobs in Gavinville and how good you were at making dresses she got real excited."

"Hart? Don't they make men's clothes? We don't know anything about making men's suits," said Hattie.

"Don't worry about that. Ms. Lacy said she'll teach you everything you need to know," said Harry. "She only asked one thing, that you stay away from union organizers. Just a bunch of Communist who can cause you to get fired. The pay probably won't be much, but with everybody chipping in, we can fix this place up in no time and rent the rest of the rooms. Lot of people out there needing a decent place to live."

"Y'all go on up and put your things away. Harry will show you around. Then come down to the kitchen and get some beans and mustards. Just took the biscuits out of the oven. Probably not as good as your mama's, but I come pretty close."

Margaret and Harry Granger had moved to Dixie Manor not long after the Hayes family got there. Their two children, Victor and Sally, had both dropped out of high school just before they moved to Chicago. Harry, a distant cousin of Jesse Hayes, could never keep a steady job in Gavinville. He was a tall man who drank heavily and always kept a cigar in his mouth, most of the time unlit. Margaret, a short, stout woman, had cooked in local restaurants, but she was known around Gavinville as "the pie lady" for the sweet potato pies, pralines, and popcorn balls that she peddled door-to-door on Saturday mornings.

After dinner, the Hayes sisters, weary from travel, quietly settled into their rooms, each separate, but with only a small cot and a dresser. Paint peeled on all the walls, the windowpanes were cracked, and boards were missing on the wooden floors. Roaches and mice crawled everywhere. Just as Harry said, they had their own bathroom with hot water, but the water pressure was very weak, and the mirror above the medicine cabinet was too cracked to see themselves in it. As modest as their home was in Gavinville, it was like paradise compared to their new home.

The sisters awoke at the crack of dawn to sounds that they had not heard that time of day—cars and trucks moving quickly, sirens screaming, and people on the streets yelling. Margaret had baked more biscuits and placed them in a basket on the kitchen table before leaving for the Country Club.

"Good morning, ladies. Sorry to interrupt your breakfast, but we've got to get moving. I told Ms. Lacy that you'd be there early today to get processed. Don't worry. Ms. Lacy seems like a good, decent woman. I'm sure she'll look out for you. She's young and has bosses, but she talked like she runs the shop. Been there eight years she said."

Hart, Schaffner & Marx had been headquartered in Chicago since the company was founded there in 1872. In 1910, they were the target of one of the most contentious labor strikes in the history of Chicago, but the company had since grown to be one of the country's largest manufactures of men's clothing.

Lacy Romano was a twenty-six-year-old Italian immigrant whose family had moved to Chicago when she was ten years old. After finishing high school, she went to work at Hart, and quickly worked her way up to supervising a section that makes shirts. She was single and seldom dated, spending much of her free time caring for her parents, both of whom had heart conditions.

"Ladies, number one, never be late. Number two, do as you are taught and told. And number three, pay no attention to the men around here wearing suits, no matter how much attention they give you. Remember, you make the suits they wear. The suits don't make you.

You take orders only from me. You do that and you'll do just fine. I know you can sew, but at Hart you've got to think time, quality, and production. That's how they make money and that's how you'll get paid and keep a job."

The sisters caught on quickly and soon gained a reputation for doing all that Ms. Lacy instructed them to do. Being only four of a dozen colored women at the factory made the quality of their work stand out even more.

Waking at dawn and returning home nearly at sunset left little time for socializing and seeing the town during weeknights. But on weekends, the sisters did what they had done in Gavinville, put on their hand-sewn dresses and pranced the downtown streets, making a fashion show of the Black business district of Bronzeville, the name given to Chicago's South Side. They especially liked State Street, sprawling with colored-owned businesses and people who patronized them. As in Gavinville, the sisters were nearly always together. Saturday nights were often spent at the Blue Note Jazz Club, where colored men in suits, ties, and hats entertained them with free drinks and stories about how they were making money and moving up in the world.

On Sundays, the sisters joined the Grangers in attending St. Columbanus Catholic Church on East 71st Street. It was there that Hattie became the first of them to fall in love with a Chicago man.

Hattie, now twenty-nine years old, was the fifth child of Ella and Jesse. She had the lightest complexion of the girls and seldom wore makeup. In spite of being the least talkative of the Hayes girls, she got the most attention from young men, but like her sisters, seldom took any of them seriously.

Thirty-three-year-old James Byrd, the only child of Dr. Thomas and Gayle Byrd, had grown up in South Side Chicago and graduated from Howard University. He worked briefly in the banking industry before starting his own insurance company. Within five years, with the financial backing of his father, he owned and operated what was considered in those days to be a conglomerate. In addition to the insurance company, he held significant amounts of real estate, including a hotel and South Side Plaza, a thriving strip shopping center, and located on State Street, the heart of Chicago's Black business district. He was, by any standard of Chicago, successful and wealthy. He and Hattie dated steadily for four months before she finally got up enough courage to say "yes" to one of his monthly marriage proposals. She had never been away from her sisters, and she dreaded the thought of not seeing them every day. The couple married on March 10, 1951, at St. Columbanus in a small, quiet ceremony attended by the Hayes sisters, the Grangers, and James' family and friends.

Considered one of Chicago's most admired and eligible colored bachelors, Byrd owned a spacious, luxurious home in Park Manor, a neighborhood once occupied exclusively by upper-class white people and now the home of many of Chicago's elite Negro residents. James insisted that Hattie quit her job at Hart and join him in managing his businesses. Hattie took business training classes at a vocational school and eventually started overseeing day-to-day operations at Byrd Insurance Company, which sold burial policies to colored families.

Carmen, Antoinette, and Rita visited Hattie from time to time after Sunday church service.

"Hattie, we didn't want to tell you before now, because of the wedding and all, but we got a letter from Mama a while back. Gladys got into some trouble," Carmen said, with her eyes looking away from Hattie.

"What kind of trouble? What happened?"

"She's okay. Actually, it wasn't her but Willie Frank, but she was with him when it happened. They were at the Oasis one night, and Willie got into a fight with Frankie Lee Garrett and stabbed him. Frankie died, and Willie's in jail."

"Oh no! What were they fighting about?"

"That's where Gladys comes in," said Carmen. "Apparently, she saw Frankie flirting with somebody and confronted him. They started arguing and Willie got in the middle of it."

"Frankie Lee? I thought she and Willie were dating?"

"You know Gladys. She likes men," said Antoinette "She and Willie were dating, but both of them were fooling around. I don't think she ever cared much about Willie, but he was always nice to her. I really feel bad for him."

"Gladys okay? And what's going on with Thelma? She still at the garment factory? What's going to happen to Willie?" Hattie asked.

"Mama didn't say much more," said Carmen. "She doesn't talk about Gladys because she never sees her. She didn't mention Thelma either, but I'm sure she's doing fine. Probably still at the factory, telling everybody what they ain't doing right, even though she's nobody's boss. Mama did say that Willie's in jail and has a trial coming up. He'll probably end up doing time in prison."

"So sorry to hear that about Willie. How's Mama and Daddy holding up otherwise?"

"Guess they're doing fine. You know Mama. She lives the good news and only talks about what needs praying for."

"Well tell me some good news. What's going on at Hart these days? Ms. Lacy found a man yet?"

"Girl, you ain't going to believe it, but she did, a colored one at that," said Antoinette.

"What? In Chicago? They're going to run her away from there."

"And rumor is he's married," Antoinette continued. "Other than that, not much happening out of the usual. Actually, it's starting to get a little boring, cutting and sewing the same pattern every day. I can do it with my eyes closed. Feeling much like the plant in Gavinville, only much bigger."

"Ms. Lacy. Sure is one for surprises. Well, give her my regards. So happy to see my sisters." Hattie paused to take a sip of her iced tea. "James and I have been talking. You think y'all would be interested in running our dress shop?"

"Dress shop? You bought a dress shop?" screamed Rita.

"No, but we're thinking about opening one, something for all women, young and old, rich and poor. You know, things like uniforms, casual wear, Sunday dress-up clothes, and a separate room with high-priced stuff for the uppity Negro women. We found the perfect spot on State Street, on a corner, a block from the Plaza. The hardware store there shut down a few months ago. The building is in good shape and big enough for a dress shop. Even got an upstairs room for the fine stuff."

"But we've never run a business. I'd be lost," said Rita.

"I know, but you know clothes, especially women's clothes, right? Not many places where colored women can find good, pretty dresses that they can afford. We're thinking big. Who knows, maybe a few shops one day. Hayes Women's Wear. How does that sound?"

"You're going to put our name on it?" Carmen screamed with excitement.

"Why not? You'll be running it and owning some of it. Won't be long before every colored woman in Chicago will be shopping there, some white ones too."

The building stood on the corner of 35th and State Street, one of the busiest intersections in the district. It didn't take much to renovate it, and with all the work done by Black tradesmen. James and Hattie used some of their savings for the renovations and got a small bank loan for working capital. Six months later, the Hayes sisters tendered their resignations at Hart, and on November 1, 1952, Hayes Women's Wear opened, just in time for the holiday season. U.S. Congressman William Levi Dawson, a friend and business associate of James, cut the ribbon. Antoinette and Rita worked the floor in sales, while Hattie and Carmen worked the cash registers.

While the sisters in Chicago were starting a new life, they had no contact with their oldest sister in Gavinville. They hadn't spoken to Gladys about what happened that night at the Oasis Lounge. All they heard was that Gladys had gotten into an argument with Frankie Lee Garrett and Willie stepped in the middle of it, killed Frankie, and went to prison. Willie served two years at Angola State Penitentiary on a manslaughter charge. When he returned to Gavinville on April 5, 1953, the first and only person he wanted to see was Gladys. He surprised her with a knock on Mary's door just after sunrise the next day.

"Hey beautiful."

"Willie? I heard you'd be coming home soon."

"Yeah, I'm back. Going to be pretty hard finding work, but my chances of surviving are much better here than at Angola. The place was hell."

"Well you look pretty fit and healthy."

"Not by the food they fed us. Nothing but slop, every meal. I'm just glad to be back home. Would have been a lot longer time if Frankie was white."

"Why'd you come here, Willie, and so early in the morning?" Gladys clearly knew the answer to that question but was subtly hinting that she didn't want to have anything to do with him.

"Thought we could get together sometime. You know, catch up on things, maybe check out a movie or just go down to the park and talk."

"I'm done talking, Willie. I've moved on."

"I know you're not married. Seeing anybody?"

"That's not your business, but I darn sure don't want to see you. Like I said, I've moved on."

"Look, Gladys, I'm not saying that you owe me anything. I'm not here to get anything from you but friendship, just some friendly conversation and maybe have a little fun. You know, like old times."

"Why me? Those old women you used to hang out with got too old for you?"

"Hey, I'm sorry about that night at the Oasis. That's behind both of us. I've done the time, now I'm looking to the future. And I'd like to have you in it. I knew that you had been seeing Frankie off and on, and I hate to say it, but he got what he deserved. I never would have played you that way."

"Now if that ain't a pile of bullshit, I've never seen one. You were nothing but a whoremonger, and I'm sure that jail cell hasn't changed you. You're just horny as hell and think I can fix that. But I can't and I won't. I've moved on."

"Now that's the Gladys I miss seeing, stubborn as hell, but I can soften you up. You know it."

"Well, we did have some good times together, but those days are long gone, Willie James Frank. You're part of the past. I'm looking forward, not backward."

"You still dancing at Harry's?"

"No, I gave that up months ago. Trying to make a fresh start with a job waiting tables at a new restaurant on Hwy 90."

"Well good for you. Look, Gladys, all I'm asking for is a little of your time."

"Heard that line before and it turned out to be nothing but trouble."

"Trouble? You just said we had some good times. Bet you haven't had that kind of fun since I left."

"Dream on, Willie, and will you please leave."

"Okay, but I'm coming back tomorrow, and the day after, and the day after that, until you open that door. If I get lucky and close enough I'll give you a hug that you'll want to hold on to forever."

True to his word, Willie went back, at first every morning, with Gladys ignoring his knock, then once or twice a week with the same result. One Saturday morning a month later he stood at the door in the middle of a downpour, and Gladys' heart softened. She opened the door, and by the time Willie left the grass had dried, birds were singing again, and the afternoon sun was starting to fade behind the trees.

Regular dating started slowly. Willie found a job on the fishing boats and eventually moved in with Gladys and Mary, helping with the bills and showering Gladys with flowers on every payday. For the first time in her life, Gladys was in love and told a man that she loved him.

Chapter 5

Hayes Women's Wear quickly grew. In the spring of 1954, they opened a smaller store on South Park Boulevard that catered strictly to upper-class colored women. The sisters' financial success enabled them to move out of the Grangers' place and buy a home of their own in Hyde Park. They bought a car, joined social clubs, and generously supported civic organizations. After the move, they saw little of the Grangers. Harry's disappointment about their moving out was resolved when they offered to buy an interest in the boarding house and convert it into a hotel. It was the first of many investments the sisters would make, all of which were successful.

By 1955, the Hayes sisters had become a fixture on the Chicago business and social scene. They were "the sisters from Louisiana," who were not only attractive and fashionable but smart. They were the standard for hairstyle and dress wear among women, never missing a social event where the colored elite of Chicago would be present. It was at one of those events that Carmen got her first lesson about Chicago politics. Dr. Elisha Stevens was one of the few colored Chicagoans who had "old money," which he inherited from his grandparents and father. He was also Chicago's oldest practicing and most successful colored physician. He had invited a large group of the city's Negro elite to his home to help celebrate his forty years in practice.

The second oldest of the Hayes women, Carmen was the most talkative and socially outgoing, using her keen business acumen and sociable demeanor to build key relationships with people who could help them to grow and sustain the business. Although she wasn't the tallest of the Hayes women, she seemed to stand an inch or two above the rest. As a single woman in her mid-thirties, her stylish, imposing appearance bordered on seduction, especially in a room filled with well-dressed married men.

"Welcome, ma'am. Can I take your coat?" asked the short, elderly woman who greeted Carmen at the door of Stevens's spacious three-story mansion.

"Well, you most certainly can. I can't wait to get out of this thing. It's pretty and all and keeps the freezing air out, but it gets mighty uncomfortable after a while," said Carmen, taking her coat off and shaking off the snow that had been falling lightly all day. "Thank you, ma'am. And you are?"

"I'm Andrea, Mr. Stevens's maid, one of them at least. The party is just down the hall. Just follow the music."

"Thank you again. Now, Ms. Andrea, your face doesn't show it, but I'd bet that coat of mine, that by the look of those silver streaks in that pretty hairdo of yours, you are a lot older than me. My mama and daddy always taught me to show respect. I know you're just doing your job, but you've got no business calling me ma'am. What's your last name?"

"Cooper. Andrea Cooper."

"Well, good evening, Mrs. Cooper. It is Mrs., right? I'm Carmen. Carmen Hayes. Call me Carmen."

"Oh, yes, yes. I've been married too long to remember, now. My husband Anthony died years ago, though, when our kids were young. Got three grown children and six grandchildren. Been working for Dr. Stevens for thirty-five years. Started when I was about your age from the looks of you."

Carmen started walking toward the room where music was playing, but, with a nod, gestured Andrea to walk with her. "My sisters and I own Hayes Women's Wear down on State Steet. You ever shop there?"

"Oh, no. I can't afford new dresses," said Andrea, shaking her head. "Dr. Stevens is a good man and pays well, but the rent takes up half my pay. Not enough left over to be shopping for clothes. Besides, since I started wearing these uniforms, ain't got too much use for dresses and blouses except on Sunday."

"Well, a pretty lady like you deserves to have a new dress every now and then, even if it's just to wear to church. I tell you what. You come on down to our State Street store anytime and ask for me. I'll make you a deal that you can't turn down. Here's my card. If you come, just ask for Carmen. I'm there every Saturday all day if you can't stop by during the week."

"Well, that's mighty nice of you, Carmen. I just might do that," said Mrs. Cooper, smiling.

"Now, I'm going to go inside and eat the good doctor's good food and drink his good wine. But I'll be expecting to see you soon," Carmen said cheerfully, as she began to mingle—hugging or shaking hands with everyone she encountered. She was the only Hayes sister to attend the gathering and was on a business mission as much as she was there to socialize. A year ago, the sisters had purchased a large plot of land on the east side of Chicago and were planning to break ground on the construction of a new store . . . the first that would cater exclusively to men. She knew that every wealthy colored man in Chicago, and a lot of middle-class men whom Stevens had cared for or mentored, would be at the party.

"Well, well, well! Royalty has finally arrived," said Dr. Stevens in greeting Carmen with a hug. "So happy you could make it. Where is the rest of the court?"

"Good evening, Doc. Thanks so much for the invitation. You know I wouldn't miss the party of the year. The others couldn't make it. You know, lots of stuff going on."

"Well, the smartest and most beautiful of the bunch showed, so I can't be disappointed. Help yourself to drinks and food. Knowing the Hayes sisters might show up, I bought nothing but the best. By the way, how are plans coming with the new store? I hope I can afford the suits."

"We're excited about it, Doc. You know it's how we got our start here, making suits for Hart. We've got a nice line shaping up through a few distributors, but we'll have a tailoring service for men who want the personal touch. It's coming along nicely. Should be cutting the ribbon by early December. We plan to give Hart a run for his money."

"I hope whoever is doing the tailoring has enough cloth and thread. This pot belly of mine seems to grow by the hour," said Stevens, laughing while holding his stomach.

"Doc, I'm going to mingle a bit, but if you can spare a few minutes, I do want to chat with you in private before the party is over."

"Most certainly. You go right ahead. Enjoy yourself."

"By the way," said Carmen, "that lady who opened the door and took my coat sure was pleasant."

"You must be referring to Andrea. She is sweet, isn't she? Been around for nearly as long as I've been practicing. But don't let her demeanor fool you. She can be mean and bossy at times . . . and outspoken, too, just like someone else I know," said Stevens, giving Carmen a wink. "Have some fun. The party doesn't end until I start yawning."

Carmen smiled and turned to mingle with a few guests as she worked her way to the bar. As pleasant as Mrs. Cooper was, something that she said lingered in Carmen's head. Knowing Stevens, he pays his workers more than a decent wage, but Mrs. Cooper said that half of it was going toward rent. Here was a widow working for one of the wealthiest Negro men in the city and couldn't afford to buy a new dress. Probably barely afforded to keep the utilities turned on. Carmen thought how difficult it must be for a colored woman who didn't work for a Negro doctor, women doing menial work that barely allowed them to put food on the table. Something was terribly wrong with the city where she and her sisters were living. As the evening grew late, she got Stevens' attention and asked if she could have a few minutes with him. Stevens suggested that they step onto a wooden deck and sit at a small table overlooking the patio.

"Looks like business is doing well," said Stevens. "The Hayes sisters have taken this city by storm. Everybody's talking about it."

"Yeah, we've really been blessed. Great locations. And, of course, we owe everything to James and Hattie for giving us a start."

"Well, you've really found a niche, but you're not just making money. You're helping a lot of women in this community, not to mention the jobs you've created."

"Speaking of which, Doc, I know you are doing the right thing and are paying your housekeepers well, but when I suggested to Mrs.

Cooper that she come by the store to buy a dress, she said that half of her pay goes toward paying the rent. She can't even afford to buy a dress, and our State Street clothes are priced for working-class women. Are things really that bad in this city? Are colored people that bad off or are white people just that greedy? Are they charging rent so high that Negroes can barely afford to live in those shacks? She's a widow with one income, and her children are grown. But what about families with young mouths to feed and have to buy clothes to put on their backs. How are colored people surviving in this town?"

"To put it bluntly," said Stevens, "barely. Look, I was born in this city, but unlike many of those folks inside who are standing around having a good time, I'm an exception. I was fortunate to inherit the blessings of my grandfather and daddy. They worked hard and with prayers and a lot of luck managed to give me a good upbringing and a good enough education to make something of myself. And notwithstanding your talent and hard work, you're one of the lucky ones, too. But most Negroes in this city aren't so lucky. They're one step from being either dead or homeless. That's the cold fact. And it's not because they want to be. It's because the system is designed to make them poor."

"What do you mean, Doc?"

"What I mean is that the white politicians of this city do whatever they can to keep the poor that way. The bosses, the people with real money, run this city. They put the politicians in office for only one reason: to make the rich richer and the poor poorer. The only way to turn that around is to change the system, and the only way to do that is to kick the bums out of office. But, talking to Negroes in Chicago about registering to vote and getting politically active is like telling a brick wall to move itself. Trust me, I've tried it."

"I don't quite know what to do, Doc, but I feel like I have to do something," said Carmen. "What Mrs. Cooper said was a real eye-opener, and what you just said opened my eyes wider. I had no idea that things were so bad for poor people here."

"Whatever you do, Carmen, just remember this . . . that when you go against the grain around here and start encouraging Negroes to stand up for their rights, it gets the bosses' attention. And they play hardball by *their* rules, not yours or mine."

"Point well taken, Doc. I'll keep that in mind."

"And don't you worry about Andrea. She's like a sister to me . . . and sister does she act like it at times. But she's family. Now if it's alright with you, I say we get back in there and do some celebrating," said Stevens, rising from his chair to return to the party. Carmen rose also, thinking to herself, that while she knew it would take some time to decide what she'll do with her new awareness of the harsh realities of being a colored resident of Chicago, the seed had been planted. She knew that at some point she and her sisters would have to do *something* to make life better for the poor and disadvantaged residents of the city.

Two weeks later, while standing at a counter, combing through catalogs, Carmen felt the presence of someone standing behind her. She turned around to find Mrs. Cooper smiling.

"Well, Mrs. Cooper, what a pleasant surprise. I was hoping you'd stop by one day."

"I don't mean to disturb you. Looks like you're busy. I just stopped to say hello, but if you're busy, I'll just browse around," Mrs. Cooper said in a soft, apologetic tone. The seventy-year-old woman couldn't have stood more than five-feet tall and looked even shorter standing beside Carmen. "Doubt that I can afford anything here, but it'll be fun to look around. Been a long time since I smelled the perfume in a department store. I used to go shopping just to get a sample of sweet stuff, knowing darn well I wouldn't buy any."

"Well, I didn't ask you to come here just to browse and sample perfume. I do want you to browse though, but don't you even think about buying. Now, what I want you to do is take as much time as you want and look around, then pick out two fancy dresses that you really like, something that makes you feel like a queen when you look in the mirror. And bring those dresses to me. And if you want a bottle of perfume, I'm fine with that too. That'll be my gift."

"Oh no, no, I can't let you do that. You're in business to make money. I'll just look around for a while. That's very generous of you, but I didn't come to buy anything. I just wanted to stop by and say hello. But if you're busy, you go on with your work. I'll just look around."

"Now, Mrs. Cooper, when we talked the other night at Doc's place, you seemed like a real nice lady. But Doc warned me that you can be a little tough. But I can be tough too. And in this store, I'm the boss! The Lord has blessed me and now I want to be a blessing to you. I don't want any fuss about it. And don't even pay attention to the price tags. Those dresses are so marked up that sometimes I'm embarrassed to ring them up at the cash register. You go on out there and pick those dresses out and bring them to me to box up. And when you're done, we're going to go across the street to the diner and get ourselves a sundae with all the toppings and sit and talk some more. You go on now. I'll be right here when you're done."

"That's so nice of you. One way or another, though, I'll figure out a way to repay you."

"Fair enough. But until then, just enjoy the shopping."

An hour later, Mrs. Cooper returned with two dresses.

"My, my, these are beautiful," said Carmen, laying the dresses out on the counter. "I must say, Mrs. Cooper, you've got good taste. These are nice. Yes ma'am, they sure are, and I bet they look great on you. Okay, as soon as I box these up and grab my coat, we'll go get a little ice cream."

"Like I said, one day I'll find a way to pay you."

"Well, I hope that day never comes," said Carmen laughing. "The Lord says give without ever expecting to receive. That's what giving is all about." Carmen boxed up the dresses and they walked across the street to the diner.

"There are two seats right there. How about we sit? You know, it wasn't that long ago when colored people couldn't walk in here and sit at the counter. They finally started letting us sit when they counted the number of people walking in and out of our store one day. You tell me money doesn't change things." Both ladies laughed. After ordering the sundaes, Carmen got down to the real purpose of her wanting to chat. "Mrs. Cooper, I don't mean to pry, but where exactly do you live?" asked Carmen, swallowing a spoonful of ice cream.

"Down on Clark Street, not far from here actually. It's not a bad place, better than I see a lot a folks living in. It's just me and Fifi, a stray cat that followed me home one day. So, one bedroom is enough. I moved there after Anthony passed and the kids grew up and married. They tried talking me into moving in with them, but I like being alone and having my own place. On weekdays, I take the L not far from where I live, then hop a bus over to Doc Stevens. I catch a ride to church on Sundays." Mrs. Cooper paused to eat a few spoonfuls of ice cream. "This ice cream sure is delicious. Don't think I've tasted any this good."

"Mrs. Cooper, did I hear you say that the rent where you live is nearly half of what Doc pays you?"

"Yes, but like I said, Elisha takes good care of me. I probably make twice as much as I would working for white people. It's a lot until I start paying the bills, the rent mostly. I get by, though. I'm not complaining. Like I said, I do better than a lot of coloreds around here."

"Have you thought about shopping for something cheaper, where the rent isn't so high?"

"I did, but to be honest, there ain't much else out there for an old woman like me. I only need a little space. The neighborhood is safe and stores are right down the street. But it's the same everywhere you go. Landlords around here are known for gouging colored people, knowing that laws make it impossible for most Negroes to live anywhere but in slums and ghettos. White people own all the decent rent property, so if you don't want to live in the projects there ain't much else you can do but pay what they charge. But I don't complain. The Lord provides. His grace is more than sufficient."

"Amen to that. He sure has been good to my sisters and me," said Carmen, reaching for more dessert. "Been better to me than I've been to myself, that's for sure." Carmen paused. "Doc Stevens told me about the corrupt politics in this city and how voiceless colored people are. I come from a real small town in Louisiana where everybody knows everybody. Things down there are bad, but not nearly as bad as what I heard Doc say, maybe because Gavinville is so much smaller. They've got one housing project, but not the high-rise ghettos I see around here. Thank God you're not living in one of those."

"It's a luxury to not be living in Cabrini-Green," said Mrs. Cooper. "There's probably ten thousand Negroes in there, stacked on top of each other. Most of them probably don't have a job and struggle to put food on the table. There's nothing there but robbing, killing, and prostitution.

Not a safe place for someone my age. I don't mind paying for a little safety and peace of mind."

"And like you said, the landlords make it a premium just to stay out of there."

"That's right," said Mrs. Cooper. "Not only that. The city got laws that don't even allow coloreds to live around white people. So, even Negroes who got decent jobs and can afford to buy a house got no place to go but around other Negroes in rundown neighborhoods. They corral all colored people into a hog pen to fight over a few crumbs they throw on the ground. And that's exactly what Negroes do, fight and kill each other."

"My Lord!" said Carmen, shaking her head. "Well, thank God, you're safe." Carmen paused again. "Mrs. Cooper, if there is ever anything I can do for you, if you ever have a need, anything, you know where to find me. Don't think twice. You just let me know."

"So nice of you to offer, but I'll be okay. My kids look in on me often and Elisha has been a godsend. He'll never let you know, but he makes sure I'm not hurting or wanting for anything. One worry I don't have is paying for a doctor when I need one," said Mrs. Cooper, laughing.

Carmen glanced at her wristwatch. "Oh my, time has really slipped up on me. I hate to end our talk, but I've got to get over to the store for a meeting. It's so nice to have gotten to know you. I'd like for us to stay in touch. I know you can cook, and I love to eat. Maybe you can repay me with a homecooked supper one day. Better than that . . . I want to be in your church one Sunday and see those men's head turn when you're wearing one of those fancy new dresses." Both ladies laughed.

"You just say when," said Mrs. Cooper, smiling.

"That I will. Promise!" Carmen said, rising to walk toward the register. "You go ahead and finish that sundae. Can I call you at Doc Stevens' place?"

"Sure, anytime."

As promised, Carmen stayed in touch with Mrs. Cooper. In the months that followed, they met periodically for chats and ice cream. To Mrs. Cooper, Carmen was a blessing, but what she didn't know was that through their relationship Carmen grew increasingly more aware of and sensitive to the plight of the city's poor and elderly residents. Mrs. Cooper sparked a quiet fire inside Carmen, and it wouldn't be long before it started to blaze.

In August 1955, news of the death of Emmett Till shook Chicago and the nation like a massive earthquake. Till, a fourteen-year-old Negro boy from Chicago, was murdered in Drew, Mississippi, supposedly for flirting with a white woman. Mamie Till, the boy's mother, was a regular customer at the dress shop, so the sisters took the incident personal. They were among the tens of thousands who lined up outside of Bronzeville's Roberts Temple Church of God in Christ to view the boy's mutilated body, lying in a glass-covered coffin. In a way, the lynching of Till reminded them that, although they had left the South, they were still a part of it and were victims of the same vicious hatred and racism that killed Till. Chicago was north, but in many ways not different from how colored people were looked at and treated in Gavinville. Most Negroes in Chicago worked as laborers and lived in run-down housing that was in much worse condition than Harry's place was the day the sisters moved in. Colored workers kept the steel factories going, but were barely making ends meet, living the blues as they listened to it, in cramped, overcrowded slums and high-rise housing projects.

To the sisters, the murder of Till was also a reminder that dollars were green but their skin was still brown, and no money or success would ever change that. Hattie's mansion on the hill, and their new cars, fancy clothes, and swank home in Hyde Park didn't change the brown color of their skin. They saw Mamie Till in the face of every woman who walked into their store, and they felt their pain and suffering, even that of the educated, bourgeoisie women who were just as much the victims of white hate. Chatting at dinner one evening, Carmen suggested that they leave Chicago for a while.

"I think it's time for us to go back home and see Mama and Daddy. It's been five years."

"Gavinville? For how long?" Rita asked.

"I don't know, a week maybe."

"We can't leave now, Carmen. We've got to get ready for the fall and winter. Those are our busiest seasons," said Antoinette.

"I'm not thinking about money and business right now. I need to go home and hug my mama and daddy."

"I agree with Antoinette. We should wait until after New Year," Rita said.

"Wait for what, to make more money and show off our fancy hairdos and clothes, while poor colored women we sell to starve and freeze to death in run-down shacks without heat and electricity? Don't y'all see what we're in the middle of here. We're in hell and don't know it because we don't feel the fire. But sisters the fire is raging all around us. You think that white people in Chicago don't look down on us because we're Negroes with money? And you think the poor colored women who buy our clothes don't think we're uppity and snobby?"

"Carmen, we're all feeling Ms. Mamie's pain. But do you honestly think that leaving here for a week is going to make things better?" said Rita.

"No, but I'm tired of standing by, watching people starve and suffer while we're making bank deposits and living like we're white, as if we're not Negroes to white folks. We're just as colored to them as Emmett and all the other Negroes they're beating, lynching, and keeping in slums with the laws they make. It's not just about us going back home. It's about us pretending that we ain't colored anymore and doing nothing to help the poor people who buy from us, who barely got a place to rest their bodies at the end of a hard day's work. I just need to get away from all this for a while and go home. I think it'll do us some good."

"Well, why don't you make the trip alone? Antoinette and I can stay and handle business."

"We all need to get out of this city for a while and get back to our roots. Besides, Mama and Daddy haven't seen us in years, much too long after all they did for us. And you know that Mama won't even think about leaving those so-called God's children who knock on her door for prayer and healing. We've got to go. That business won't fall apart just because we're not there. Hattie can look after things while we're gone."

Carmen prevailed, and on Labor Day of 1955, she, Rita, and Antoinette went back home for the first time in five years. Time had stood still in Gavinville. Except for the Grangers, the same families lived in Dixie Manor. They just got larger. The colored school at the edge of the housing project had grown to include all twelve grades. Mount Calvary had bought an old school bus to pick up the children at Dixie Manor. No new industry had moved into town. Most of the colored women were still doing domestic work, cooking in restaurants, or working in the garment factory. Most men still worked in the fishing industry—on the boats or at the icehouse—or did odd jobs like gardening and yard maintenance for white families. Dennis Jackson, an Army veteran, had become the first Black postal worker, delivering mail in the colored sections.

Ella and Jesse Hayes hadn't aged a bit. In fact, without a close look, one would think that they looked younger. Jesse was just as fit as the younger men at the icehouse. Ella, even with a slight limp, still carried the regal aura that was the envy of most women in town, colored and white. Her popularity as a faith healer had extended far beyond Gavinville. People traveled from as far as Texas, Arkansas, and Mississippi to have her lay hands on their broken or sick bodies. White people stood in the quadrangle of Dixie Manor from sunup to sundown, spawning neighborhood businesses like a convenience store, a snowball stand, vegetable truck, and front-yard kitchens selling fried fish and barbecue.

Ella had officially become one of the town's most influential citizens without leaving her home and while living among Gavinville's poorest residents. She and Jesse talked about moving out of Dixie Manor, but Ella felt strongly that it was only right to stay. "These are God's children," she told a local newspaper reporter who interviewed her for a feature story. "I have to stay with God's children. His power won't work anywhere else. They're sicker than any devil I heal from other parts of town because they've suffered longer. But God doesn't sleep. Dixie Manor is his temple. I'm just a vessel."

The Hayes sisters arrived late at night. Ella and Jesse were asleep.

"Who on God's earth can be knocking this time of night?" Jesse asked, stepping out of bed to get dressed. "Must be mighty sick," he mumbled. "Souffie, get up girl. Hurry!" Jesse shouted. "We got three angels at the door!"

Ella put her robe on and slowly made her way down the hallway to the front door. "My Lord, what has gotten into that man?"

"Well, praise Jesus!" Ella thought her heart would burst with joy at seeing her daughters standing at the door. "My babies have come home. My Lord, I don't believe what my eyes are seeing," she screamed, waving her hands to the sky before flinging her arms around the girls.

They all embraced and kissed. There were no words for the moment.

"Jesse, go wake up Thelma. Tell her who's here."

"Thelma ain't here Souffie. She didn't come home this evening. Probably sleeping at Terrell's."

"Terrell? Who's Terrell?" Carmen asked.

"Child, your little sister's in love. Some guy she met at the Oasis. They've been dating for six months or so. Haven't seen much of him, but he seems like a nice fellow—a dentist who moved here from Patterson a while back. Seems to be doing well for himself."

"Thelma? In love? I can't wait to hear more," Antoinette said. As they sat for hours talking about Chicago and reminiscing about the girls' childhood days, the question of Gladys hung like an albatross. Jesse and Ella waited until it was asked.

"How's Gladys, Mama?" Rita asked.

"Well, I wrote y'all about the incident with Willie. Gladys hasn't said much more to us than what we read in the newspaper. I think Willie got out of jail a while back. Last I heard she was still living with Mary but she's not dancing at Harry's anymore. I saw her three or four weeks ago at the beauty shop, but we didn't talk much. You know Gladys. She keeps things to herself. She did ask about y'all. How long you planning to stay?"

"A week, Mama," said Antoinette. "Then, we'll have to get back to start planning for the holiday season. That's our busiest time of year."

Jesse and Ella knew that their daughters had left Hart, opened a clothing store, and bought a home, but had no idea how wealthy they had become. The sisters had sent money to their parents every month, but they never talked about their wealth in the letters they exchanged over the years. "We heard about the store y'all opened," said Jesse. "That enough to pay the mortgage? I hear the cost of living is pretty high up there."

"Yes, sir, more than enough," said Antoinette, chuckling. "We're doing fine. Much better than we expected."

"We're still waiting for you to come to Chicago," said Carmen. "The invitation still stands."

"Well, I might if somebody will give me a grandchild to go see," said Ella laughing. "But seriously, I can't leave God's children to go off gallivanting around some big city like Chicago," said Ella. "They need me right where I am, every day of the week. So, how's Margaret and Harry? You see much of them?"

"I'd say they need you too much," said Jesse without looking at Ella. "I think all the sick people in Louisiana are right here in Gavinville. Even grandbabies wouldn't pull that woman away from this place."

"Margaret and Harry are doing okay," said Rita. "Harry's got the place fixed up real nice. They added rooms. It's a hotel now, and they say business is good and steady. Margaret is still cooking at the Country Club, but Harry works full-time at the hotel."

"I'll be darn. Sounds like Chicago turned out to be a good move," Jesse responded. "Give them our regards the next time y'all see them.

We really appreciate them for taking y'all in and giving you a start." Jesse paused. "Sweet darlings, as much as I love seeing you, somebody around here got to make a little money to pay the rent. I'm going to have to leave you. Plenty boats going out early in the morning. I need to get a little shut-eye."

"Good night, Daddy," the daughters said in unison. Jesse hugged each of his daughters before leaving to go to bed.

"How about we go visit some of the neighbors when y'all wake up," said Ella. "I'm sure they'll be excited to see you. Then we can go downtown. Not much new, but window shopping could be fun. Guess we should get some rest. You've had a long day."

After settling in for some much-needed sleep, Antoinette and Rita awoke to Carmen's nudge around mid-morning. Carmen had been awakened by the smell of her Mama's cooking an hour before, lying in bed thinking about Hattie, Gladys, and Thelma, and wondering how the business was doing. She missed Gladys and wanted so badly to see her. They'd have to go to Mary's, but first there would be a day with Mama.

"I didn't want to wake y'all, but I was beginning to wonder if you'd sleep all day. Felt good didn't it, being in your little beds again?" said Ella, stirring a pot on the stove. "As soon as this stew is done we'll make our rounds through the neighborhood. Wouldn't surprise me if a few folks show up for some prayer, but I'm sure the Lord won't mind if I put them off until tomorrow. Today, it's just me and my babies."

So they made the rounds, knocking on nearly every door at Dixie Manor, surprising everybody—The Singleton, Carter, Brown, William, and Guillory families who lived in duplexes in the quadrangle, even the families who lived in the two-stories close to Railroad Street. The sisters didn't know them as well, but everyone knew and admired their mama.

Many of them had gone to work, but somebody was always home to answer the door. Lucy Daniels had moved to Dixie Manor, and Ella especially wanted to show her the fine women that her daughters had become.

"Ella, dat you?" Lucy asked, standing at the front screen door.

"Afternoon, Lucy."

"What brings you here dis time of day?"

"Wanted you to see my babies. They're visiting from Chicago. Just going around saying hello to the neighbors."

"Hey, Ms. Lucy," the sisters said, knowing how much Lucy Daniels had spoken meanly about Ella and them over the years.

"How've you been, Lucy?"

"Oh, I'm fine. Nothin to worry about."

"I heard you had to stop working because of kidney problems. You need to come see me. Jesus can heal that you know."

"The medication seems to be helpin."

"Well, you know like I do that ain't no doctor like the Lord."

"I appreciate it, Ella. I'll think about it. Girls, good to see y'all."

Ella and her girls had to hurry to catch the stores on Front Street before they closed, but they managed to get a little shopping done, turning every head they passed on the sidewalk. Thelma had gotten the news of their arrival and tracked them down at Big John's Barbecue Shack just in time for dinner.

"Sis, tell us about that tall, handsome dentist you're dating. When are we going to meet him?" Rita asked.

"Terrell? Girl, I admit. I love that man. Never thought I'd be saying that after Frankie Lee Garrett strung me out and started cheating. Now, he hasn't popped the question yet, but I know he will," said Thelma smiling. "And y'all are going to have to come back to be my bridesmaids, Hattie, too. I want a big wedding with lots of flowers."

"You seen Gladys lately?" Antoinette asked. "How's she doing?"

"We talk from time to time, but she doesn't like to talk about herself. She seems to be okay though. Mama, it sure would be nice if we could all get together."

"Child, you know your daddy. He's two mules in one."

"We're going to Mary's tomorrow," Rita said excitedly. "Mama, Thelma, let's say we make it a girls thing and surprise her. Be nice for all of us to be together again."

"The last time that happened turned out to be a disaster," Carmen said.

"Yeah, but that was years ago. Daddy might not have changed, but she's still my big sister, and I'm sure she's missing us just as much."

"Whatever you do, don't tell your daddy. He'll have a fit if he knew I went to see Gladys."

The next day, Ella and her daughters surprised Gladys with a visit. It was mid-day, and the knock on the door woke Gladys up.

"Oh my God!" Gladys screamed, seeing her mama and sisters standing on Mary's front porch. "Is this about Daddy? My God, oh no, what happened?"

Before Gladys could utter another word, she was in the arms of Carmen, Rita, and Antoinette, who were shedding tears of joy for seeing their big sister for the first time in five years. So much time gone by. So many moments and memories lost.

"Your daddy's fine, Gladys. Your sisters just couldn't take another day in Chicago without seeing us."

"Look at y'all. Looking pretty as ever. And Mama and Thelma. What a pleasant surprise."

Antoinette, Rita, and Carmen talked about Hattie and James, the wedding, and life in Chicago. There was much to catch up on, and they all sensed the shortness of time before they'd be separated again. They couldn't possibly fill the gulf that time had built between them in so short a visit. Gladys' past hung in the air.

Antoinette quickly brought it down to the ground. "Sis, what happened?"

"I really don't want to talk about it. I just want to put it all behind me and move on." Gladys paused to think how she might quickly change the subject of the conversation. "So Thelma, I don't see much of you these days. Tell me about this Terrell. Have y'all set a date?"

"Not yet, Sis, but you've got to promise me that you'll be there . . . maid of honor."

I wouldn't miss it, but I don't want to come anywhere near that bouquet," said Gladys, drawing laughter from her sisters. She paused before changing the topic. "I heard that y'all are now successful businesswomen. Imagine that. Gavinville women in business in Chicago."

"And what about you, Sis? What are you doing with yourself these days?" asked Carmen.

"Well, I'm not dancing anymore. Guess I got too old for the old men. I took a job waiting tables at Sonny's Grill. And I can't believe I'm saying this but I got a steady man."

"What? Steady? Who's the lucky fellow?" Rita asked.

"Like I said, I can't believe I'm saying it . . .Willie Frank."

"Willie Frank?" Carmen asked with a tone that sounded more like a scream.

"Yeah, Willie. When he got out of jail we just started hanging out again and one thing led to another."

"Well, I'll be. That man always was crazy about you. Must be serious if it's steady," said Antoinette.

"I don't know. We'll see how it goes. Mama, how's Daddy?"

"Nothing new with that man, although I kind of wish he'd do more fishing and hunting and stay out of my business."

"So what's going on in Chicago other than y'all making a lot of money?"

"Hattie sends her regards. She's picked up a few pounds. Married life must be good," said Antoinette.

"Yeah. I hear that husband of hers is quite a catch. Can't wait to meet him."

"Girl, you've got to come and shop. And don't worry about money. We've got more than we can spend. And bring Willie."

"Thanks, Sis. Maybe one day. Be nice to see what a big city looks like, but not in the winter. I hear it gets pretty cold up there."

"We best be going, Mama" said Carmen, turning to look at Ella. "I know you want to make another round in the project to catch the folks who've gotten home from work. Daddy's taking the day off tomorrow to take us out on a boat. I haven't seen a live fish in six years. Should be fun."

"Well, if you get lucky, don't forget your big sister. Tell Daddy I said hello."

Everyone embraced with hugs, saying good-bye, relishing the moment of being in each other's arms with the sadness of knowing that time and distance might pull them even farther apart.

After a week in Gavinville, the sisters were homesick for the fast-paced life of Chicago and were anxious to get back to their stores. Hattie had managed the business while they were gone, but she, too, was anxious to get back to her work at the insurance company. They arrived on a Friday afternoon in much more pleasant weather than they experienced the first day they arrived in Chicago over five years ago.

"Let's say we take Hattie and James out to the Blue Note tonight and catch up, that's if they're up to it. We can fill them in on how everyone's doing back home," said Carmen. "Can't wait to tell them about Thelma and Terrell."

The Oscar Peterson Trio was warming up the crowd and Miles Davis would soon follow. Seated at the table always reserved for James and his guests, they sat sipping cocktails, talking about Gavinville, family, and business.

"Guess who's getting married?" said Antoinette.

"Oh no. Don't tell me that my little sister is in love."

"Terrell, a dentist, but we didn't get to meet him. He hasn't really proposed but it's a forgone conclusion as far as Thelma is concerned. Just a matter of when. We promised that we'll all go to the wedding, you two included."

"Well, it better be soon because I won't be up for travelling in a few months. Did you see Gladys?"

"We did, all of us, except Daddy at least," said Carmen. "She seems to be holding up well, but still won't say much about the incident. She's not working at Harry's anymore, and she and Willie are dating again."

"Willie?"

"Yeah, I had the same reaction, but who are we to question love."

Hattie was grinning with excitement. "I suppose this is as good a time as any to tell everyone. James and I are having the first Hayes boy in the family."

"What! You're pregnant?" Carmen screamed.

"But that's only half of it. Twins," said James. "James Jr. and Jesse. We already named them."

"Boys? Suppose they're girls," said Antoinette.

"Boys, I'm telling you. I can feel it. Byrd men," said James excitedly.

"The doctor says they'll be spring babies. I wish we had known before you left for Gavinville. We kinda knew but we hadn't gotten word from the doctor. I called Mama and Daddy this morning. They were so excited. I'm sure the whole town knows by now. They said the children are going to call them Pops and Granny. I sure hope James is right. Lord knows we've got enough women in this family."

"So happy for both of you," said Rita, raising her cocktail. "In fact, I'd like to make a toast to James Jr. and Jesse Byrd, the future of Chicago."

The following day, the sisters went to work and settled back into the business of running a business. As usual, the holiday season got busy in early November. By December 1st they had already surpassed last year's sales.

Four months after the lynching of Emmett Till, news of an incident in the South once again made headline news. Rosa Parks, a seamstress in Montgomery, Alabama, had been arrested for refusing to give up her seat on a bus to a white man, sparking a boycott of the buses by colored residents. Reverend Martin Luther King Jr. a young Baptist minister, was leading the boycott.

White citizens of Chicago paid little if any attention to the boycott. But for the colored community, the boycott was a lightning bolt. For decades, Chicago had been practicing Jim Crow through racial housing laws that restricted colored people from buying property in predominantly white neighborhoods and kept them confined to overcrowded slums of public housing and over-priced rental properties owned by whites. The laws went unchallenged. This "closed society," as King would call it years later when he brought his fight against racial discrimination to cities of the North, was the product of the same vicious hatred that colored residents of Montgomery had decided it was time to stop.

Once again, Carmen decided it was time that the sisters did something, but not by leaving town to go visit their parents. Sipping coffee at the café where they sat every morning on their way to the stores, Carmen suggested that they get more involved politically.

"You know, I hear that Rosa Parks is a seamstress, no different from where we started and where the colored women who do our tailoring are today. But she decided that it was time to stand up to the white man's hate. I'm proud of what she did, and I think we should do the same."

"You mean start a boycott?" Antoinette asked, stirring her coffee.

"No, I mean we stop pretending we're all that and start doing something to help those who don't have the money to shield themselves from the hatred and injustice in this city. They can't buy their way out of it, and neither can we if we be honest with ourselves. Whites in Chicago don't look at us any different or treat us any different than they do the folks living in Bronzeville. In fact, many of them are jealous that we have it and they don't, and they despise us for it."

"Don't forget that we're dependent upon those white people to sell us the supplies and inventory and give us the mortgages we need," said Rita.

"Right," Carmen said, holding her cup half-way to take a sip, "which means we're just as much a slave to them as those women we give jobs to are to us. But Rosa Parks and women like her down South, women who don't have nearly the wealth that we have, are standing up for equal rights, while we're sitting down counting money the white man lets us make."

"What do you have in mind, Ms. Rosa?" Antoinette asked.

"I say we join the NAACP and get active in the work they're doing. Not saying we have to be out front protesting, but we could attend meetings, see what's going on, and lend our support."

"But we've got a business to run," said Rita. "How are we going to find time for all that?"

"I agree," Antoinette chimed in. "We don't have time for politics. We can barely find time now to handle business with all that we've got going on. Politics will be too much of a distraction."

"Right," said Rita. "I'm already over my head with meetings. All we seem to do these days is sit around conference tables. Now you want to pull us into more meetings that will be completely unrelated to our business. I'm all for supporting the NAACP, but I don't have time for meetings on politics."

"It seems unrelated," Carmen said, "but politics has got everything to do with whether we succeed or fail in business. What good will it do us to succeed if we fail to take a stand to help the folks who help us to succeed? Without civil rights, we can't achieve real economic progress, and we darn sure can't protect what little we do manage to get from white folks. Our getting politically active isn't just some extra pastime. It's something we have to do, not just to protect our interests, but to help our people. It's something we should do out of conscience because it's right. We have to make time to do it."

The sisters did just that, tended to business, while taking quiet, small steps into the political arena. They joined the NAACP and donated to local political candidates who advocated better education, jobs, and housing for poor, colored people. Raising their twin boys,

Hattie and James continued to grow investments in real estate and insurance but remained relatively uninvolved in the civil rights struggle. For Carmen, it was just the beginning of a long journey.

Chapter 6

Six months after Carmen's eloquent and passionate plea that the sisters begin to stand up for the civil rights of Chicago's poor, something unexpected happened in Gavinville. On June 1, 1956, Gladys Hayes and Willie Frank married.

Willie proposed in the most dramatic way, going to the restaurant one evening and sitting at the counter to eat a burger and fries. He walked over to the table that Gladys was serving and dropped to one knee, then told everyone there that he had been up all-night thinking about a woman who worked there whom he wanted to marry. He said that he hesitated to come because he was afraid that she wouldn't say yes, but he knew in his heart that there could be no other woman.

Gladys said yes, and on a breezy early summer morning they went to the home of the Justice of the Peace and exchanged wedding vows. Gladys had just turned thirty-seven years old and Willie was three years older. They lived at Mary's for two months before renting a one-bedroom house on Farrel Street. It seemed like another world compared to the life her sisters in Chicago talked about, and to Thelma's dream of moving into the five-bedroom house that Terrell had bought anticipating lots of children. But for once, Gladys was happy and at peace with herself. Music was in the air when it wasn't playing. Her humble home was a castle and she was its queen.

Gladys hoped that her new, settled life would mend the wounds between her and her father. Jesse didn't think much of Willie Frank, a man who had no education and spent time in prison. He saw Willie from time to time packing ice for the boats and avoided being near him. Christmas was approaching, and Ella suggested that they invite Thelma, Gladys, and their men over for Christmas dinner. Jesse could only think about the last holiday that Gladys had spent with them when she angrily stormed out of the front door. But things had changed. Gladys no longer danced at Harry's, had taken a more respectable job, and gotten married.

As much as he despised Willie Frank, Jesse was willing to bury the past. He agreed to extend the invitation. He, too, hoped for reconciliation and a new beginning between him and his oldest daughter. Seeing the two men seated across from each other, Terrell, a successful dentist who would one day marry his baby girl, and Willie, the ex-con who had married his oldest daughter and could do little to lift her out of poverty, Jesse struggled to find words to speak. He sat as if he weren't there or the men and his daughters weren't there. He thought about days when he was paralyzed and lying helplessly on his back, and about the vision and the miracle of his recovery, that moment when he stood on his legs for the first time in three years. He thought about all the years that he and Ella had struggled to make a good life for their children, the sacrifices they had made expecting nothing in return but that his girls would grow up to be decent, strong women and make a good life for themselves.

Looking into Willie's eyes for the first time, Jesse bluntly asked, "Willie, how could you kill a man?"

"Jesse!" Ella shouted.

Jesse's voice rose. "No, I need to know what's in this man's heart!" he said, slamming a fist on the table. "He killed a man, went to prison then married my daughter, without asking for my blessing I might add, and now he's sitting at my dinner table."

"Daddy, we've put all that behind us. Please. First it was me, now it's the man I love? Or is it still me you hate? Don't take it out on Willie. He's done his time and started a new life."

"Let the man answer the question, Gladys."

"Mr. Hayes, I'll admit. I made a big mistake, and I'll pay for it the rest of my life. I was just trying to protect Gladys, that's all. Listen, I love your daughter. I would have done anything for her then, and I'll do anything for her now. I'd do anything to make her happy."

"Let's not forget that there's another man sitting here," interjected Thelma. "And just last night he asked me to marry him, and I accepted."

"What! Congratulations, honey. Terrell, welcome to the family. We're glad to have you. And pay no attention to your father-in-law. He's all bark and no bite."

"Thank you, Mrs. Hayes. I'll do my best to make your baby happy."

"Congratulations, Sis. Now remember what you said, I'm maid of honor. Girl, wait until Chicago hears about this."

"I already told them. Called them last night and said I'll let them know as soon as we set the date. They're all coming down, Hattie and James, too."

"Terrell, I know you are a good man. Now, Hattie's got my two grandsons up there in Chicago. Guess I'll finally get to see them when they come down for the wedding. So, you got to promise me. Don't pack up and take my grandbabies two thousand miles away."

"Grandbabies! Daddy we're not married yet."

"No need to worry, Mr. Hayes. We plan to settle down right here in Gavinville. I hope to build a strong practice here."

"Willie and I already decided. We don't want children. It'll just be the two of us, growing old together, sitting on the porch, rocking the time away."

"Alright, since we've gotten all that behind us, let me say a blessing so we can get on with the business of eating Souffie's good cooking."

Jesse blessed the meal and they ate, reminiscing and laughing about Gladys and Thelma's childhood and high school dating years. Jesse made homemade ice cream and Ella brought out her lemon cake. It was the happiest moment that Gladys had shared with her parents in years. She and her Daddy were daughter and father again. She felt redeemed, as if a cross had been taken off her shoulders, but it wouldn't be long before an even heavier burden would be felt.

Thelma and Terrell were married on Saturday, February 9 1957, eight months after Gladys and Willie secretly tied the knot. The family didn't know much about Terrell Williams, except that he grew up ten miles down the road in Patterson, graduated at the top of his high school class and went on to Stanford, where he obtained his undergraduate degree and graduate degree in dental medicine. He moved to Gavinville to be the town's first colored dentist. Thelma quit her job at the garment factory not long after Terrell's proposal and joined him at the dental office as a receptionist and office manager.

This was not to be a small, quiet ceremony. Thelma wanted it to be the biggest wedding that Gavinville had ever seen. The sisters of Chicago agreed to come down and be bridesmaids and Gladys was maid of honor, all wearing dresses they made just for the occasion. The wedding was held at St. Paul, with every bit of what Thelma dreamt and wanted—plenty guests, flowers, food, and wine. The youngest of the Hayes sisters, Thelma, was closest to her father. Jesse tried to look dignified but cried during the entire ceremony, tears rolling down his cheeks as quickly as he wiped them away.

The reception was held at Mount Calvary's community center, large enough for the crowd that showed up, most of whom didn't attend the wedding but wouldn't miss Gavinville's biggest party. Sitting at several tables reserved for them, the Byrd and Hayes entourage seemed out of place when the records started playing and friends of Thelma and Terrell started dancing. Their reserved demeanor grew even more noticeable when nearly everyone was half-drunk, and they were the only folks not on the dance floor. When the record player spun Fats Domino's "I'm Walking," Thelma went over to James and Hattie, grabbed them by the hands, and pulled them onto to the dance floor. Before long, every seat was empty on every record played.

The evening was long, but there would be little time for talking with old friends and neighbors. Thelma's sisters and their families all left for Chicago early the next morning. Thelma and Terrell promised that they would visit Chicago before their first child.

Toward the end of their first year of marriage, Willie started drinking heavily, coming home later than usual, and hanging out at the gambling shack, sometimes winning but sometimes losing his whole paycheck.

One early Saturday morning around 3:00 a.m., Gladys sat in bed waiting for him to walk in. She spoke calmly but with anger in her voice.

"Where've you been all night?"

"Just down at the shack."

"That's a damn lie. I smell that whore all over you."

"Honest, honest, honest, baby. I . . . I was on a roll, and . . . I . . . I forgot what time it was."

"Willie, some things have got to change. You're in the street more than you're home. I know you're sleeping around."

"Now why would I be sleeping around when I've got the finest, prettiest woman in Gavinville right here at home?"

"That's what I'd like to know. Must be more out there than at home. How would you feel if the shoe were on the other foot, Willie? What if you were going to bed every night alone and I was out gallivanting around town shaking my tail in front of some man? I'm beginning to feel like I'd be better off alone than sitting around here worrying about where you are or what you are doing at three o'clock in the morning."

Willie's late-night escapades slacked off for several months, but the wildness in him couldn't be tamed. Gladys moved out and went back to Mary's, but as usual Willie's sweet talk brought her back home. When he was caught jumping out of a casket half-naked with Betty Cole on the day of their second wedding anniversary Gladys swore she'd never take him back, but she did. In their frequent arguments the name "Betty Cole" always came up, either by Gladys accusing Willie of still sneaking around with her, or Willie accusing Gladys of not letting go and harboring old, unpleasant memories.

In the years that followed, their breaking up and making up became a way of life. Although Gladys didn't give any serious thought to a divorce, she started doing what Willie was doing, being unfaithful in marriage. They grew farther apart, but there were still moments when Willie made her laugh and feel like his world revolved around her. He was never physically abusive, mainly out of fear that Gladys would slit his throat one night in the middle of his deep, drunken sleep. He had seen that side of her at the Oasis Lounge. Strangely, it was a side of her that he found attractive, her unwillingness to back down from any man's threat to physically harm her. As much as Willie tested her patience and tolerance with his infidelity, he was not about to push her to the edge by striking her.

By 1970, they had been married for fourteen years and still lived in the one-bedroom shack they moved to when they got married. Willie was fifty-four years old, extremely overweight, and nearly bald. The only women he could pick up were the prostitutes standing outside the gambling shack on Friday and Saturday nights. His drinking started taking a toll and his health declined, first a failing liver, then kidney problems. But he continued to drink. He refused medical attention and was not about to humble himself and ask Ella Hayes to lay her healing hands on him. The only reason he wouldn't stop working was to support his addictions for drinking, gambling, and picking up prostitutes. Oddly, perhaps because he saw his end nearing, he became physically abusive toward Gladys, but not in a way that could do her much harm, an occasional slap to her face that always resulted in her hitting him back. Some days, Gladys got so angry with him that she flirted with the thought of killing him, but she wouldn't think seriously of slitting a sick man's throat in his sleep.

Gladys had reached a stage of life when love and a happy marriage were no longer a dream. She yearned for something more but didn't quite know what it was, something that no man could give her. The emptiness and yearning gave her a strange sense of peace, a feeling that she was just a child with a whole life stretched before her and yet to be lived. One Sunday morning, without thinking or knowing why, she stepped into St. Paul for the first time in decades and started attending every week.

Jesse and Ella were now in their mid-to-late seventies but showed no signs of growing old. Battling with a failing marriage, several years had passed since Gladys had seen her Mama and Daddy. She felt the distance widening between them with each passing day but didn't quite know how to narrow it. When they met unexpectedly at St. Paul's annual bazaar in late February 1970 none of them could have imagined the outcome.

Gladys had taken up quilting as a hobby and to earn extra income. She laid out a collection of quilts more impressive than any other craftwork at the bazaar.

"When somebody told me that my girl was here with the best quilts they'd ever seen, I said, 'well, that doesn't surprise me. That girl was the best of my girls at sewing.' I couldn't wait to get over here to take a look."

"Mama, what on earth are you doing here? And when are you going to start looking your age? And you, too, Daddy. I hope I've got your blood."

"Well of course you do, half mine and half your daddy's."

"Hi Gladys. Does look like some mighty fine quilts. You made all of these?"

"Jesse, what kind of question is that to ask?"

"Yep, these are all mine."

"Well, what got you started. Why quilts? Everybody knows you are the best dressmaker in town."

"Don't know. One day, I was sitting at home feeling cold and lonely. I looked at my old raggedy blankets and decided to make my own. I picked up a needle, thread and some old sheets, and couldn't put them down."

"My, my, my. Look at this one, Jesse. Child, this is really something special. Best I've seen, and you know I've seen plenty."

"Thank you, Mama. Ain't but four left, but you can have any that you like."

"Like? I'll take all of them."

"Mama what are going to do with four quilts?"

"How's Willie, Gladys?" Jesse asked. "I hear he's been pretty sick lately."

"Just taking one day at a time, Daddy. If I could just get him off the bottle . . ." Gladys sighed, then shook her head. "So good to see both of you looking well."

"Girl, this is art," said Ella, still admiring the quilts. You've got a gift for sure."

"Oh, Mama, they're not all that. Just some pieces of cloth sewn together."

"I bet folks in Chicago would pay a lot more money than what you're selling these for in Gavinville. Gets mighty cold up there. And they're so pretty. Look at these patterns. I'll tell you what. I'll buy all four of them and ship them to your sisters. Make nice gifts. They'll tell you what they think. And you know they've got connections with people who've got money. Who knows, could be the beginning of something. Folks who've got money don't look at price. They'll see art and they'll buy it just to say nobody else has it."

Gladys' quilts were a big hit with her sisters in Chicago. Hattie was convinced that there was a market for them. The quilts were not only practical for Chicago's very cold winters but were beautiful and artful. With so many Black people living in Chicago who had migrated from the South, they would market the quilts for what they were: hand-sewed by a Southern woman, with patterns that Chicagoans had not seen before. Gladys shipped a half-dozen more quilts, and the sisters stocked them in their specialty shop on State Street that sold home decor, art, and antiques, catering to upper-income buyers. The quilts sold quickly and Gladys shipped more, with the same result. Demand grew so rapidly that Gladys quit her job at the restaurant to make quilts on a full-time basis, but even that wasn't enough to keep enough quilts on the shelf. Hattie began to think big, the development of an entirely new product line consisting of bedding products—spreads, blankets, and pillows—under the brand name of G's Quilts & Bedding, something colored folks in Chicago could only find in large department stores. James, Carmen, Rita, and Antoinette supported the idea. Hattie called Gladys and gave her the good news, that they would support her starting a quilting business in Chicago. Gladys would have to leave soon to begin planning the startup.

Gladys couldn't leave Willie. As unhappy as she was being married to him, she couldn't leave him, knowing how sick he was. She mentioned the idea of the business and the move to Chicago one night over dinner.

"Chicago, uh? I always knew you'd pack up and leave one day, but I never thought it would be Chicago. Guess I've been too good for you. You can't appreciate a man giving everything he's got to make you happy. You've got to run off to Chicago to find happiness hanging out with those boogie sisters of yours."

"It sounds like a good opportunity, Willie. Could be a new start for us."

"New start? Doing what? Maybe a new life for you, but I don't sew. Who's going to give a man my age a decent job? I was born and reared in Gavinville, and I'm going to die and be buried here. If Chicago's where you want to go, don't let me stop you. Plenty women around here would love to lie in your bed."

"You old, sick bastard. Can't you see I'm trying to make this marriage work?" Gladys yelled.

"Trying? You're *trying*, alright. By doing what, packing up to move on the other side of the country to live with rich Negroes? Well if that's trying, you'll have to do it without me. I always said I was too good for you. Wasn't for me you'd still be down at Harry's shaking your ass in front of them old white men."

"You know damn well that ain't true, Willie. I had already quit Harry's when you came begging me to sleep with you when you got out of jail."

"Well, guess I begged too much. Guess I shouldn't have shown you a man who cared about you. I should have been like those crackers who tossed dollar bills at your feet for a ten-minute thrill. Go on, then. Go on up to Chicago with your fur-coat wearing sisters. I'll be just fine. Maybe I'll find a woman who'll appreciate the man I am to her."

"Appreciate what? This dump you call a house? You staying out all night, sleeping around, and coming home drunk?"

Willie's voice rose to a screaming yell. "Well, maybe if I felt some appreciation and got more respect, I wouldn't be in the streets. Bitch, you were a whore when I met you and you're still a tramp. Them quilts might cover a bed but they won't cover your filthy ass. You ought to be thankful that I cleaned you up a little. Who knows what you would have turned out to be if it weren't for me. I saved your ass and this is the thanks I get. But go on. I'll be fine. Get the hell out!"

Willie's words cut deeper than he knew. He was half-drunk and would probably wake up the next day not remembering most of what he said and regretting what little he did remember. But Gladys had seen and heard enough to know that their differences were irreconcilable and the damage was beyond repair. Willie was sick in too many ways to be helped even if he wanted assistance. More days spent with him would only bring more tension and argument. She knew that it was time to move on. She needed to fill the emptiness she felt inside her, and she finally came to the realization that the only way to do that was to leave Willie Frank.

It hurt her to have to leave so abruptly, not because of Willie's poor health but because she didn't get to say good-bye to her mama and daddy and to Thelma. She left Gavinville on the morning of March 6, 1970. By the time she arrived in New Orleans to board a train, Willie was still asleep. She didn't say good-bye to him, and she never looked back. Riding to Chicago, she wrote her mama and daddy a letter filled with words of regret and apologies, thanking them for their love and patience, and asking for their prayers. She was excited about the unknown, the new suns that would rise and set, as if her past life was being told to her in a story while she sat listening until the book was finished. And when she closed it, she would begin to write a story of a life she had yet to live. When she got news six months later that Willie died, she went into the bathroom, ran warm water into her cupped hands, and washed her face. She didn't attend his funeral.

Chapter 7

The late 1950's were quiet but productive times for the Hayes sisters in Chicago. Now a part of the city's elite, they did the things that rich folks did, accumulated more wealth, dressed stylishly, bought bigger, more expensive homes and cars, and took vacations to places that most Chicagoans only dreamt of. By the early 1960's, the sisters' business ventures were highly profitable and poised for growth. With the primary focus on business, they watched the unfolding of the civil rights movement largely from their television sets.

On January 7, 1966, Reverend Martin Luther King Jr. made a major announcement that he was taking the Civil Rights Movement to the North to end conditions that created slums in urban America. Chicago would be his first battleground. In Chicago, King met a level and intensity of racial hatred that he had not seen in the South. On August 5, 1966, King and others were stoned and beaten by whites who protested his being there. The months that followed were marked by protests and protests against protests, as King and other Black leaders pushed for an end to Chicago's racially-biased housing restrictions.

The Hayes sisters didn't attend marches and protest rallies, but they were there, unseen and quietly funneling money into SCLC to help fuel the campaign. While it was widely acknowledged that the agreements reached between civil rights leaders and the city fathers went largely unenforced, the Chicago Freedom Movement, as it had been called, was credited with Congress's passage of the 1968 Fair Housing Act.

Through all the protest fire of the mid-sixties, the Hayes sisters remained silently active in "the movement," effectively wielding their financial influence. They began to turn their attention to national issues like the Viet Nam War and were strong supporters of New York Senator Robert Kennedy's bid for the Democratic nomination for U. S. President. King's assignation in April 1968 and Kennedy's violent death a few months later brought a period of withdrawal from politics, a time to focus more closely on their business and the explosion of a new consciousness of Black identity that had begun to permeate all aspects of Afro-American culture.

The inspiration for launching a new line of clothing aimed at tapping into the wave of "Black Beauty" attire came one evening in the summer of 1970, while the sisters were drinking wine and listening to music at Carmen's new place. Gladys, who had seldom socialized with her younger sisters since moving to Chicago in March, had decided to join them. After several bottles of wine, the sisters got loose.

"Play that Aretha record, Carmen," said Antoinette.

"Which one?" Carmen asked.

"You know, the one where she sings about how much she loves that man."

"Child, all Aretha's records are about some man. Which one are you talking about?" asked Gladys.

"You know the one," Antoinette said, "the one where she sings about how natural that man makes her feel." Antoinette stood up with a glass of wine raised in the air and started swaying as though the record was playing.

"Hold on, Aretha Hayes, hold on, I know the one you're talking about," said Carmen, reaching into a stack to find the record. When Carmen put the record on, Antoinette started singing, then the other sisters joined in.

Before the song ended, Rita stood up and said, "Now play that other one, Sis—the up-tempo one about how she loves that man so much that she can't pack up and leave him even though she knows he's whoring around. You know the one I'm talking about." Rita started singing.

"Why that song, Sis? You got a man like that?" Carmen joked.

"Girl, just put the record on. You know the one she's talking about. I can definitely relate to that song. On the flip side it's got that song about how that man stays on her mind all the time—and go get a couple more bottles of wine," said Gladys.

When Carmen spun the record, Rita started singing again. Then the other sisters jumped to their feet and started clapping and singing along. As Aretha sang and the piano and horns chimed in, the sisters locked arms and rocked from side to side.

The night went on that way. Carmen played song after song by Aretha Franklin, and the sisters drank, sang, and danced.

When they had settled down to the last bottle of wine, Antoinette uncrossed her legs, leaned forward, and proposed an idea. "You know, there's a new awareness out there about how beautiful Black people are, a new consciousness. Black folks are expressing pride in their heritage. It's in the music for sure, but it's really everywhere, in hairdos, movies, books, even in clothes. Blacks, young and old, have their own style, and white folks are cashing in on it. I say it's time for us to get in it, too."

"What do you mean, Sis?" asked Rita.

"Well, we've got the customer base. Women and men love what we sell, but it's mostly conventional. Not many young people come in to buy, because we're not selling what they wear.

"Why not launch a Black beauty line of what Black people call fashion these days? Dresses and miniskirts are fine, but pants are really hot these days, so hot that half the butt cheeks are hanging out. Women like wearing them short and men like watching them. And they like them tight. Bell-bottoms have gone in and out but they're mainstream now. It's time for us to get in on it. Let's put some color in Hayes."

"You know, it's funny that you mention it," said Rita. "Just the other day I was thinking how Hollywood is way ahead of everybody. The west coast is modeling, and people buy what they see being modeled. I agree."

"Girl, I love those hip-huggers, and I sure got plenty to hug," said Carmen, twisting in her seat and putting her hands on her hips.

"Too much, judging by my eyes," quipped Antoinette. "Call me old fashion," said Gladys, "but I'll stick with my dresses. Nothing against the hip stuff, but it shows a little too much of what I don't want nobody but me to see."

"And since when did you start caring about somebody seeing too much?" joked Carmen.

"Seriously, there's plenty money to be made," said Antoinette. "I say we look into it."

"Well, I'll drink to that, Sis," said Rita, raising her glass and bobbing her head from side to side. "Let's get hip!"

The sisters followed up on Antoinette's idea. Hayes Enterprises, as the business had become known, soon partnered with several leading manufacturers and distributors to establish their own brand of "hip attire," everything from blouses and pants to clog shoes. They simultaneously launched a new brand of conventional dresses for both working and middle-class women, branding it "Ella Hayes." Not only did it sound white, it sold white, and quickly penetrated the national women's apparel market. They opened a music and bookstore, and another clothing store on Chicago's west side that catered to Chicago's younger, more racially conscious and educated women. Like everything else they had invested in, the stores were a big success.

The sisters also got squarely in the middle of Chicago's Black Renaissance of art and literature, promoting the literary work of Margaret Walker and Gwendolyn Brooks, and the visual art of Archibald John Motley. As avid lovers of jazz and blues, they frequented Chicago's jazz clubs and helped to promote some of the city's top Negro musicians. Savvy enough to know the power of advertising and effective media relations, they established close personal ties with John H. Johnson, founder of *Ebony* and *Jet* magazines, and became a silent investor in *The Chicago Defender*, the country's leading Black-owned newspaper.

On July 20, 1970, Rita had married Charles West, a forty-eight-year-old Baptist minister. Charles, a native of Chicago, had been pastor of several small churches but would later head one of the largest Baptist churches in the city. The ceremony was attended only by close members of both families. The second youngest daughter, Rita was the tallest of the sisters, a trait she inherited from her daddy. If Thelma was Daddy's girl, Rita was Mama's. Because she and Ella were so close, it surprised her older sisters that she agreed to move to Chicago. Before meeting Charles, she dated men but had never gotten serious about any of them. Her sisters joked that she looked down on men too much, literally and figuratively. She was forty-five years old when she and Charles started dating and they married two years later. A month after the wedding, Rita and Hattie, the only Hayes sisters to marry in Chicago, chatted about married life over tea.

"So, what's it like?" asked Hattie, stirring her tea.

"Lord, I still pinch myself to believe that I found that Negro. I love him so much. After all these years, I found the love of my life. He's such a good, sweet man. Every day I ask *why me, Lord*. What did I do to deserve such goodness? You know, I met Charles not long after we moved to Chicago, in a bar of all places. Actually, it was a quaint little café that had a bar. I had slipped away from you all one evening just to have some time to myself. I looked up and there he was standing beside me, looking like it was his first time at a bar. He didn't know the brands of liquor or the names of any drinks. The bartender suggested something, but he ordered a beer, which he only took one swallow of. He introduced himself as a student studying to be a preacher and we chatted a few minutes. I didn't see him again until a few years ago, when he walked into our men's store to buy a suit. The rest is history I suppose." Rita paused to sip her tea. "How are James and the boys?"

Hattie sighed. "Oh, same old thing. James lives and breathes business. I never knew a man so driven. I think he wants his legacy to be the richest Negro to ever live in Chicago. The boys are doing well in school, very well in fact. You thought about what it's going be like to be a preacher's wife? Are you ready for that?"

"Yeah, we've talked about it a lot. It'll pull me away from the business a little, but Charles supports my staying active. I'll figure out a way to juggle both. The only thing that worries me is having to tone down the way I dress. You know, got to do everything in moderation. But I'm okay with that. What I'm really going to miss are those Saturday evening sister flings, but we're all slowing down. Lord knows its time."

"I'm sure it makes Mama happy. I think she wanted all of us to marry preachers," Hattie said. "Who would have thought that you'd be the one? It's a shame she and Daddy couldn't make it."

"Yeah, I miss Mama and Daddy so much, especially Mama. Guess she's still laying hands on the sick and being fussy about Daddy doing too much fishing. They gave us a good life, you know. Wasn't easy for poor folks in Gavinville to raise a house full of girls. Charles and I plan to go down there sometime soon."

"I miss them, too," Hattie said. "When I count my blessings, I put Mama and Daddy at the top of the list. I often think that the good we reap is the goodness that Mama sowed. To think we were living with an angel all those years and didn't know it. So, how are Carmen and Antoinette? Any talk about men sweeping them off their feet? And what's my big sister up to?"

"Child, no way. Carmen dates every now and then. But Antoinette? No way. They're the brains and workaholics of Hayes Enterprises . . . arguing all the time about this and that. Carmen is determined to change the world, and all Antoinette wants to do is design the best-looking dress wear in Chicago. But they're fine." Rita paused and sighed. "Gladys is Gladys, mostly keeps to herself. Don't see much of her, but her quilting line has really taken off. She's come a long way from Willie, though, and seems to be at peace."

"That's so good to hear," Hattie said. "Of course, I'm not surprised about how that turned out. She deserved better. In due time, I'm sure she'll find out."

"But I don't think she's looking for it, Hattie. Big sis seems to be content just being all to herself. We see her every now and then, but I always have the sense that she's holding back, you know, like there's something there that's heavy on her mind but she'd rather not talk about it."

"Well, we've all got that in a way," said Hattie. "The most we can do is love and support each other."

Hattie and Rita shared a lot of stories that afternoon. It had been a while since just the two of them had been together, and they vowed to do more of it. But there was a haunting spirit between them—dark, hidden secrets that would create more distance—hovering. Only Rita felt its presence. She felt the weight of words that should have been said years ago but weren't. When she spoke about Gladys holding something back, she might well have been thinking of herself. As time passed, she spent fewer and fewer days at the stores and even less time alone with Hattie.

By 1971, the Hayes sisters had been in Chicago for twenty-one years and were now clearly and unquestionably some of the city's wealthiest residents, Black or white. Hattie and Rita had settled comfortably into married life, and Gladys was content to run her quilting business and spend her leisure time reading and sewing.

Carmen, age 51, and Antoinette, age 50, had no intention of settling down. They spent more time traveling, mainly to Europe, observing new fashions and meeting with designers. They dated, of course, and on occasion found men that interested them, handsome men of wealth and power, but something was always lacking, not enough of this or too much of that, causing them to keep a distance, to pull back before plunging. They were both at a stage of life when friendship and intimacy came easy, but love was more like a song, a story, or a movie, something to have but not to hold. They were women of power and prestige who bought anything and went anywhere they pleased, but they were long past the stage of having children and couldn't imagine being married. Neither of them felt the emptiness or void of not being a mother.

Antoinette, known for her fashion consciousness and dry, quick wit, had always dated infrequently. Of all the sisters, she had the least to say about the men she had met and gotten close to. In younger years, the sisters kept short-cut hairstyles, but as they grew older they took on the popular hairstyles of the day, like afros and long-hair wigs. Antoinette went the other direction. She never wore a wig, and the older she got the shorter she cut her hair, which was now starting to be salted with strands of gray. She often teased her sisters that one day they would stop following the looks of other people and catch up to her style.

While Carmen still had the beauty of Ella Hayes, like Hattie, she had gained weight and lost the stunning figure of her younger years but still had enough curves in just the right places to turn men's heads. One Sunday afternoon, as the two of them strolled through a park, Carmen dropped a bombshell. "Remember that boy, Bebo, whom Mama talked about years ago, the one who apologized for throwing rocks that morning she was walking to the bus stop? You remember, the day of the miracle when Daddy was healed?" Carmen asked, fidgeting with the keys in her hand.

"I sort of remember him, Ms. Eliza's son, right? I remember her mentioning him a few days later, how Bebo and some bird were a sign that something special was going to happen that day. Ms. Eliza had diabetes and one leg. I think she eventually lost the other one."

"Yeah, that's him."

Antoinette, turning toward Carmen with a look of interest if not surprise, asked, "That was, what, thirty years ago? What makes you think of Bebo?"

"Turns out that Bernard, that's his real name, is living in Chicago. He must have been a real smart kid. Got a scholarship to Morehouse and ended up getting a Ph.D. at Princeton. Now he's a professor of sociology at the University of Chicago."

"Bebo from Gavinville? In Chicago? A professor? How do you know? You talked to Mama?"

"No. Believe it or not, Bebo went to the bookstore the other day and was asking about us. He had read about these women from Gavinville who were in business and he wanted to make the connection. I happened to be there. He had no idea that we were Ms. Ella's daughters."

"How long has he been here?"

"He just moved up from New Jersey. Said he starts teaching in September."

"Sounds like he's turned out to be a really fine young man. I'm sure Mama would be glad to know. His wife and kids here too?"

"Doesn't have any. Single, and good looking, too. He asked if I could show him around, help him get to know the city."

"How old is this good-looking child?" Antoinette asked.

"I don't know. I'm guessing thirty-six or thirty-seven. Far from being a child. Talks like a man much older in fact." Carmen paused. "That's not all."

"What?"

"He asked me out to dinner."

"Dinner? That's his idea of you showing him around, going to dinner? Carmen, he's thirteen or fourteen years younger than you. Please tell me you said no."

"I didn't say I was going to bed with the man. He's a professor at the university. From Gavinville. New to the city. Just going to have a little dinner. Folks will think it's all business, me having dinner with a tall, handsome man discussing business. And if they think any more than that, I say why not stir up a little curiosity."

"My, my, my. If that ain't a sign of change of life. Robbing the cradle. Girl, that's scandalous. You better hope Jesse Hayes doesn't hear about it."

"It's not really a date, Antoinette. Besides, like you said, Mama would be glad to know how fine a man Bernard turned out to be, and glad to hear that we're helping him to get to know his way around this big crazy town."

"But not that her second oldest child is about to christen him."

"Girl, you need to stop."

"What restaurant?"

"Don't know. He's picking me up."

"Picking you up? Carmen, since when did you let some man drive you around, and a young man at that? I can't wait to see this Bebo, excuse me . . . Bernard."

Carmen and Bernard did more talking than eating that evening. He was different from other men she had known. He had grown up poor, without a father, and valued education as a way out of poverty instead of as a doorway to privilege. He was also politically conscious, having marched with the SCLC as a student at Morehouse. He was only 22 years old in 1955, when Emmett Till was lynched and Rosa Parks made her grand sit-down against injustice, but like Carmen he took a stand, leading protest marches while doing post-graduate work at Princeton University. He was the first intellectual that Carmen had met and a true man of letters who had published books and scholarly articles. But he was also humble and down-to-earth, never talking about his education or status. Carmen's wealth was equally unimportant to him. He showed more interest in her feelings and thoughts than the things she owned.

Carmen felt the strong mutual attraction. In time, Bernard told her that he loved her, but, cautiously, she was hesitant about telling him how she felt. She thought about the scandal and problems that their age difference would cause, personally and professionally. The more they dated and talked about the age issue, the closer she got and the more comfortable she grew with him being much younger. Eventually, she accepted the fact that she was deeply in love and was willing to take the leap. She understood the risks, social complications, and potential business consequences, but her heart spoke louder. Bernard exhibited a self-confidence that she had not seen in any man. He wanted to be the father that he never had, but he accepted the fact that Carmen could not bear children. He was willing to let her shine and follow her dreams, knowing where her heart was. One Christmas Eve, after they had been shuttered in his apartment for nearly a week by one of the worst blizzards to hit Chicago, he proposed to her, and she accepted.

The Hayes sisters had not gotten together in months, so when Hattie's sons, James Jr. and Jesse, came home from Harvard for spring break in April 1975, it was as good a time as any for a family gathering. James Sr. fired up the barbeque pit for steaks and burgers. It would be the first time that Hattie, Rita, Gladys, and Antoinette met Bernard Hawkins. Several of them had heard their mother speak of Bebo but they were all anxious to meet the young man from Gavinville who had spun Carmen dizzy. The afternoon turned out to be quite pleasant, with everyone sitting and lounging around the swimming pool, sipping wine while talking business, sports, and politics. Everyone danced around the topic of Carmen's new beau, and his age.

Rita couldn't resist getting personal. "Bernard, how are they treating you at the university?"

"Just fine, thank you. Chicago has turned out to be the best move of my life," Bernard answered, smiling while reaching to hold Carmen's hand.

"Well, I'm happy for both of you. Lord knows it's past time Carmen settled down. You know, she snores louder than all of us, and she's prone to spend hours in the mirror. You ready for that?"

"Oh, and tell him about the toilet," Hattie chimed in. "When Carmen went in there, we had to go next door to use the bathroom."

They all laughed, but Bernard didn't miss a beat. "Yeah, I'm ready for all that. But those are just rooms. This woman and I will be living in a mansion built on a foundation of love and understanding. Besides, she already knows how long it takes me to shave and shine my favorite shoes."

"So when's the big date?" Antoinette asked.

"October 11th, a Saturday," said Bernard. "But we're not getting married here. We're flying to New Orleans and then on to the Bahamas for the honeymoon."

"New Orleans," Rita said. "Why New Orleans?"

"I don't know," Carmen said. "We just thought it would be good to get away. Do it our way. Go back South to our roots. Things have gotten a lot better there since we left."

"Sounds like you're running away instead of getting away," said. Hattie "Why not Chicago?"

"Neither of us is up for fanfare and panache. We just want to marry quietly."

"Among strangers, without family?"

"I didn't say without family. I said New Orleans. We're flying all of you down, expenses paid. You know I wouldn't marry without my sisters being there. Besides, it's only a couple of hours drive from Gavinville. Bernard's brothers and friends might want to go."

"Damn, brother-in-law! I'm liking you better by the minute," said James excitedly, standing to pour Bernard another glass of wine.

"What about Mama and Daddy? They haven't been to New Orleans since the day they married. You think they'll be up for travel?" Gladys asked.

"We've already talked to them. Took an hour-long telephone conversation, but they agreed. Daddy said he'll only go if we promised to take him to see the New Orleans Saints. Turns out that they're playing in the new dome stadium that Sunday."

"Sis, what did Mama and Daddy have to say about, you know?" Rita asked without really asking.

"About me marrying Mama's little Bebo?"

Bernard quickly jumped in. "Look, Ms. Ella came over often when Mama was sick, and she always carried a bag of groceries for my brothers and me. She stayed in touch over the years after Mama passed, even dropping in from time to time at school to talk to our teachers about how we were doing. I owe a lot to her. I think she feels the way we do, that fate, maybe God himself, brought Carmen and me together. And nothing's going to put that asunder, not even age. I can't wait to see her again."

"Spoken like a man who knows the way to a woman's heart," said Hattie.

"What about Thelma and Terrell? Are they going?" Gladys asked.

"Thelma couldn't contain herself. You could probably hear her screaming with excitement a mile away. Said she was going out to buy a new dress as soon as she hung up."

"Mama wasn't happy when we told her that we weren't going to marry Catholic. Charles has a pastor friend at a Baptist church there who agreed to officiate."

"Charles, I can't believe you didn't tell me," said Rita.

"Sorry, honey. I promised Carmen," Charles said. "She wanted it to be a surprise. I almost slipped up a couple of times and mentioned it, but for once the Lord kept my mouth shut."

So the planning began. Carmen reserved rooms for everyone at the Fairmont Hotel, a few blocks from the French Quarter. They would have a dinner party at Dooky Chase's on Friday evening and hang out in the French Quarter before settling down. They would start the next day with breakfast at Café du Monde, known for its famous beignets, then, do some shopping on Canal Street. They would marry on Saturday afternoon at the First African Baptist Church—the oldest Black church in Louisiana—and have a small reception there with friends and family, including many who had come down from Gavinville. As a compromise with Ella, they would attend Sunday worship service at St. Augustine Catholic Church, then cap off the weekend with a Sunday afternoon Saints game in the newly-build Superdome. To Jesse's delight, the Saints beat the Green Bay Packers by a score of 20 to19.

The New Orleans wedding was the first time in decades that all the Hayes sisters were together. They acted as if they had never been separated by time and distance, and they were happy to be together with their mama and daddy. Three of Bernard's brothers and their families were there. Now was not the time for disagreements and arguments. It was a time for counting blessings and celebrating success. The weekend could not have been more perfect.

After dinner at Dooky's, Ella and Bernard managed to get a few minutes alone and talk for the first time since he had gone off to Morehouse College twenty-four years ago.

"Bebo, you sure have turned out to be a fine man. But I'm not surprised. Your Mama was a strong, God-fearing woman. Her prayers were answered, even though she's not around to see it. I know she'd be proud."

"Couldn't have gotten here without you, Ms. Ella."

"No, I can't take credit. You worked hard to get where you are. Not many boys come out of Gavinville and make a mark in the world the way you have. I always knew you were a gifted child, but it's one thing to have a gift and another thing to use it. All I did was pray. You plowed the ground and planted the mustard seed. God did the watering."

"Ms. Ella."

Ella raised her hand to interrupt. "Now let me stop you right there. I'm not Ms. Ella anymore. You're my son, and I'm your Mama, just like I am to the rest of my children."

"Okay, Mama. It means a lot to Carmen and me that you and Mr. Hayes—excuse me—Daddy, have accepted and blessed our marriage. I promise that I'll do everything in my power to make her happy."

"I know you will, son. Just remember that there are lots of small-minded people out there. They don't see things the way we do because they don't know your heart. They look at love as something that's seen but not felt. They see love as something with boundaries, something to be packaged and wrapped with a bow. For years, Jesse and I had no idea that our daughters in Chicago were so well off. They didn't call to brag about it. They've always known that money is a means to an end, but not *the* end. Jesse and I raised them to understand that. But I'm sure that there are people in Chicago, colored and white, who think different and who'll look down on you even more than they look down on my girls. But pay them no mind. They see the bird but not the wings that make him fly. They might even watch the bird flying but that's all they see, not the wings and air. Sometimes, the air is wet and cold, but the bird flies anyway. I know that you love my Carmen and will do well by her. You're a decent, strong man because that's how Eliza raised you."

Ella and Bernard embraced. Holding him, she felt something different. She couldn't quite explain it. She had held him as a child and embraced many people over the years, saying a prayer as she held them, but had never felt such burning warmth. She sensed something different but pushed it aside to get back to the ground she was standing on, knowing that they had talked longer than either of them thought, and that it was time to get back to the wedding party.

After four days in the Bahamas, Carmen and Bernard returned to Chicago and moved into a lavish but relatively small dwelling in Hyde Park. She got back to the business and he got back to his teaching duties at the University of Chicago.

Chapter 8

During the late 1970's, economic recession fueled by high inflation and rising oil prices began to spell doom for Chicago's steel manufacturers, the city's industrial base. As factories began to scale back and shut down, jobs were lost. The city's Black community, particularly its poor, suffered most. The negative effects were especially disastrous for the South Side business district. Without the buying power and patronage of Black residents, many businesses began to fail. They had weathered the recession of the mid-seventies, largely on the strength of a still vibrant steel industry, but the late seventies brought a new economic reality of deindustrialization that Byrd Enterprises and Hayes Enterprises were not prepared to deal with. Both were highly leveraged with bank debt. They had no choice but to scale back. Their real estate and insurance ventures remained viable, but retail, the base of the sisters' operations, had to be reined in.

By then, James Jr. and Jesse Byrd had graduated from Harvard Business School and taken executive roles in running both enterprises. James Sr., Hattie, Gladys, Carmen, Antoinette, and Rita remained active but left strategic business decisions to their sons and nephews. In one of the family's regular Monday morning executive meetings, James Jr. and Jesse laid out a plan.

"After carefully weighing all options," said James Jr., "we propose that we sell off the less productive real estate properties and close the less profitable retail operations. We'll also have to make some operating adjustments in the stores that remain open, including some layoffs. We need to build a stronger cash base and concentrate on our strengths, which is insurance and our larger retail shops."

Jesse stepped in. "Many of our commercial and residential tenants are struggling to make rent payments. We should narrow our profit margins and give them some relief to help them to stay in business."

"But what about our workers?" Hattie responded. "We can't just abandon them. Many are already struggling with the loss of one income due to the factories closing. Laying them off would be devastating."

"Mama, we're aware and certainly sensitive to that," said James Jr., "but we've got to stay focused on the bigger, long-term picture. We'll have to lay off a lot more workers in a few months if we don't act now. We should certainly study the financial condition and market outlook of each store very carefully and do only what is absolutely necessary at this point."

"Exactly," said Jesse. "Keep in mind that our retail operations are not labor-intensive. It's the debt and non-personnel costs that are killing us. We've got fixed expenses that have to be paid, no matter how little revenue is coming in. Sales are down and falling more each month. Inventory is not turning over quickly enough. Lowering prices on some lines will help, but we've got to keep margins at levels that will cover all costs. And we need to shore up cash—working capital. Unfortunately, in cases where our margins are already thin, that might not be enough. We will have to shut down. We'll come back to you all very shortly with detailed analyses and specific recommendations, but we think that's the general direction we should go."

"Well, I'm just relieved to know that we've got Harvard men at the helm," Antoinette joked.

"I'm on board," said James Sr. "We'll have to make some tough decisions, some unpleasant ones, but all for the greater good. We're stronger than many small businesses, and I have all the confidence that we'll get through this. The good news is that the insurance company is cash-strong and in much better position to handle the downturn without these types of measures, although we've got to stay on top of collections and investment income."

James Jr. and Jesse steered the ship, lowering rents, selling off less profitable assets, and closing stores. The decisions they made provided a cash flow cushion that enabled the base operations to weather the storm.

Gladys had moved to Chicago and begun operating the bedding line not anticipating the sudden economic downturn. The quilting and bedding operation was shut down, along with other specialty stores that sold items that Black folks no longer had the luxury of buying. Gladys talked of moving back to Gavinville. Jesse and Ella were in their mid-eighties and could use some help being cared for. Thelma, she knew, would look out for them but was more focused on Terrell's dental practice.

"Sis," she said to Rita while visiting Rita and Charles one Sunday after church. "I've been thinking of going back home. Things didn't quite turn out the way I expected here, and Mama and Daddy can probably use the help."

"Girl, don't you worry about Jesse and Ella Hayes. They'll probably outlive all of us. I don't know what they've got in their blood, but it sure ain't death. Mama and Daddy are doing well enough."

"I'm not so sure. They'll never talk about what's ailing them, but we know they've both got heart conditions."

"What would you do Gladys, sit around and play nurse, if Mama and Daddy would even let you? You're sixty-one years old, too old to be tending to rich white folks' needs or standing inside somebody's restaurant cooking and waiting tables. You can't live off of selling a few quilts every now and then. Chicago's your home now."

"I know, but I don't want to be a burden to y'all. The chances of somebody hiring me here are no better than in Gavinville."

"But we agreed to have you stay on and help with the other stores."

"I know and I really appreciate it, but I feel like it's charity, like y'all are just trying to keep me off the welfare roll. I'd feel better if I did something else, if I could pull my weight instead of being carried."

"Sis, let me tell you something, You're a Hayes and you're our big sister. We all have something or someone bigger than us who've helped us to get where we are. Do you think we'd be who we are if Mama and Daddy hadn't worked hard and sacrificed for us? You think we'd be in business if James and Hattie hadn't given us a start? And do you think James would have been able to do that if his mama and daddy didn't sacrifice to give him a start in life? We're family and that's what family does. We stick together, hell or high water."

Gladys agreed to stay on, helping guide the stores in the recovery. In time, she started making quilts again, selling them at farmers' markets and crafts shows. As economic conditions improved, G's Quilts again became hot, popular items, especially among high-income white collectors of Black art. Her work was featured in a Sunday edition of *Chicago Tribune*, free advertisement that spawned more sales.

The Hayes sisters grew closer in those days. James Jr. and Jesse were completely in charge of the businesses and hired other executives as chief operating officers. By 1980, the sisters, now in their late fifties, assumed roles of consulting on important buying, advertising, and strategic partnership decisions. They were even more strongly involved in public relations and building relationships important to the business. Socially, they grew more active, giving to charities, attending important community events, and hosting monthly dinner parties attended by five or six of Chicago's most powerful, successful, and admired Black residents—politicians, musicians, professional athletes, artists, and business leaders. That year, and those that followed, brought another major challenge, this one more political than economic.

In November 1980, Ronald Reagan was elected the 40th President of the United States on an agenda of restoring America's economic vitality and shrinking the size of government. Reagan literally declared war on social programs that many South Side Chicago residents depended on for survival. Carmen voiced her concerns about the impact that Reagan's agenda would have on poor and middle-class residents who supported their businesses. In early 1982, she let her feelings be known in a weekly executive meeting, now attended by the men whom James Jr. and Jesse had hired as operating officers.

"This country and city deserve better. Too many people are being hurt. We can't just stand by and let him tear lives and families apart. And it touches us too. If we're going to survive as a business and as a community, we've got to get more politically active. Mayor Jane Byrne is only interested in padding the pockets of her cronies. She's playing up to the white vote. She's even taken Blacks off the Board of Education and the Housing Authority and replaced them with whites. We've got to use our influence to get her out."

"And how exactly can we do that?" asked Hattie.

"The only way to do that is to get more active. Encourage and help Black people to register to vote and go to the polls. We know that Congressman Harold Washington, a native of Bronzeville who has served this community better than any politician, has jumped into the mayor's race, not the first Black man to run for mayor of this city, but the first to have a chance of winning. We need to get solidly behind him."

Before Washington's announcement, the Hayes sisters had already quietly supported registration drives led by white liberals and grass-roots Latino community organizers, but Carmen was suggesting more—that they also publicly endorse Washington and help raise money for his campaign.

Rising to his feet, James Jr. spoke business. "With all due respect, Aunt Carmen, we've got to tread carefully here. We've built business relationships that cross party lines, relationships that are important to our sustainability and future growth."

"I agree with Junior," said James Sr. "It's one thing to write a check but another thing to go public. Putting our names on Washington's campaign could be damaging. Besides, Carmen, you're talking about going against an incumbent mayor. Washington can't win."

"I disagree, but the only way that Washington can beat Byrne is for Black and Latino people to step up their game. And those of us who've got the means need to use every ounce of power we have to help him win. He can't win without the Black businesses of Chicago standing with him, pledging support, and being actively involved. Big checks will help, but nobody touches the lives of Black people more than we do. We need to stand with Washington and tell everybody in Chicago, including the whites we do business with, that we've had enough of white leaders of this city keeping Blacks in slums and ghettos. It's time for us to stand up. Sitting down will keep our pockets full but it won't do anything for poor and middle-class Black people."

"What if Washington loses?" asked Hattie.

"And in this city, that's a more likely outcome," said Rita. "Negroes don't vote."

"They will if we join Washington in getting them registered and to the polls."

"I don't know, Sis. That's easier said than done," said Antoinette.

"I disagree. With the Black and Latino population here, we've got the numbers. We've just got to get them registered and to the polls. That's going to take a lot of work and money."

"Hattie's got a point," said James Sr. "If we lose, you can bet that the Byrne machine will come after us. That's how they do it when they win, reward their friends and punish their enemies."

"Lord knows we don't need to be fighting politicians," said Hattie, looking at Carmen. "We've barely come through a recession with our heads above water. We've got competitors copying everything we do that makes money. And many of those same Negroes that you're trying to save are running over there instead of buying from us. We'd be playing Russian roulette by backing Harold, and sooner or later that bullet will come around."

"Is this all about making more money?" asked Carmen, looking at James and Hattie. "Is this all about us?"

"No, Sis. It's not about us making money," said James Sr. "It's about surviving. We've invested a lot in all this. And we've weathered some storms. Now is not the time to risk it all on some political pipedream.

Harold's a good man. I'm with him, but we can't afford to go public. It's just too risky."

"What about this community?" asked Carmen. "What about poor people and old folks who live in the projects or who spend half their pay checks on high rent that goes into white folks' pockets? Whose taking risks for them? You think Mayor Bryne and her cronies give a damn about poor people? Washington cares and is willing to fight the bosses. I say let's stand with him and push as hard as we can to get her out and get him in."

Jesse, who had been quietly listening while jotting down notes, decided to speak. "You know, there's truth to both sides of this. Aunt Carmen is right. Our community needs and deserves better leadership. Daddy . . . Mama, I clearly appreciate your concern about the fallout if we go public and Washington loses. But think about it. Suppose he wins. Think of how that will position us, not only in helping to change the system that we all know is corrupt, but we'll be better positioned strategically, you know, in a business sense." Jesse paused to take a sip of water. "But there is an alternative. We don't have to go public now. We can wait and see how the Washington campaign shapes up, wait to see if he starts moving up in the polling, and how effective the voter registration drives are. Meanwhile, we can support him quietly, with donations. We can decide later whether our going public would make any difference. Mr. Washington might or might not need our public endorsement, or it might be that we need him more. I say, let's just wait and see."

After a brief silence in the room, Carmen responded. "I never thought I'd see the day when a boy whose butt I spanked would spank me back . . . and teach me a lesson while doing it," she said, drawing laughter from everyone. "Thank you, Jesse. If that's a compromise that we can all agree on, I'm in. In fact, I offer Jesse's suggestion as a motion. If anyone disagrees, let's hear it." No one disagreed, and Jesse's recommendation stood.

So, they waited, and when Washington's candidacy started building momentum, they joined a dozen of Chicago's wealthiest Negro business owners and publicly endorsed Washington in his bid for mayor. The Byrd and Hayes families spoke at rallies and hosted fundraising events, including monthly dinner parties that raised a substantial amount of money for the campaign. When Washington won on April 12, 1983, the sisters found themselves squarely in the inner circle of the political, business, and civic leadership that was now running the city of Chicago.

By 1986, all the Hayes sisters, including Thelma, were at least sixty years old. All had married except Antoinette, who had buried two fiancées along the way. The Hayes women still looked much younger for their ages, showing little visible signs of growing old. And they certainly didn't dress like women their age, always seen in hairstyles and dress wear that were not common to Chicago, even to other rich Black women. They took pride in being the vanguard of fashion and made a conscious effort to keep things that way at any expense, sometimes flying to London and Paris just to shop. Gladys had not been in Gavinville since the day she left Willie. Rita and Carmen had gone only twice since Thelma's wedding in 1957, but all the sisters were beginning to talk about taking another trip home, this time to celebrate Jesse and Ella's seventieth wedding anniversary.

Both in their early nineties, Jesse and Ella had been showing signs of aging for quite a few years. Jesse, long since retired and spending most of his days watching television and tending to his gardens, was much thinner and completely bald. He had suffered one heart attack and undergone bypass surgery. Ella, hair white as snow, was confined to a wheelchair, but never stopped healing the sick, even though her hands trembled when she laid them on people's bodies, rubbing holy water and chanting prayers. When she heard that her girls were coming home to visit, she couldn't contain her excitement, telling everybody whom she prayed on that her babies were coming home again. She asked her daughters to bring their husbands. James Jr. and Jesse stayed in Chicago to handle business while the others were gone. It would be another Hayes family reunion.

James Sr. and Charles had been to New Orleans for Carmen's wedding but never to Gavinville. For Bernard, it would be a trip back to his roots, which he had not seen for a number of years. On the morning of July 8, 1987, they all flew to New Orleans and from there rented cars for the drive to Gavinville, arriving just before sundown in pouring rain. James and Charles saw a Louisiana much different from the big-city, urban life of New Orleans. Gavinville had grown and was now fully racially integrated but was still a step back in time compared to the noisy urban congestion and thriving commerce of Chicago. After checking into the hotel, they made the short drive to Dixie Manor. Suddenly, there were circles of hugs and kisses, everyone pressing in to have a moment embracing their mama and daddy, telling them how happy they were to see them and congratulating them on a long, happy marriage.

The daughters of Jesse and Ella had more than enough wealth to buy their parents a new home, one of the finest in Gavinville, but Ella refused to leave Dixie Manor, insisting that God's healing powers would not work anyplace else, especially if she and Jesse began to serve material wealth more than they did the Lord. She and Jesse hadn't thought about how many family members would be coming from Chicago and the need for more living room space and chairs, but everyone settled in comfortably, some grabbing sofa pillows to sit on the floor. Thelma and Terrell would join them at the church service the next day. Bernard remained standing, never taking his eyes off of Ella.

They talked for several hours about Gavinville, Chicago, and how Jesse and Ella were spending their golden days. Jesse drew plenty of laughs when he recounted the story that he had told Big John forty-eight years ago about how Ella got the nickname "Souffie."

"Mama," said Bernard, "tell us about the miracle, that day Daddy was healed."

"Oh Bebo, you and I had walked together that morning on my way to the bus stop. You were about six years old. Not sure if you remember, but you came up behind me while I was walking and praying. Between you and that sparrow flying over my head, I felt that God was speaking to me in some mysterious way. It was a miracle for sure. Jesse had been paralyzed from the neck down for three years, and he stood up and walked, been walking ever since. I had stayed up all night praying for him, but I didn't raise your Daddy up out of that bed. That was all God's doing. Jesse and I both saw the figure in the porch screen. We saw God's hands clasped together like He was praying, then he opened them. I reached in and touched the image of His hands on the porch screen, and I felt the scars where the nails had been driven. I saw and felt the flesh of Jesus."

Ella continued. "My papa had the gift of healing that his grandmother, his mama's mother, had passed down to him. Papa was born in 1877. His mama, my grandmother, was pregnant for him when they stole her from Africa and brought her to New Orleans. My papa's grandmother lived on the Ivory Coast. She could interpret dreams and see into the future. Years later, my papa learned that his grandmother lived to be 120 years old. I never got to know my papa, but the gift passed from him to me. Years ago, I heard the Lord say that after me the gift would be passed to a male."

"I can't speak for Thelma and Terrell, but you only have two sons with James and me, and all they think about is getting rich. So I hope God has a Plan B," Hattie joked.

"God has his own way and does things in his own time, child. If the gift is meant to pass on, he's already done it."

"Speaking of grandchildren, Mama," James Sr. said, "you're the first to know that you'll be a great grandma and grandpa in seven months. Junior's wife Margie is expecting." Hattie and James Sr. had kept the news a secret for just this moment. Everyone voiced their surprise and happiness, congratulating Hattie on becoming the first grandmother of the Hayes sisters.

"Congratulations to both of you. I just hope the Lord lets me hang around long enough to see them," said Jesse.

"Oh Daddy, don't talk that way. You've got plenty more years to grow tomatoes," said Gladys.

"Child, don't get that man talking about his gardens." "What else do you have growing out there, Daddy?" Rita asked.

"Something you don't find much of in Chicago. I just cut the last okra, but the mustards and collards I planted in the spring are spreading like crazy. Probably end up giving them all away, though. Souffie forgot how to cook."

While everyone laughed, Charles looked at his watch. They had made dinner reservations at Pierre's Café, Gavinville's finest restaurant. "Mama, Daddy, we don't want to be late. We best start moving. And don't you worry, Mama. We can handle that wheelchair."

On Sunday morning, the family attended St. Paul's 9:30 service before heading back to Chicago. Ella Hayes always attracted attention in public, but that morning all eyes were on her daughters, whom most church goers had heard about but never seen. As would be expected, the Hayes women looked elegant with their hats and scarfs, the sight of which was all new to the Negro residents of Gavinville and was talked about long after the sisters were gone. It had been thirty years since they were all together in their hometown, sitting in St. Paul Catholic Church. But unlike Thelma's wedding, this was not a time to drink and dance. Their mother and father were celebrating seventy years of marriage, more years than most Black people in Gavinville lived from birth. The sisters sat basking in the incredibleness of that achievement and being a part of it. Chicago and the wealth they had accumulated seemed small and irrelevant. This was a time to show love and appreciation, a time to reflect on where they had come from, and the sacrifices their Mama and Daddy made for them.

Gladys wished she had more time to spend with her parents. She sat thinking about the afternoon at the church bizarre when Ella bought her quilts. She thought about the subsequent argument with Willie, and the freedom she felt when she quietly closed the door to not wake him up. She had closed a door to a life of mistakes and regrets and had entered another room where the rest of her life was just beginning. More than any of her sisters, she felt loved when Father Wicker acknowledged Jesse and Ella's achievement, and the entire congregation stood and applauded.

It had been decades since Gladys and her father had really talked to each other without fussing and arguing, but she loved her daddy and had always hoped for reconciliation. When everyone gathered to say good-bye to their mama and daddy before heading to New Orleans for the flight back to Chicago, Gladys walked up to Jesse and hugged him tight. Ella and the others, knowing that the father and daughter needed a moment alone, walked away. Gladys looked into her daddy's eyes. It was a long stare, without words being said.

"I love you, Daddy," she said. "We've had our differences. I've done a lot of things that I regret, and I'm sorry if I hurt you in doing them. I've never stopped loving you. Please forgive me."

Jesse didn't quite know what words to say. He, too, had made mistakes in how he had spoken to and treated his oldest child. Over four decades had passed since Judy's death. In his heart, Jesse had never forgiven Gladys for it. Her becoming a strip club dancer and accepting Stone's car had all led to the tragic accident. His resentment had softened over the years, but it hadn't gone away. There was still a part of him that had not forgiven, but he had long ago known that it was past time for the wounds to be healed. He knew that only he could do that.

"Gladys, I haven't been perfect, either. I've made mistakes that I've regretted and been too proud to admit. I might have given you the best I could when you were a child, but I haven't given you what you've needed most as you've grown and matured. I haven't given you the love of a father. Forgive me. I'm so sorry."

"Daddy, you've been the best father any child could have. I didn't see your love because of the blindness of my selfishness. I'm so sorry for the pain I caused."

Jesse stood stiffly and looked his daughter in the eyes, then put his arms around her and held her tight. They both cried soft tears that streamed down their cheeks.

Upon returning to Chicago and going into the office, James Sr. was told by Junior that an FBI agent had gone to the insurance company to see him.

"What did he want? What did he say?" asked James Sr.

"He said that he needed to speak with you about reports he had gotten from underwriters, something about premiums not being sent."

"Premiums? Which underwriters?"

"He didn't say. He left his card and said that you should contact him as soon as you got back."

"Well did you look at the books? You see anything wrong?"

"No sir, I didn't look. I only look at the books when you give them to me to give to the accountant."

Speaking at a pitch that could now be heard by everyone in the office, James Sr. was visibly upset. "Well, I'll be damned. I leave town for two days and the FBI comes knocking on my door. Why didn't you call me?"

"I knew you'd only be gone for the weekend. I thought it could wait until you got back."

"Damn government. Man can't do anything good without them up his ass."

James Sr. met with the FBI agent two days later, a meeting in which he emphatically denied withholding premium payments. Two weeks later, three FBI agents showed up unannounced at the insurance company with a subpoena for all the financial records of Hayes and Byrd Enterprises. They carted off a half-dozen boxes of files.

News of the investigation leaked and became public. Suddenly, James Sr. was faced with a public relations nightmare, if not a possible indictment on charges of insurance fraud. The insurance company had always been the most profitable of James and Hattie's businesses and the only one in which he remained hands-on after bringing Junior, Jesse, and other executives in to oversee the other operations. The accusation was that James Sr. was embezzling premiums for personal use or to funnel cash into other operations, a practice which, according to the FBI, started during the recession of the late 1970s and continued for at least five years. James defended his innocence at a Monday morning Board of Directors meeting with all the sisters present.

"These allegations are absolutely false!" said James Sr., slamming his fist on the table. "I was afraid this might happen when we went public with Harold Washington. The Byrne machine and our own Democratic Party are coming after us, and the state Republican Party is carrying the rope and kerosene. Probably going after every other major Black business that supported Washington. I warned y'all about this. Chicago politics is wicked. Thank God we've got the best lawyer in the city. Murphy Paine will get us through this."

"James, they say the records support their allegations," Carmen said. "How do you defend that?"

"The records don't lie unless they've doctored them up somehow to support their ridiculous and preposterous claims. I'll admit, funds were moved out in the form of short-term loans, but they were all paid back, every penny. This is nothing but a witch hunt designed to destroy our credibility in the Black community and bring us down. It's purely political."

"It certainly is stirring a lot of attention," Rita said. "People are talking, wondering if the company is going under, wondering if you won't be able to pay claims."

"Well, that's not going to happen, I assure you. The company is strong, liquid, and has solid investments to back any and all claims, now and in the future. I'm confident that we'll get past this."

"Is there anything you can do to deal with the negative publicity and calm people's fears?" asked Carmen.

"We had that discussion with Murphy. About all we can do to mitigate the public relations fallout is control our own message," Junior said calmly. "We can do that with a heavy investment in radio advertisement, positive messages about the company's viability and its long-term service to the Black community. We should also meet with *The Defender* to lay out the case that this is all politically motivated, and it certainly wouldn't hurt to meet with a few influential insiders in Mayor Washington's organization."

The investigation continued for another three months. While the advertising campaign helped to mitigate some damage, it was clear that much of it was irreparable. As rumors continued to spread that the company was in trouble and might not be able to honor death claims, policy sales dropped substantially.

In November 1987, nine months after winning his mayoral second term, Harold Washington suffered a massive heart attack and died. Though later proven unfounded, allegations surfaced that cocaine use might have been a contributing factor. Fearing that the Washington camp would have no choice but to distance itself from the insurance fraud scandal that had rocked Bronzeville, James Sr. stepped up the advertising campaign.

The stress of the investigation was affecting him in other ways. He had already gained considerable weight in recent years. He was a heavy smoker, workaholic, had high blood pressure, and suffered frequent bladder infections—for which he didn't seek medical attention. He drank more and slept a lot less than when the investigation started.

Hattie grew increasingly concerned about James' health and pleaded with him to seek medical attention, particularly for the persistent cough that grew worse over time. James said he would but didn't.

"Honey, when are you going to see the doctor about that cough?" Hattie asked as they sat eating breakfast. "It's getting worse by the day."

"Oh, I'll be alright. Just need a little rest."

"What you need to do is put those cigarettes and that liquor bottle down."

"Now, Hattie, don't go preaching to me. I hear enough of that on Sunday morning. Don't worry. I'll be fine."

"How can I not worry, James? This business is killing you. And it all started with that damn investigation. There's a lot more to life than making money. Besides, you won't see a penny of it if you keep this up. You need to retire. Let Junior and Jesse handle things."

"Junior and Jesse have come a long way, but they aren't ready to take the reins, especially with the Feds breathing down our neck. Just settle down. It's not that bad. A little rest over the next few days and I'll be good as new."

"Well, if you aren't, I'm going to call the doctor myself and get him over here."

"I'm okay with that, but trust me, I'll be fine."

On the afternoon of February 3, 1988, James started coughing up blood and was taken to Michael Reese Hospital. Test results showed an advanced stage of incurable lung cancer. At most he had six months to live. It was devastating news to the family but especially to Hattie and their two sons. Just weeks before, James Sr. had celebrated his 70th birthday, the same day that Karry, their first grandchild was born.

On July15th, James was readmitted to the hospital and immediately brought to the intensive care unit and put on a respirator. Thirty-six hours later, a doctor went to the waiting room shortly after midnight and told the family that James had died. Hattie felt devastated that she was asleep and not with him when he took his last breath. She cried uncontrollably for so long that the medical staff had to give her a sedative. Junior and Jesse took the loss equally hard.

James' death was not the first in the Hayes family. The memory of Judy dying in Gladys' car accident at the age of twenty-three still lingered. Willie had died thirty-eight years ago but Ella was the only member of the Hayes family who attended the funeral. At age 70, James Byrd was remembered as an intelligent, strong-willed man who helped to build the Bronzeville business district. Thousands lined up outside Charles S. Jackson Funeral Home to go inside and pay their respects. His funeral brought Bronzeville together, poor and rich, business owners and politicians, hustlers, and those who were hustled, all coming together to pay homage to one of Bronzeville's leading Black citizens.

The Byrd and Hayes families sat in the four front pews of St. Columbanus. The Hayes sisters mourned the loss of a brother who had given them the opportunity and support to not only survive and become successful in Chicago, but to grow into a powerful and influential catalyst for change that bettered the lives of an untold number of other Black residents of the city. They cried as much as Hattie and felt nearly as much of the void and emptiness that James' death created. James was laid to rest in Oak Woods Cemetery, the burial place of many of Chicago's most prominent Black citizens, including Ida B. Wells, Jesse Owens, and Harold Washington.

Ironically, a month after James' death, the FBI closed the case, having found no wrongdoing. While James' practice of borrowing from the insurance company to support the cash flow of other operations was deemed an inappropriate practice, financial records confirmed his claim that the loans were repaid and never diverted for personal use. The investigation alone had not caused James' death, but it probably hastened it. Hattie and her sisters could find no solace in the government's decision. It was not a victory and cause for celebration. The only consolation was that James' character as a decent man was vindicated. At the appropriate time, Junior and Jesse called a special meeting of the Board for Murphy Paine to present James' will.

"James' will and testament bequeaths his entire estate, including Byrd Enterprises, to Hattie, and upon her death to James Jr., Jesse, and their heirs. But he stipulated that all of his financial interest in Hayes Enterprises, which constitutes forty-nine percent of Hayes stock, be equally divided among each of you, Carmen, Rita, Antoinette, and Gladys. We'll have to compute what that means monetarily, but that essentially means that collectively the four of you are now one-hundred percent owners of Hayes Enterprises. Congratulations. What profits you earn going forward will be entirely yours, assuming the company will continue to be profitable. Of course, this also means that collectively you are now responsible for all debt of Hayes Enterprises, short and long-term. Again, I'll provide a detailed accounting of all that at a later date. The good news, as you know, is that having recovered fully from the downturn some years ago, Hayes has minimal debt obligations."

Murphy continued. "Regarding the transfer of his interest in Hayes to you, the will has one last stipulation and a very important one. It stipulates that upon your deaths, what was James' forty-nine percent interest and is now yours will not revert to your heirs, but will go to charitable purposes in perpetuity, meaning that when all of you pass, that portion of your wealth that is attributable to James' gift will not go to your husbands, children, or grandchildren. It will transfer to a separately created philanthropic, non-profit organization that will exist solely for the purpose of donating funds to religious, educational, and social services. He stipulated that it be called the Ella & Jesse Hayes

Foundation and that it only serve the people of Southeast Louisiana. If possible, it would be his wish that the Foundation always be operated either by you, your heirs or those of Hattie and him, but he wisely left that open."

"James and I often talked about his business interests, but as you know he was quite a visionary, not just a business owner. He saw his support to your start and eventual success in business as a gift to him. He'd often joked, 'I'm a blessed man to be married to Hattie in more ways that I can count, but especially because she has those smart, good-looking sisters!' James felt that it would only be appropriate that, through you, his gift to you will live on in perpetuity to help those most in need, and through the names of your mama and daddy."

"And don't y'all worry, Aunties," said Junior. "We'll work closely with Mr. Paine to work out all the details of this."

"But Murphy, only Hattie and Thelma have children." said Carmen. "The rest of us have no heirs other than our husbands, those that have them anyway, and they'll probably go before we do."

"Well, if it does happen that either of your husbands outlive you, the profits from that forty-nine percent will not go to them. It will go directly to the Foundation."

"It sure will make Mama and Daddy proud to have the Foundation in their names," said Hattie. "After all they've done for the people of Gavinville, they'll leave a more permanent legacy of helping people."

"Indeed they will," said Murphy. "You would think that James would have wanted the gift to be in his family name but naming it after your mother and father says everything about the man he was. You all should be proud. We credit much to James' hard work, generosity, and vision, but without your talent and sacrifice the good work wouldn't be there to carry on."

"Lord, I still can't believe he's gone," said Hattie, tearing up.

"Take comfort in knowing that he's in a better place, Mama," Junior said. "He'd want all of us to be strong and carry on."

"Yes, even in his passing, he was thoughtful and giving," said Carmen. "He's in a bigger mansion now for sure."

The meeting was nearly as solemn as James' homegoing celebration. He would be sorely missed by Hattie and her sisters. Fortunately, he left behind two highly educated sons to carry on the work. Under their leadership, Byrd Enterprises would continue to flourish and grow and would eventually establish its footprint in the skyscraping landscape of Chicago.

Chapter 9

After James' funeral, the Hayes sisters were slow to get back to business, quietly mourning in ways that they didn't show publicly. They made no social or political appearances and visited each other more frequently, spending long evenings talking. They had always been like peas in a pod, but James' death brought them closer together, giving each other emotional support that each of them so badly needed. Several months later, somewhere between the third or fourth bottle of wine after dinner, Antoinette suggested that they do something they had never done before together—have a get-away, take a trip abroad to Paris, London, maybe Florence, for at least a week, all of them. Gladys, Carmen, and Rita agreed to it. A few days later, Thelma said yes, and got so excited about the trip that she flew to Chicago to join them in making plans. Hattie, still mourning the loss of James, decided not to go. They met over lunch one afternoon to plan the itinerary.

"Girl, what will five old women in their sixties, some almost seventy, do in Paris and London?" Rita asked, smiling at Gladys and

Carmen. "And Antoinette, you've got more gray hair than any of us and move the slowest. Don't you think you're too old for this?"

"Old? Child, speak for yourself," Antoinette said. "When the sun goes down, I'm like a hot light shining on the back porch . . . bugs swarming all around me."

"I guess that explains why you never married," said Gladys. "You're too busy flaunting and flirting."

"Amen to that, sister," said Carmen. "I've got plenty of pep left in me, too, and then some. Never mind that I'm married. I've yet to pass a man on the street, young, old, or in between who didn't look back to take a look at these hips, even with a woman at his side."

"Do they look when Bernard is with you?" Rita asked.

"You darn right they look."

"And what does Bernard say about all that?" Rita continued.

"What can he say? He knows what he's got. Gets down on his knees every night to thank the Lord for it."

"Lord, help that child . . . please," said Antoinette, lowering and shaking her head.

"You know, the more I think about this trip, the more I'm liking it," said Gladys. "It'll be like the days when we walked down Front Street wearing our hats and new dresses, twisting just to be noticed. I think it'll be fun. God knows we need a change of scenery and something to lift our spirits."

"Well, I wouldn't have flown up here to make plans if I weren't ready. I can't wait. But Antoinette, you've got to promise to behave yourself."

"Girl don't worry about me. Carmen is the wild one. She talks all that political stuff but when she cuts loose, it's like a runaway caboose."

The sisters had not spent time together since before Gladys left home to live with their cousin Mary. Their plans included three days in London, on to Paris for two days, then two days in Florence. Six weeks later, they flew from Chicago to New York, and then to London. For seven days, they spent lavishly, lodged in the finest hotels, dined in the finest restaurants, shopped in Europe's most luxurious stores, and visited famous museums and historic sites, including the ancient cathedrals and castles.

After being abroad for a week, the highlight of the trip was the last night, when they capped dinner off with desserts at two of Florence's oldest restaurants. Their last stop was the famous, Trattoria Buzzino, established in 1844 and a must-stop for every tourist. None of them spoke Italian, but they had managed to enjoy two days of Florence without it.

"First things first," said Antoinette. "One more bottle of wine. I have no idea what it says on this bottle, but it's just wine. I'm sure we can afford it."

"Not for me," Carmen said. "I'm starting to feel woozy. I've had enough."

"Since when did you ever get enough of anything, especially food and wine," Rita said. "Girl, you gotta drink. One way or another, we'll get you back to the hotel. Besides, this is our last night. We gotta get in the mood for some partying!"

"Partying?" Gladys chimed in, "I'm pooped, and my stomach is about ready to pop. I can't wait to throw myself across the bed."

"Come on Sis, it's our last night," said Rita, looking at Carmen.

"Alright, but just one glass," Carmen said. "They'll probably end up carrying the four of you out on a stretcher. One of us needs to be a little sober."

"I can't believe it. Girls from Gavinville in Florence, Italy," said Thelma, looking out onto the cobbled street filled with people. "To be honest, I had heard about London and Paris, but the last time I even thought about Italy was when I peeped on David Hebert's test paper in geography class to answer some stupid question about Mussolini."

"So, who do y'all think has the finest looking men, Paris, London, or Florence?" asked Carmen.

"Child, as old as you are, I'm surprised you know what a man is," said Antoinette, laughing.

"Well, I ain't seen a man all week that wasn't good looking, but I can't wait to get back home and see me some Negro," said Thelma. "Ain't nothing like a tall, handsome, dark skin man."

"I'm with that," said Carmen softly. "I miss mine to death."

"Which one, Sis?" Gladys asked jokingly.

"Every one of them," Carmen said, bobbing her head and snapping fingers on both hands.

"Yeah, you sure have had enough to drink," said Antoinette, looking up from the menu. "Can any of you make out any words on this dessert menu. I sure hope the waiter speaks English. To be honest, as good as it tasted, I have no idea what I ate at the other restaurant. All I remember is that it was sweet."

"I've got a taste for meringue pie. Don't know if it's on here, but I sure will ask," said Thelma.

"Okay with me," said Antoinette. "At least I'll know what I'm eating."

"Same for me," said Carmen.

"Not a bad choice, Sis, I'll do the same if they got it," said Rita. "Lemon in fact. If they ain't got it, I'll ask them to make one . . . Gladys?"

"Good enough for me, Sis," said Gladys. "I'll take the same, but not if they have to make one. I don't want any part of that discussion. Lord knows where it'll end up. We'll be sitting here half the night with Antoinette ordering more wine."

The waiter came and guided the sisters in a selection of one of Italy's finest cabernet sauvignons. As things turned out, lemon meringue pie was one of the restaurant's most popular dessert offerings. No one talked business and Carmen was too tipsy to think politics. The sisters simply had fun. They ate, drank, and reminisced. For Black women from the small town of Gavinville, Louisiana, the world that they had lived in for nearly seventy years quickly became larger than they could have ever dreamt or imagined. More importantly, they had discovered it as sisters, the daughters of Jesse and Ella Hayes. In some ways, the trip proved to be transcendent, not just of the boundaries of where they lived, but of the limits of their dreams and aspirations. They returned home with a renewed sense of purpose and destiny, and a realization that there was still much more required of them, not just in building more wealth for themselves, but in helping those who were less fortunate and poor.

In April 1989, the sisters met with Murphy Paine and proposed the idea of establishing the Jesse and Ella Hayes Foundation now rather than when their inheritance of James' gift would pass on to their heirs. They would capitalize and support the organization with cash savings and profits from their fifty-one percent share of Hayes Enterprises. They wanted to do it now, while their mama and daddy were still alive to know that the fruits of their hard work and sacrifices were helping others. Three years later, the Jesse and Ella Hayes Foundation made its first charitable investment, the construction of a new elderly housing project in Gavinville. They named it Vermilion Place. Thelma would be there but the sisters in Chicago insisted that Gladys go alone to represent them at the ribbon cutting.

"But people will remember me as a strip club dancer. I don't think I should go, let alone represent the family. It wouldn't be right. It would detract from the good that Mama and Daddy are doing."

"Sis, that was your past, over forty years ago," Carmen quickly stepped in to say. "If anything, your being there to represent us would show that you've risen above all that. You're a strong Black woman who made mistakes, but by God's grace you've overcome them. You've beaten back the odds against you, including a bad marriage, and you've gone on to make a great mark in the world. And now you're going back to show other young Black women that they too can rise when they fall."

"Besides, you're the oldest, our big sister," said Rita. "Who can represent us better?"

Ella and Jesse were on hand to cut the yellow ribbon on September 18, 1992. The ceremony drew the attendance of every politician in Southeast Louisiana, Black and white, and nearly every politician holding statewide office. It was a proud day for Ella and Jesse, a perfect day of cool weather and blue skies. As expected, Ella drew attention as the old Black woman, who for over fifty years had healed the sick with God's hands. But all she could think about was her daughters, the little girls from Gavinville whose hair she used to curl, her babies who grew up, moved to Chicago, became wealthy, and gave back by building a housing project for some of Gavinville's oldest and poorest residents.

On October 18, 1992, a month after he and Ella held the big scissors to cut the ribbon on Vermilion Place, Jesse Hayes died quietly in his sleep. He was ninety-seven years old. He and Ella had been married for seventy-five years. Ella was lying beside him, in the place where she had slept every night since the day of their marriage, cuddled inside Jesse's big arm, her head resting on his chest. Even in the years when Jesse was paralyzed she'd lift his arm to put it around her. She'd listen to hear his heart as if it were the only birdsong in the air when the sun went down, and one star stood beside the moon. That night, the bird stopped singing, and Ella knew that morning would not come. She lay there for a long time against Jesse's chest until the sun rose, listening to the quietness that he had brought, a silence that even the birds outside must have felt, because they made no sounds, as if they knew that one of their own had passed, gone on to another sky far away.

Much to Gladys' disappointment, her daddy was waked at Cole Funeral Home. The crowd was standing room only all afternoon and well into the night, prompting Phillip Cole III, the son of Phillip Cole Jr., to extend visitation hours until midnight. By most estimates, the entire Black community of Gavinville, and many white people who had either worked with Jesse or been healed by Ella, stood in line to pay their last respects. Families brought their children and grandchildren to gaze down on the face of a man who had lived longer than anyone in the history of the town. Many went just to cast their eyes on Mama Ella, some hoping to get near enough to be touched by her healing hands. Ella graciously obliged, sitting in her wheelchair a few feet from the coffin, her hands never resting, constantly reaching out and touching those who passed by.

Joining the Hayes daughters on the front pews were their husbands, children, and close relatives. As expected, the sisters were dressed fashionably, though in black, and were the only women wearing hats. Even sitting, they looked dignified and statuesque. Unlike James' funeral, none of them wept publicly. They needed to be strong for their Mama. The solemn, stoic looks on their faces was their only show of pain and grief.

The celebration mass at St. Paul was customarily brief but with a flair of veneration to those who knew Jesse Hayes more personally and intimately. He was an unusual man, not only to have lived so long but to have been entirely faithful to his loving wife for seventy-five years, a strong Black man who worked hard, never tilted his hat to white people, never stepped aside to let them pass, and never hesitated to speak his mind. Though living in the shadow of a legend, his quiet strength had not gone unseen and unappreciated.

The interment at Gavinville Cemetery was followed by a repast in which the whole town, Black and white, seemed to have made plans to attend. In anticipation of a large crowd, the Mayor of Gavinville had personally visited Ella to express his condolences and offer the Municipal Auditorium as a place for the repast at no cost to the family. Restaurants donated cooked food, and bars slipped cases of liquor through the back door. The procession of cars caused a major traffic jam on Hwy 90, larger than any of the seafood festivals that were Gavinville's largest tourist attractions. It was the first time in the history of the town that so many Black and white people had come together under one roof.

Many of the white people there had heard about the miracle of 1939. Most of them had not seen or met Jesse or Ella, but they all knew that something old and godly, like a stately oak, had left them and would never be seen again. They wanted to be a part of its passing, if only in a small, quickly forgotten way. They were drawn, unconsciously perhaps, by the universal archetype of the wise old man, who in the minds of many of them was not Black at all. To them, Jesse was more symbol and myth than reality, but they clung to it as if it were something needful and redeeming. Ella and her daughters took it all in stride, greeting and thanking as many people as time would allow.

The day after their daddy's funeral, Antoinette, Carmen, and Hattie returned to Chicago with other members of the family. Gladys and Rita stayed behind to spend time with their mama. Ella's health had declined as much as their daddy's had in recent years. They knew that she could not live alone. Jesse would not be there to care for her and she needed regular medical attention. Ella had already told Thelma that she would never go to live with her because she needed her own space and her own time to do God's work.

It pained Rita to leave her mama in Gavinville at a time when she most needed help. Thelma would be there, but she knew that Thelma would be more focused on Terrell's dental practice and tending to her own family matters. Rita told her mama that she would speak to Charles about them moving to Gavinville.

"Why would you want to move back to this town?"

"One of us needs to be here with you, Mama. You can't live in this house alone."

"Child, don't worry about me. I'll be okay. The neighbors around here will help. We're all family here. And Thelma's in town."

"Mama, you need professional care. The neighbors can't give you that. And Thelma's in Gavinville but she's not in this house. With Daddy gone, you need someone here twenty-four hours a day. I think I can convince Charles to move. We'll buy a home here. In the meantime, we can move you to St. Aloysius Nursing Home."

"A nursing home? I can't go there. I've got to be where God's children will come for help."

"St. Aloysius is a new facility and it's on the lake. You can have your own suite, the kind reserved for people who don't need government assistance. We'll pay for everything. You can even have your own living room and a patio with a view of the lake. More importantly, you'd have around the clock nursing care."

"My Lord, now you're trying to put me with the rich white people. God's children will never go there for help."

"We just want you to have the best care, Mama. You deserve that. And it'll only be for a while, probably six months, nine at the most, just long enough for us to settle our business in Chicago and buy a home here."

"Well, I suppose I can go, but only for a while. And only if they don't stop God's children from coming by, anytime they want to. People show up here all hours of the night. Sometimes death is knocking at the door. I've got to be there for them."

"I'm sure we can work something out with the nursing home, Mama. And don't forget, you'll be living in a place where a lot of people need prayer and healing."

Gladys stayed in Gavinville long enough to help Rita and Thelma settle their daddy's funeral expenses and plan their mama's move. Murphy Paine had advised them to get Ella to sign a Power of Attorney, giving them complete control over her financial and medical decisions. Ella agreed to that also, as well as having her mail routed to them in Chicago. They returned to Chicago a month later.

Charles was a native of Chicago. Rita knew that it would take some persuading to get him to leave. He had been pastoring over forty years and was already talking about retiring. Money would certainly not be an issue. They'd probably be the wealthiest Black people in Gavinville. More than anything, he was concerned about moving to the South, particularly a town as small as Gavinville. Reluctantly, he agreed to go, but the other sisters pushed back.

"Sis, Mama will be in good hands at the nursing home," Carmen said. "She'll be taken care of. She's lived a long life, but we all know that her days are numbered, as precious as each one is. Your moving to Gavinville isn't going to change that."

"I know, but I don't want to leave my mama there without one of us around. Thelma is there, but you know Thelma. She cares as much about her big house and fancy car as she does about Mama's health. She loves Mama but she was Daddy's girl, and with him gone Mama won't see as much of her as she should. Mama deserves more. She has given us her life. The least we can do is be there for her in her last days. Besides, it took some persuading just to get her to leave Dixie Manor. She only agreed to the nursing home on the condition that it be temporary, until Charles and I buy a home in Gavinville."

"So, Charles has agreed to moving?" Gladys asked.

"He's not happy about leaving Chicago, particularly about moving to the South, but we've talked and prayed about it and he's on board. We both think it's the right thing to do."

"What about your work, Sis?" Antoinette asked.

"Y'all know that we'll be retiring soon. I'll just be the first. I'm pretty sure that things will run just as smoothly without me being around. Besides, now that the Foundation is up and running, it would be good to put an office in Gavinville. Charles and I can run it from our home until we hire support staff. Remember, that was one of James' conditions, that if possible a member of the family would always run the Foundation. None of us know much about running a foundation, but Charles has good experience being a church pastor. With some help from Murphy, we'll figure it out."

"But Gavinville," said Gladys. "I can't imagine me ever moving back to that place. When I left I said I'll never go back, and I won't."

"I'm not asking any of you to go. Chicago is your life now. I understand. But Charles and I have decided. We'll be leaving as soon as his church finds another pastor and we buy a home. Now, what I need is a big hug from all my sisters." With that said, they all embraced and pledged to support Rita and Charles in whatever way they could.

Charles and Rita bought a historic but luxurious home on Burbank Avenue, the most upscale white neighborhood in Gavinville. Needless to say, the purchase caused quite a stir among the neighbors, who wondered how any Black family could afford a house there. Much to Rita's surprise, it happened to be the first home of Dr. and Mrs. Edwin Stanford, whom her Mama had done domestic work for during the 1930s. The Stanfords had sold the house to a young attorney and moved into a smaller home while Ella worked for them. When the attorney passed away, his family decided to put the house up for sale. Rita couldn't wait to give her Mama the news.

"The Stanford's old home?" asked Ella, speaking in a voice that was now almost a whisper, so low that Rita had to get closer to hear. "Child I can't live there. What will people think, me sitting behind those tall, white columns? They'll say I got rich off the Lord's work. And what will the Lord say? He told me years ago that I was a vessel to heal his children. I need to be where they will go, not on that hill looking down on them."

"Mama, you can barely lift your hands to pray for yourself, let alone somebody else. Maybe it's time you start thinking more about you, not in a selfish way, but by letting us help you to be more comfortable."

"I'm comfortable enough here. I just can't see myself living on that hill while poor people are starving and dying because they can't get help."

"The Foundation will work on that, Mama. You and Daddy are giving this community a gift that will help now and for many years to come. You've healed a lot a people for over half a century. God knows the good you've done. You always told us, 'It's not about where you live but how you live.' The people here will know whose house this is. I think it will matter a lot to them and to God that you're living with your children and being taken good care of."

Ella agreed to move. She hadn't given any thought to the irony of it—that she would be living in the house that she rode the bus to every weekday morning, crossing the flat, wooden bridge where Jesse's horse bucked and caused him to be paralyzed for three years, the home of the white family she had to clean, iron, and cook for.

Two days before the moving van was scheduled to arrive and begin packing their belongings for the move to Gavinville, Rita got a phone call from Carmen one early evening. She didn't give any details, but in a tone that conveyed concern and urgency Carmen urged Rita and Charles to go to Hattie's home as quickly as possible.

"What happened, what's going on?" Rita asked.

"I'm sorry but I can't say much more right now. Just get over here as quickly as possible, both of you. I've got to go now. It's very important. Come quickly."

Rita couldn't imagine what had happened. She could only think the worst, that something terrible had happened to Hattie. Her concern was heightened when they arrived and saw no lights on in Hattie's home and cars were lined on both sides of the street. Upon ringing the door, the door swung open to the sound of "surprise!" The sisters had secretly planned a going away party, but this was more than a party. It was a gathering of Bronzeville's wealthiest, most influential and powerful residents, all there to bid Rita and Charles farewell. Knowing that Rita would probably not come dressed as she normally would for such an occasion, Hattie had instructed the invitees to dress casual. It would be a pool party in Hattie's lush, exquisitely landscaped backyard, catered, of course, with fine food and wine. A jazz quartet began playing when Rita and Charles arrived. It was a special night filled with dancing and laughter among friends and close associates, each one hoping to get a moment with Rita and Charles to say good-bye. Jesse was there and James Jr. called to say that he, Margie, and Karry, their five-year old son, were on the way.

At 9:30 that evening, while most guests were still present, Hattie answered the doorbell to find Clarence Mason, a Chicago police officer and friend of the Byrd family standing there.

"Clarence don't tell me one of the neighbors complained about the noise. We're having a going away party for Rita and Charles."

"Good evening, Hattie. No, I'm afraid it's much more serious than that. I would have called but I thought it best to tell you in person. May I come in?"

"Yes, please. What happened? What's going on?"

"Hattie, there's been an accident. Junior and his family."

"Oh no. What? What happened? Are they okay?"

"From the facts we were able to gather, a drunk driver traveling at high speed lost control of his vehicle and entered the lane in which Junior was traveling in the opposite direction. The collision was head-on and fatal. Unfortunately, Junior and your grandson didn't survive. They were pronounced dead at the scene."

"Oh my Lord. Oh my Lord." Hattie fainted, and was immediately attended to by Dr. Pendleton, a physician present at the party.

Jesse and his aunts screamed and cried. Suddenly, the atmosphere was filled with grief too heavy for words to comfort. The guests cried and comforted each other.

"How's Margie?" Charles asked Officer Mason.

"Margie appeared to have suffered a severe head injury from crashing into the windshield and was rushed to University of Chicago Medical Center. I have no information beyond that. I don't know how to reach other members of her family. If you or any others have that information, I'll contact them."

When brought back to consciousness, Hattie was hysterical. "Take me to my children. Take me to the morgue," she screamed. I have to see my children."

"Mrs. Hayes, it's best that you don't go there now," said Dr. Pendleton. "What you need right now is rest. I'll get you a sedative for that. Please, stay home and rest."

Jesse, stricken and crying over the loss of his brother and nephew, had enough composure to suggest that they go to the hospital. Other family members followed. Gladys and Carmen stayed with Hattie. It was a devastating blow for a family that in the last four years had already experienced the deaths of two men closer to them than any men they had known.

James Jr. would have been thirty-seven years old in two months. He and Jesse had steered the Byrd and Hayes businesses through their roughest times. After the death of James Sr., they shared the titles of President and CEO, and were poised to lead both businesses to even greater heights for many years to come. Like his father, Junior was eulogized as a bright, visionary business leader that Bronzeville would long remember. He was buried in one of the Byrd family plots in Oak

Woods Cemetery on a frigid day in late February. Karry was laid to rest a few feet away.

Doctors had recommended immediate brain surgery for Margie on the night of the accident. Her condition remained critical. Lying in a hospital bed under heavy sedation, she mourned the loss of her husband and son. Her mother and father, Joseph and Denise Bradford, left the funeral with the Byrd and Hayes families and went directly to the hospital to begin the long vigil of waiting and praying for Margie's recovery. Still overcome with grief, Hattie felt that it was best that she not go. Jesse drove her home.

A week later, Margie went into a comatose state and was put on a respirator. The doctor asked for a meeting of the families to discuss their options for treatment. He stated that Margie's chance of recovery was close to none, and if she survived, she'd live the rest of her life in a severely vegetative state. He advised that they consider taking her off the respirator, assuring them she would be given morphine to relieve any pain in the final minutes of her life. He left the families to talk it over. Margie was the only child of the Bradfords. Everyone felt that they should make the decision. A day later, the Bradford's returned with the decision to terminate Margie's life support and let her go peacefully.

Bernard, who had been mostly a bystander throughout the vigil, sat quietly in the waiting area, comforting Carmen while reading his Bible. Bernard was a prayerful man of strong faith, and Carmen often joked that he had missed his calling by not being a preacher. He asked the Bradford family if they would join him in prayer at Margie's bedside before speaking to the doctor. They agreed, and everyone, including the Hayes family, went in, filling up the small room. Bernard opened his Bible and read a scripture, then laid his right hand on Margie's head and began to pray. It was a short prayer, but when he said "Amen" and everyone lifted their heads Bernard stood still, his head still bowed and his hand still resting on Margie's head. Several minutes went by and he remained in that position, prompting Carmen to speak.

"Bernard, are you okay?" He didn't answer.

"Bernard . . . honey."

"Bernard?"

The moment that Bernard took his hand off Margie's forehead, tears streamed from his eyes. He remained silent, then turned to the Bradfords and said, "Let the doctor know when you are ready." He left the room and walked toward the waiting area. Carmen, concerned and somewhat baffled, followed him. Stricken with grief, the Bradfords asked for a moment to be alone with their daughter. The Hayes family left and stood outside the door as Mr. and Mrs. Bradford said good-bye to their only child. By then, everyone was in tears. When the Bradfords gestured, they went back inside, sobbing and comforting each other.

Two nurses entered the room, followed by the doctor, who spoke to the Bradfords once more and told them that they could be present when he removed the respirator and gave the injection. The Bradfords motioned the Byrds to come closer. As the nurses moved toward Margie to remove the tube from her throat, something pushed them back, and one of them screamed. Everyone looked down to find that Margie had suddenly opened her eyes.

"My God!" the doctor said in shock. "What in God's heaven has happened?" He asked the families to leave the room for a few minutes and closed the door. No one knows what went through the minds of the nurses and doctor in that moment when they saw Margie, surreal as it must have been for them to be looking at a patient who for all practical purposes had been dead and was now alive, breathing on her own, with her eyes wide open. After examining Margie, the doctor called the family back inside. He and the nurses stood silently against the wall, watching everyone's joyful reaction to what was simply unexplainable. They had all witnessed a miracle. Margie did not speak at that moment, but further examinations would conclude that her brain damage was minimal and with therapy she could live a long, productive life with no cognitive or physical impairment.

Feeling weak and somewhat disoriented when he left Margie's room, Bernard had asked Carmen if they could go home. He wasn't there to see or know what had happened, and he didn't have to be told. He knew. He had felt the power pass to him the day he and Carmen were married when he and Ella talked and embraced. Ella, too, had felt the strange, indescribable warmth that had passed through him to her. Bernard knew then that he had been given the treater's gift of healing that Ella's father had over a century ago and that Ella was given in 1939. But this was 1993, Chicago, not the small town of Gavinville. Bernard knew the power of faith. Still, he was as confused about why the miracle had happened as he was certain that it had. He had to go see Mama Ella.

Three days later, after Carmen had gone to spend a few days with Hattie, Bernard flew to New Orleans. Charles picked him up at the airport for the trip to Gavinville. Bernard was the least talkative of the sons-in-law. He sensed that he had a spiritual calling but was content teaching at the university. Not once did he give any thought to entering the ministry, even after feeling the strangely warm spirit that had flowed through his body that afternoon of his wedding when he and Ella talked. Rita started the conversation.

"Bernard, everyone is still a little baffled about what happened, but no one doubts that Margie wouldn't be alive if you hadn't prayed and laid hands on her. Looks like Mama was right about the gift passing on to a man."

"I'm not so sure about all that. To be honest, I'm searching for answers like everyone else. All I did was pray and believe. Like Mama Ella always said, 'God does the healing.' How's she doing by the way?"

"Mama is doing fine. She took it all pretty hard, losing a grandson and great grand. She never got to see Karry. She's spending more time in bed these days, not wanting to sit up as much as she used to. We're a little worried about that. You'll have to get real close and speak loud. Her hearing and voice are getting worse, but her mind is sharp as a razor, too sharp for an old woman her age. You can't get anything past her."

"I'm excited about seeing her again. It's amazing that our paths crossed this way after so many years. Not sure if she can help me find some answers, but it'll be good just to see her again."

"How are Hattie and the others holding up?" Charles asked.

"Hattie's resting better. Carmen's there with her and Gladys and Antoinette drop in every day."

"Caring for Mama is a thirty-six-hour day. Lord, that old woman is something. All day long, she complains that no one stops by for prayer and healing, blaming Charles and me for moving her to some mansion on a hill."

Bernard closed his eyes and dozed off about halfway to Gavinville. When he awoke, the first thing he saw were the tall white columns and big porch that wrapped around the three-story antebellum mansion. "My, my, looks like slaves really put their heart and soul into this one."

"Thank you, Bernard," Charles said. "A bit much for just Rita and me to keep up, but it's home. Thelma's here, looking after Mama while we took the drive. She'll be glad to see you."

Thelma had taken Ella out of bed and moved her to the side porch facing the rose garden. After exchanging greetings and hugs with

Bernard, she brought him over. Hattie and Charles stood at a distance but close enough to watch Ella's reaction to seeing her Bebo. Bernard walked toward her from the back of the porch, so Ella wouldn't see him coming. He grabbed one of the rocking chairs, hurriedly pulled it close to the wheelchair, then reached down and put his arms around Ella, startling her momentarily until she realized who was there. He held her face in his hands, letting their eyes say the first words as he watched them twinkle like the first two stars of evening, then he pulled the rocker closer to face her.

"My Bebo!" she whispered, reaching to put her arms around him. "What a beautiful day the Lord has made."

"Hi Mama."

"My Bebo. Boy you're starting to get gray as me. And what's that gal feeding you? Still the most handsome man in the family, though."

"Thank you, Mama. How've you been?"

"Oh, you know. Same old thing. Trying to make better women out of those daughters of mine. Thank God they've got strong men like you who tolerate their nonsense." Ella paused for a moment to catch her breath. "I know what brings you here. Rita told me what happened. I felt it you know. I felt the spirit that day when you and Carmen got married. I knew."

"Mama, I'm as thankful as everyone that Margie lived, but all I did was pray and believe."

Ella's whisper grew louder and clearer. "Son, that's the gift. It's not you. It's not your hands. It's your faith. It might sound simple, but it's not easy to believe in the greatness of God. People say they do, but they always come up short. The troubles of life always get in the way of pure faith in God. Few can believe the way you do, the way the Lord taught us to. Margie was your first mountain, but there will be plenty more if you let God speak. You've been given the gift of healing. Don't try to understand it. Just listen to Him and be the vessel. He'll tell you what to do and when. He'll point the way."

As simple as Ella's words sounded, they were as profound as any that Bernard had ever heard spoken. Suddenly, he had become Bebo again, the six-year-old boy who apologized to Miss Ella for flinging rocks while she walked toward the bus stop. Her words had become the song of the sparrow that had flown over their heads as they walked and talked about his mama's health.

Bernard spent the rest of the day with Rita, Charles, and Thelma, with Ella joining them for dinner, before he settled in for the early morning ride back to New Orleans. The days and months ahead would be a period of introspection and quiet reflection, listening for answers to questions that Margie's miraculous recovery had posed. He returned home to find his wife and sisters-in-law still mourning. Hattie had worn black every day since the funeral and hadn't left the house. Carmen went home but was uncharacteristically quiet most of the time. The only time that Antoinette and Gladys left home was to visit Hattie. Margie was released from the hospital and being cared for by her parents.

Fortunately, Jesse remained collected enough to go back to work and tend to business. The economy was booming under the leadership of a young U.S. President from Arkansas who had been elected in November 1992. The closing of U. S. Steel's South Works marked the end of an already declining steel industry, but service industries such as those in which the sisters had invested grew rapidly. High-poverty, high-rise housing projects, and high-crime continued to pose major problems for South Side Chicago, but there were encouraging signs of redevelopment. At the end of 1993, Hayes Enterprises was poised for another year of record-setting profits.

Slowly, the sisters, now in their early to mid-seventies, returned to their roles as socialites and civic engagers. Although they had not formally retired, they spent hardly any time in their business offices, showing up mostly for Board of Directors meetings and important lunch or dinner meetings when Jesse thought their presence would be helpful. About the only fun they really seemed to have was shopping and attending White Sox and Bulls games. They hadn't paid much attention to sports in their younger years, but for some strange reason they got interested when they grew older. Of course, they'd always have some of the best seats, and over the years took photos and got autographs of all the star players. They especially loved to watch Michael Jordan and Scottie Pippen when Jordan came out of retirement and the Bulls seemed invincible

Always socially and politically conscious as businesswomen, the sisters continued to promote causes for Chicago's economically disadvantaged, and quietly worked to reshape the landscape of Chicago politics. In 1994, they supported the candidacy of Roland Burris, an African American state attorney general, in his unsuccessful bid for the Democratic nomination for governor of the State of Illinois. They again backed Burris in his unsuccessful run against long-time Mayor Richard M. Daly. Just when it seemed that their political influence had diminished, a dynamic young civil rights attorney and political newcomer, who had previously led a major voter registration campaign in Chicago, declared his candidacy for state senate in the fall of 1995. Only thirty-four years old, Barack Obama, struck a chord among Chicago's South Side residents, whom he would represent in the State Senate. The Hayes sisters were especially enamored for reasons that were as much personal as they were political. Like James Jr. and Jesse, Obama was a Harvard graduate, and he was young, courageous, and visionary. They quickly got behind him. Obama would go on to win the race in November 1996. It would be the last political campaign that the sisters supported as residents of Chicago.

Chapter 10

Christmas was always the most special and exciting time of year for the Hayes sisters. Even now, when they were no longer involved in the day-to-day operations of their stores, they made rounds regularly between Thanksgiving and Christmas, mainly to talk with employees, mingle with shoppers, and look at displays and decorations. Needless to say, they always attracted attention—four Black women, old by some standards, wealthy by any, walking the streets of downtown Chicago with flamboyance that made everyone they pass stare and wonder.

Saturday, December 16, 1995, was cold enough for them to wear the fur coats and hats that they bought in London years ago but only wore when they were all together, prancing down the streets to make a show of themselves. After a half-day of sightseeing, they returned to Carmen's house to find Bernard standing outside the front door. He had spoken to Carmen by phone and knew that they were on their way. He had bad news but needed to tell them in person. Their mama had died. Like their daddy, she passed quietly, without pain. Rita had wheeled her to the porch to have breakfast in her favorite spot, facing one of the gardens. While Ella waited for Rita to bring coffee, she closed her eyes and never opened them again.

The sisters cried but not in the way they had done for their daddy and James Sr. Their mama had lived a long life, ninety-eight years. Her death was sudden but not unexpected. They took comfort in knowing that, like their daddy, she didn't suffer. Still, it was painful to lose the woman who had given them birth, nurtured and taught them, and prepared them to go out into the world and rise above all its bitterness and brokenness. Their tears seemed joyful, as if they had already begun to celebrate their mama's passing into the only life that really mattered to her. Unlike their daddy and James, their mama was a woman, and they were women. With her, they shared the fun and laughter of girlhood and the meaning of womanhood and motherhood—all the ways of being a woman. In some ways, she was a sister with whom they had so much more in common than they could have ever had with a brother, even their father. To everyone in Gavinville, she was Ella Hayes, the great Louisiana traiteus who healed the sick, but to them she was simply Mama.

Ella had often spoken about the kind of funeral she wanted. She knew that she would live to be so old that nearly everyone she had healed would be gone. She didn't want the town's people who never knew her to put her on a pedestal and make a spectacle of her service to God. She wanted the whole church to be filled with children. She wanted her life to be history to them, not some high-flown eulogy about the good she had done. She wanted someone to tell the children about the hate and injustice she had to endure growing up and living in the South. "Tell the children," Ella would say, "where my mama, papa, and their mama and papa came from and what they had to go through for me to have breath, marry a good man, and raise beautiful children."

Lastly, she didn't want the repast to be a party with people pouring in off the streets just to grab a free plate of food. "Feed the children well," she'd say, "and give them cups of cold water."

And so, the sisters made another trip to Gavinville to lay their mama in the ground beside their daddy. People stood in line for hours outside Cole Funeral Home to go inside and pass by her coffin. The funeral at St. Paul would be on a Saturday. The local superintendent of schools sent an invitation to all the public-school children of Gavinville to attend. They would be picked up at Gavinville High School and bused to the church. After the family processional, the children would enter the church, followed by adults if there were any empty seats remaining. There were few. The only gown-ups present were Ella's family and a few former neighbors from Dixie Manor. There were no politicians and civic leaders, no reporters and television cameras. Ella had her way, and Bernard gave a eulogy exactly as she had asked it to be spoken. Rita and Charles hosted the repast for family members, close friends, and the children in their back yard. Each of the children was given a balloon, and in one bright moment, when the sun broke through and the birds were singing, they released them into the sky.

Death seemed to have stalked the Hayes daughters over the last four years, first James Sr, then their Daddy, then James Jr. and Karry, and now their Mama. The sisters were starting to wonder if a curse had befallen them or whether it was just God's way of talking. They were growing old, albeit gracefully. Though unusual for Black people their age, none of the sisters had any serious health issues to worry about. Still, they thought about what dreadful disease might be lurking, dormant deep down inside, waiting to come alive. Both parents now gone, they were alone, not knowing what they didn't know and couldn't feel, masking a world broken by grief.

There were moments when they talked about their fears and insecurities, the thoughts that weighed heaviest on their hearts when they lay awake while the world slept. Sitting on Gladys' patio one Friday evening, chatting, sipping wine, and listening to John Coltrane's tenor sax wailing in the background, Carmen posed a challenge. "Let's tell the darkest secret we have, the one thing we did that we regret doing but haven't told anyone in the family. Let's shine the light on the one thing we did that we are most ashamed of and have kept a secret. Now, the only condition is that what we say here must stay here, not to ever be told to anyone else, not even Rita and Thelma."

"Why not Rita and Thelma?" Antoinette asked.

"Because they're not here to tell us theirs," said Carmen.

"I don't know if I'm ready for that kind of truth, Sis," said Antoinette. "I love y'all but I ain't ready to hear about times you worshipped the devil. And I damn sure don't what you to hear mine."

"I'm with Antoinette," said Hattie. "Some things are just between Jesus and me. I don't have to broadcast it to the world. I've repented and He's forgiven. Case closed."

"I'm not talking about confessing," said Carmen. "I'm talking about sister truth, sister sharing, and sister love. What's there to fear or be ashamed of?"

"Y'all know I could never keep a secret. How could I with y'all being one step ahead or one step behind me all the time."

"Come on, Hattie. We all know it's there," Gladys said. "If we're going to tell it, you've got to be first. Tell it!"

"Come on Sis," said Carmen. "Let it out. There's got to be something. We weren't always around, especially when you and Rita went tipping out late at night."

Hattie paused to think. "How big a secret?"

"You know, big, the biggest, so big that if anyone found out, you'd be so ashamed and embarrassed that you'd want to die, maybe kill yourself, even now."

"Well since you brought it up, why don't you go first, Carmen?"

Carmen looked up into the trees, then down without looking at anything. "Well, I didn't show it, but the first couple of years of my marriage were hard. Bernard and I were having differences. He'd complain about everything, me not responding to him, my cooking not being right, me spending too much time with my sisters, and on and on. I suspected that he was having an affair with a woman at the university, a white woman in fact, who was much younger than he was. I confronted him about it and he denied it but the charade continued. Eventually, I ended up having an affair myself. I don't know, maybe it was my way of retaliating, paying him back. It didn't last long. When we got to the point where both of us were ready to call it quits, we decided to seek counseling to try to get back on track. We did, but I'm still very ashamed of committing adultery."

"Girl, didn't I tell you that man was too young for you to marry?" Hattie joked, "but there's nothing to be ashamed of. He was the first to act a fool."

"Why didn't you come to us, Sis?" Gladys asked. "You know we would have been there for you."

"I know, but in marriage, sometimes you feel that it's all about the bedroom and that's where it needs to stay. I gave a minute's thought to leaving Bernard, but I loved that man, still do. I always felt that somehow we'd work things out."

"What I want to know is was it worth it?" Antoinette asked, smiling.

"What do you mean?"

"Now, I know it's been a while, old woman, but I think you know darn well what I mean."

"Oh, Antoinette. I thought your mind would have gotten cleaner by now. But I see it's still in the gutter. Well, all I'll say is that I've never met a man who can light my fire like that sweet, charming Negro of mine, but he's lucky to have a brick house rather than that little wooden thing he was fooling around with."

"Gosh, Sis, that one's going to be hard to follow," Hattie said, "but I'll give it a try." Hattie sighed, pausing to ask herself if she really wanted to confess. "Well here goes. James Jr. wasn't the first child of mine to die. Remember Jerome Jackson, the boy I dated a few times in high school? I got pregnant by him. We both knew that I couldn't have that baby, so I got rid of it."

"Oh Hattie. How? Who?" Antoinette asked.

"That's not important. I'd rather not say, but today I still see that child. I see her in my dreams. Yes, a girl, although I didn't know it at the time."

"Why didn't you tell us, Sis?" Gladys asked.

"Telling y'all would have been telling Mama and Daddy. I was too scared. I couldn't. Lord knows I regret getting rid of that baby. I often think about her, you know, who and what she might have become. But I didn't love Jerome. I wasn't ready to be a mother, and Jerome surely wasn't ready to be a father. More than anything, I was afraid of how Daddy and Mama would react."

The sisters paused in silence for a while to process Hattie's story, which had shocked them much more than the secret that Carmen told. "Okay, only two of us left and I don't want to be last. I'll just get right to the truth," said Antoinette. "No dancing around it. I used to be a lesbian."

"What!" Hattie stood up and shouted.

"Yep. Loved me some hoochie."

"But Antoinette…" said Gladys.

"Wait, wait, wait a minute. I wasn't slutty about it. They were hoochie but they had to have class and style. I wasn't cruising through Robert Taylor Housing Project at two o'clock in the morning."

"But Sis, you dated men," said Carmen.

"I did, fine ones at that, but they always left me feeling empty. I'd put them down as fast as I picked them up, because they never gave me anything I could hold on to or wanted to go back to. I didn't know that I was lesbian. The first time it happened it just felt normal. I felt like a real woman for a change. I didn't know that something in me wasn't living until that girl and I touched each other. I went back to men but always with the same result. So, I did what felt normal, what made me feel whole."

"I can't believe it," Hattie said. "All these years and we never knew. So, that explains the long engagements."

"It's sad when you stay engaged so long that your fiancé dies of old age," Carmen joked.

"I really can't explain why. It's just who I was and what I felt. I wasn't ashamed, but sisters or not, I couldn't bring myself to tell you. Like we all are, I was just fearful of the truth being known."

"And now?" asked Carmen.

"I'll always be who I am, Sis. Like each of you, I'm just a child of God, imperfect but blessed and thankful for the blessings."

Gladys knew that she had to speak up. Her sisters had opened doors to their darkest rooms, and they all entered, including her. She had many secrets, but she could never tell the biggest one, not at seventy-six years old. It was a past that she had buried over fifty years ago and she wasn't about to resurrect it. Her sisters knew about the wild, promiscuous life she lived in her twenties when she danced at Harry's, especially after she left home to live with Mary. They knew that she and Willie had a marriage made in hell, and that she did a lot to keep the devil smiling. "Big secret." That was pretty normal for her in those days, but "biggest" weighed too much, heavier than anything the other sisters had said. She wasn't about to go there.

"All y'all know my dark secrets, so what's the point in saying one of them. I've been the black sheep of the family all my life, so nothing's hidden that you haven't seen or heard about. Telling one is telling all of them, which y'all know are pretty awful and embarrassing. I've done a lot of things that I regret."

Carmen, feeling the weight of the burden on Gladys' heart, lightened the mood. "Gladys, I thought I'd never say this, but you've left me speechless. Now can we all please get off the edge of this cliff, drink the rest of this fine wine, and start talking like old women again?"

As the youngest of the sisters, Rita and Thelma had always felt some distance between them and their older sisters. When the older ones started talking about boys that they had met in high school, it was just chatter to Rita and Thelma, who were still making doll dresses and building houses with blankets. Although they didn't think about it much, being in Gavinville so far away from the others, particularly since their Mama and Daddy had passed, widened the gulf between them as the younger siblings.

Rita called Chicago from time to time, but it could never be like those days when she was there, and they were all together. She especially missed the shopping sprees and them sitting around uncorking wine bottles one after another. Without Ella to tend to and fuss with, she and Charles now had the house all to themselves. They spent the day hours doing the Foundation's work, but the evenings brought the whole mansion into one room, where they sat reading or watching television. There wasn't much to see or do in Gavinville on weekends, so they often drove to New Orleans just for the ride, seldom getting out of the car except to dine.

Rita was in as good a physical shape as her sisters, with not much to complain about except gaining too much weight, but Charles was beginning to show early signs of dementia. He'd have periodic lapses of memory and had begun to horde things that should be thrown away. Rita stayed closer to him, never leaving him alone and certainly not letting him drive the car, but he wasn't at the stage that caused her to be too concerned. She had eventually hired Daniel Broussard, a recent business graduate of Southern University in Baton Rouge, to manage the Foundation on a full-time basis.

Thelma, the youngest of the sisters, turned seventy-three years old on March 18, 1997, not long after she and Terrell celebrated their fortieth wedding anniversary. Their third and last child was born in 1961, but they had yet to be grandparents. All the children were married, living out of state, and building successful careers in medicine. With only her and Terrell in the large home that Terrell bought before they married, they, too, were feeling overwhelmed by empty rooms. They decided to sell the house and move into the newly built, lush condominiums on Lake Street, with a patio view of the river. Terrell was still practicing dentistry but had made plans to retire in two years. The two sisters visited each other often and celebrated every holiday together, always with Thelma's children coming home and livening up the occasion with youthful energy and loud music.

If age and geography weren't enough to create distance between the sisters in Chicago and those in Gavinville, the memories of past relationships with men had locked some doors that none of them dared to open. For years, Thelma was quietly bitter toward Gladys for sleeping with Frankie Lee Garrett when she and Frankie started dating. Long before she and Terrell met, she had dreams of marrying Frankie one day, in spite of his much talked about indiscretions as a "lady's man." Although she never talked about it, she was deeply hurt when she learned that Gladys had slept with Frankie and more hurt when he bled to death lying on the ground outside the Oasis Lounge that night in December 1950. Content with Gladys' desire to move on and put it all behind her, Thelma never confronted Gladys about the incident, but she knew that Gladys was to blame for Frankie's death. Thelma wasn't there that night, but she later heard that Gladys had seen Frankie flirting with Clarissa Charles earlier and confronted him about it, which led to the argument. More than that, Thelma harbored a dark secret about the whole story of that night that she had not told to anyone, a secret too dark to tell anyone.

Rita, too, harbored bitterness toward one of her older sisters that she never openly expressed. She wasn't there the night Hattie talked about the abortion, but she knew about it and she knew that the daddy was Jerome Jackson. In all the years that passed, Rita never told Hattie that she knew. She respected her sister's decision to keep it a secret from the rest of the family, so she made sure that the truth was never told. Jerome had confessed it to her years later when they started dating, not long before she and her sisters moved to Chicago. Knowing that Hattie and Jerome had dated at one time, Rita felt uncomfortable about telling Hattie that she was spending time with him, although he never picked her up at home. She was about to do that when Jerome told her about Hattie's abortion.

Rita and Jerome had only dated a few times, but she was growing to like him, maybe falling in love. His confession about Hattie's pregnancy and her secrecy about the abortion virtually closed the door on any serious relationship between them. She knew that the door would never open again, leaving only questions of what might have or could have developed between them had she not known the truth. More distressing to Rita was the burden of being the only member of the family who knew Hattie's secret. Although she would not admit it to herself, she felt a quiet resentment toward Hattie that she had to carry that burden alone, keeping it from her mama, daddy, and sisters for all those years.

It would be years before the two sisters stood together in one room, facing doors that had remained shut for decades and that only they held the keys to open.

Chapter 11

In October 2000, just prior to the start of the holiday season, the Hayes sisters announced that they were officially retiring at the end of the year. They had been in Chicago for fifty years and in business nearly that long. They all felt that it was time to completely relinquish the reins to Jesse and the other top executives. That came as no surprise to anyone, but what rocked the boardrooms of State Street, and the entire business community of Chicago was the news that Carmen, the second oldest of the Hayes sisters, was leaving Chicago and moving back to Gavinville.

Carmen was viewed as the conscience and political strategist of the Hayes business empire, tactfully and effectively wielding political influence to grow the business and improve economic conditions for the poorest residents of South Side Chicago. Bernard Hawkins, now retired from his teaching position at the University of Chicago, had decided to follow a call to the ministry. He had not attended any school of theology and had no formal training in religious studies or church administration. He would simply do what Mama Ella had told him to do, and what he heard God say was that the harvest that needed laborers was in a small field banked by a levee that ran along a deep, wide river. Bernard interpreted that to mean Gavinville.

Rita and Charles insisted that Carmen and Bernard move in with them, in their spacious three-story mansion on a hill overlooking the lower parts of the city. Carmen and Bernard agreed. A second daughter of Ella and Jesse Hayes would now be living in the home that their mother had once kept as a maid seventy years ago and where Ella had lived in the final days of her life while being cared for by her daughter and son-in-law.

Bernard and Carmen could have easily afforded to build one of the finest churches in Gavinville, but they bought a small, abandoned building that had once been the grocery store where Ella and her neighbors at Dixie Manor regularly shopped. It was not uncommon to residents of Dixie Manor walking along Railroad Street on Saturday morning, carrying bags of groceries, and stopping each other along the way to catch up on the latest gossip. The building had been boarded up for a number of years. They gutted the walls and shelves, built a few makeshift pews, and erected a sign on the front lawn that read "Refuge Tabernacle." For several weeks, Bernard and Carmen went into the building every Sunday morning at nine o'clock and read their Bibles out loud, just the two of them. One morning, the door opened, and two elderly Black women walked in. It was the morning that Bernard and Carmen officially became "Brother and Sister Hawkins" and when the torch of Ella Hays relit itself.

One by one, the poor and sick people of Gavinville, Black and white, found their way to the little wooden building where miracles were reported to have taken place, people parking their walking canes and wheelchairs at the front door as they left church, singing, dancing, and shouting praises. It hadn't been a year since Carmen and Bernard had left one of the country's largest cities, where they lived more than comfortably, enjoying the power and prestige of being among the wealthiest residents. Suddenly, all their status and wealth paled against the life, peace, and joy they were giving to the poorest people of the small town of Gavinville. Needless to say, the ministry grew rapidly, with hundreds of members, and a new, modern building flush with the fineries of any big church in the South. Bernard remained humble and faithful to the source of the gift that had called him. He built the new church in the same location as the original building, near "God's children."

At the age of eighty, Carmen had returned home, the place where she grew up. Many people of Gavinville knew that she was the daughter of Jesse and Ella Hayes and the sister of Rita West, another of Ella Hayes' daughters who had moved there from Chicago. Some knew the extent of her wealth and how she acquired it. Rumor was that the old woman had come home to die and be buried next to her mama and daddy. But no one in Gavinville knew of Carmen's convictions to social justice and civil rights. No one knew the story of Andrea Cooper, and how the lynching of Emmett Till and the civil disobedience of Rosa Parks and Reverend Martin Luther King Jr. stirred a fire in her gut. No one knew of her political activism against the Jim Crow housing laws of Chicago, and how strongly she supported causes to end racial injustice and discrimination. No one was prepared for an old, wealthy Black woman with a holiness preaching husband to be so vocal and active politically, in a town where most Black people were poor, illiterate, and didn't vote, and most white people pretty much did whatever they wanted to do in order to keep things that way.

Carmen soon made it clear that she was neither close to death nor willing to spend the golden days of her life sitting quietly on the porch watching butterflies dart between the flowers. On the morning of May 4, 2002, she drove herself to Town Hall, stood upright as a woman half her age, walked into the building, and asked to see the Mayor of Gavinville. Mayor Sonnier, knowing who she was and the wealth she held, quickly obliged. After exchanging the typical pleasantries, peppered with small talk about the cool, spring weather, Carmen got to the business at hand.

"Mr. Mayor, I know your time is precious, so I won't keep you long. First of all, I want to be clear that I'm not here to speak for any so-called civil rights group. I speak for myself and for the poor, uneducated people of this town. I am here to make demands, not to ask for political favors. Number one, that confederate flag you've got flying over the courthouse needs to come down, right away. Number two, that Black housing project near the railroad track is falling apart. Either fix it up or tear it down and build a new one. And lastly, do something about the schools in this town. Looks like the only purpose they serve is giving jobs to white folks."

The Mayor hadn't really listened to the elegantly dressed old woman. His hearing went deaf after the first ten words came out of her mouth. What he couldn't get past was her shockingly youthful appearance and her audacity and boldness, not to mention the clarity and sharpness of her mind. Everyone her age that he knew was either lying in bed or putting big-piece puzzles together at St. Aloysius Nursing Home. There she sat, demanding change and telling him how to run the town. He thought it was a bit comical, and the moment he broke a smile, Carmen fired again.

"I'm not here to entertain, Mr. Mayor, so you can wipe that smile off your face. And don't think for a minute that I'm just blowing hot air.

I've got the wind at my back, and I'm moving forward, faster than you think."

Sensing now that he wasn't facing something light and ordinary as the passing morning breeze that flowed through his raised windows, Mayor Sonnier politely apologized and assured Carmen that he would take her concerns under advisement with the Town Council and Board of Education.

"Well if you don't, I will." Carmen thanked the Mayor for his time, shook his hand, and left his office.

There would be more meetings between Carmen and Mayor Sonnier, and eventually with other town elected officials. It was apparent to them that Carmen's outspokenness and financial independence made her a force to be reckoned with. Carmen had no interest in joining organizations and building coalitions. She had long ago passed the point when she felt that those things mattered or were necessary. She was simply going to speak her mind, but she clearly understood the power of her wealth and lone voice. She regularly attended Town Council and Board of Education meetings, advocating change. The confederate flag never came down, but the Mayor requested assistance from the federal government to address the deteriorating condition of the housing project. Schools remained a major problem, particularly the high dropout rate among Black children, but in the months that followed, Carmen pushed on, demanding that the Board of Education address the issue.

Rita was growing increasingly concerned about Charles' health. He had been diagnosed with Alzheimer's and his memory was completely gone. At times he would be disoriented, not knowing where he was or what he was doing. He was prone to leaving the house and wandering down the street, so Rita padlocked all the doors and kept a constant eye on him, doing her best to keep him confined to parts of the house where she could see him. When he stopped eating, she admitted him to the hospital to have a tube inserted in his stomach to be fed. When he was brought home, she hired a nurse to care for him during the day. Even with Bernard and Carmen helping, evenings and nights were more than she could handle. Bernard's prayers and healing hands could do nothing to stop the advancing death of Charles' brain. Still, Rita refused to put him in the nursing home. She was totally committed to caring for him herself. "Charles's home," she'd say, "is where I am."

Charles died of a sudden, massive heart attack on August 2, 2002. He and Rita had long ago decided that he would be buried in Chicago, the city that had been his home for nearly his entire life. He had pastored churches there for over forty years and felt that it would be appropriate to be where his former flocks could pay their last respects. Rita hired a private jet to transport Charles's body to Chicago. Bernard, Thelma, and Terrell flew with her.

Charles was waked at Evergreen Baptist Church on the morning of August 10th. His going home celebration was held there at 1:00 p.m., followed by the interment at the church's cemetery. The Hayes family had decided to meet at Hattie's home after the repast.

For the first time in seven years, since their mama's funeral, all the sisters were together. The four oldest, Gladys, Carmen, Antoinette, and Hattie, were now at least eighty-years old. Rita and Thelma were in their late seventies. Age had finally begun to show. Gray hair, wrinkles, and skin blemishes had erased their doll-like appearances. They even seemed to look shorter. Still, they looked and dressed like women many years younger. They walked slower, but none of them had any serious health issues, none of the problems that Black women much younger than them were dying of.

After Terrell and Bernard retired for the evening, the sisters moved to the den to catch up on what everyone had been doing.

"That was a beautiful service, Rita," said Hattie. "I felt Charles smiling."

"Yes indeed," Gladys remarked.

"That church was standing room only. Charles was deeply loved by a lot of people. He touched a lot of hearts," said Carmen.

"I don't know what I'll do without him. Even with you and Bernard there, that house is going to feel so much bigger with him gone. His spirit filled so much of it."

"Well, he's resting now. And his spirit will still be there. He's eternal now, everywhere and forever," said Thelma.

"Amen to that, Sis," Antoinette said.

"So how are things in Chicago," Rita asked, looking at Gladys, Hattie, and Antoinette.

"Well, I guess you heard that the Bulls had a nightmare season," Antoinette said. "I don't think this year's will be any different. The Bears were just as bad. Thank God they finally fired that head coach, whatever his name is. About the only good news is that after a hundred years the Sox are finally starting to win, but they still trail the Twins by a lot. Even better news is that according to our nephews, business has been good and profitable. We're all still making tons of money."

"And what about the three of you?" asked Rita. "Anything new and exciting?"

"I can't speak for Antoinette and Hattie, but I'm feeling young as ever," said Gladys, smiling. "I'm starting to wonder if the Hayes curse is on me. I feel like I'll live as long as Mama and Daddy, maybe longer."

"Well, the three of you still look like you can turn some heads, still got that Ella Hayes glow and charm about you," responded Rita.

"Thank you, Sis," said Hattie. "I'm still climbing the stairs, so I guess that's a good sign. Can't help but say the same about you, Carmen, and Thelma. Y'all are looking great."

Carmen had been noticeably and unusually quiet. "Sis, what's on your mind these days?" asked Antoinette, looking toward Carmen.

"Well, if you must know, I've been thinking."

"Oh, here we go. Carmen's got a thought . . . about changing the world no doubt," Hattie interjected before Carmen said another word, drawing laughter from the other sisters.

In her usual outspoken way, Carmen suggested something that none of the sisters living in Chicago would have ever thought of doing. "Well, if you must know, I've been thinking. You can laugh if you want to, but it's a very serious thought, and I think we should talk about it. Let's face it, we're all old women now. We've done a lot of good in this city, had great fun, and got rich doing it, but is there any reason why the three of you should live the rest of your lives in Chicago, even die here? I mean, what purpose will it serve for you to stay? You've got more money than you can possibly spend for the rest of your lives. Why don't you go back home, go back to where we started in Gavinville, and use the power of your wealth to really make a difference?"

"Gavinville? You can't be serious. Is it still on the map?" joked Hattie, drawing chuckles from Gladys and Antoinette.

"No, I'm very serious. Why not?" Carmen quickly responded. "As I said, what else is there for you to do here except grow older and die? We've all got a lot left in us. Why not be where we can make a difference? Gavinville is in worse shape than when we left it over fifty years ago. It's a disgrace. Reminds me of Bronzeville fifty years ago, only a lot less people. Lord knows, I don't have the spunk to fight white people the way I did back then, but I'll use my last breath to tell them that it's time for them to take their feet off the necks of Black people. And most Blacks there have bought into it. They're content to gather up the crumbs falling from the white man's table. I could use some help."

"Help? Doing what? You've got as much money as the rest of us," said Hattie.

"Now hold on, Hattie, hold on," said Antoinette. "Let's be honest. The rest of us don't come close to having what you got. I'm not complaining; I'm just explaining."

"My money can make a difference. Rita's and Thelma's can, too," said Carmen. "But I'm talking about sister power, us coming together to be one voice, not speaking out for change and being as active as we were in Chicago, but quietly stirring shit up with the power of all our purses."

"Like I said, there she goes," said Hattie. "Talking about helping Negroes who won't do a damn thing to help themselves. I stopped thinking about saving Negroes years ago. It's time you do the same."

"But that was Chicago, Sis. Heck, with the money we've got, we can have every politician in the state of Louisiana eating out of our hands. Money talks in Chicago. In Louisiana it sings *and* talks. We can help turn those backward ass schools around and give Black children a proper education, and we can help Black people to live in decent, affordable housing."

"And how exactly are we going to do that?" Antoinette asked.

"For one thing, we've got the Foundation, and there aren't many more Black people in Louisiana whose pockets are as deep as ours. Politicians have tax money that can help poor people. It all boils down to how they choose to spend it. I'm not talking about buying politicians, but I haven't met one yet who won't get up and dance when somebody with money tells him to get up out of his seat. Most of them can't dance a lick but they get up."

"Carmen, Chicago is home now. I've lived here for over fifty years. I married here, raised a family here, and buried a husband and grandson here. It's where I want to die and be buried," said Hattie. She paused, then looked at her other sisters. "What do y'all have to say about this?"

"Well, I'm the only one that's never left Gavinville, and if I hadn't met a good man to raise a family with I probably would have ended up here in Chicago. There just aren't any economic opportunities in Gavinville, even for educated African Americans. Thankfully, Terrell's practice has done well over the years, but it hasn't been easy. African Americans don't have the jobs to buy insurance and pay doctors and dentists to keep them healthy. I'm not sure what the answer is, but I'd welcome having my old sisters back home stirring shit up."

"I'll say this," said Rita, "in the few years I've been back it's been pretty depressing. Before Charles got sick, we couldn't wait to get out of there on weekends. Of course, you old women don't need the excitement and attention that you craved years ago, but the point is that the town is really one step from the grave. Like Thelma, I'd count it a blessing to be there with all my sisters. We *are* getting older. Tomorrow isn't promised to any of us, and we *are* still family. Y'all coming down will help, but what concerns me most is the money going the other way. The damn conservative business community in Louisiana has most politicians in their back pockets. We've got deep pockets, too, but ours alone won't be enough to fix all the brokenness in Gavinville and Louisiana. We'd have to align ourselves with the money that's pushing in the right direction, but some kind of way we'd have to broaden the base."

"And that's all the more reason why we should go," said Carmen. "Money will always go the other way. Why not use what we've been blessed with to collectively wield some real power and influence and make Gavinville a better place for future generations? We might not turn things completely around, but we'll make a difference."

Antoinette hadn't spoken. She was on the fence and wasn't sure which way to lean. Listening to her sisters, she thought about her mama and daddy in those years when they struggled to feed their children, put decent clothes on their backs, and made sure that they got a high school education. When Judy was alive, Antoinette was in the middle, the fourth child of seven. She wore hand-me-downs of her older sisters and never got the attention that her mama and daddy gave the youngest ones. Maybe, she thought to herself, maybe that's why she never felt that she fit in. Chicago had been no different. She enjoyed the success, the money and material things it bought, but, more than any of the sisters, she had felt an emptiness that money hadn't fulfilled. Sensing that her voice would count and that Gladys would more than likely not agree to move, she felt compelled to disagree with Hattie.

"I'm in. I say let's go. Carmen's right. What good does it do for the world if we die with our money sitting in the bank vault while children are starving and suffering? Sure, the Foundation will help, but what about our voice? People need to know where we stand. Here in Chicago, we're just Black women with money. Hell, there are hundreds, thousands like us. But in Gavinville and Louisiana we can be kingmakers. Imagine that. Queens making kings, and all for the good of poor children and families."

Gladys saw more of the past than the future. Going back to Gavinville, even at the age of eighty-three, when nearly everyone who had heard about her past was dead, seemed pointless. There were bad memories and fears that still haunted her. She'd have to think more about it before answering. On the other hand, she dreaded the thought of being alone in Chicago, of not being with the sisters who looked beyond her faults and mistakes, believed in her, and gave her a chance to put the past behind her and make a new start. Her silence was long, but she answered. "I've said a thousand times that I'll never go back to Gavinville. There's nothing back there for me, especially at my old age, but if nothing else I think we owe it to Mama and Daddy. I'm in."

Reluctantly, Hattie got on board. It took nearly a year for the sisters in Chicago to settle their business. They sold their homes and furniture, said good-bye to Jesse and Margie, and made one last visit to their stores. They visited the graves of James Sr., James Jr., Karry, and Charles. There would be no grand going away party. The moving vans, which barely had enough room for their wardrobes, was already en route when they boarded an airplane at Midway Airport on July 7, 2003 to go back to the town they had always called home. They would all live at Rita's mansion, which had more than enough room to accommodate them. They hadn't all lived together since 1947, before Gladys moved out and went to stay with Mary. Thelma wouldn't be there, but she'd be living in Gavinville, not far away. The sisters of Chicago had become successful, quite wealthy in fact. They had traveled the world and come full circle to the place where their journey started, in the small, Louisiana town of Gavinville. They were now the sisters of Gavinville, and neither South Side Chicago nor Gavinville would ever be the same again.

The home that Charles and Rita bought when they arrived in Gavinville sat on a wooded four-acre hill and was the largest pre-Civil War antebellum house in the region. Built in 1861 as a replica of a much larger plantation home in White Castle, Louisiana, the 20,000 square foot mansion stood on the highest ground in a town that was below sea level and surrounded by wide, deep waters. Nearly all the eighteenth and nineteenth century furniture had remained with the house when Charles and Rita bought it. Most of the rooms were flush with brightly lit crystal chandeliers and all the intricate, hand-crafted finishes one would find in an antebellum mansion. It was as grand a place as any that the sisters had seen in Chicago. The three-story, wooden frame mansion had nine bedrooms, four on the second floor, four on the third, and a separate master bedroom at the rear of the third floor. Each of the second and third floors had two bathrooms, with the exception of the master bedroom, that had a bathroom of its own, all of which were fully modernized. Each suite had a fifteen-foot-ceiling, a fireplace, and French doors leading to a private balcony and porch. Two winding, double, mahogany staircases led to the second and third floors. The first floor housed the kitchen, dining room, utility room, and sitting rooms.

Rita and Charles never slept in the master bedroom. It meant having to climb too many flights of stairs. Until Charles got ill, they slept in one of the second-floor bedrooms, but they eventually moved into the largest sitting room on the first floor. Bernard and Carmen had taken the master bedroom. Where the other sisters would sleep was the first of many disagreements they would have while living under one roof, but they worked it out by age. The younger sisters would climb the most stairs, at least until some years later when none of them had the strength and fortitude to climb any.

The mansion had always attracted tourists visiting Gavinville, but when the sisters from Chicago moved in, the locals started parading up and down Burbank Avenue from sunup to sundown, hoping to catch a glimpse of the women who were unquestionably the most unusual and strangest residents of the town. The fact that they were wealthy and from Chicago stirred enough curiosity, but to know that they were old, Black, and female, and living on Burbank Avenue was a bit much for Gavinville to absorb. And it wasn't just the ordinary poor Black people who made the drive-by on a regular basis, at least once a week—especially on sunny Sunday afternoons—the rich white residents drove by also. Burbank Avenue was the only street in Gavinville where on any given day every make, model, and year of automobile since 1970 could be seen. One minute you're cruising behind a brand-new Mercedes Benz and the next you're watching a dented, half-painted 1975 Pontiac with no inspection sticker going the other direction. Of course, the sisters never went out to the front balcony or the front lawn, and when they drove away they always took their private rear alley to the main road. Occasionally, it was rumored that there was a sighting of one of them sitting in a rocking chair on the second or third floor balcony.

That rather mysterious, seemingly mystical presence of the sisters had the whole town talking about them. In the early months after the move, they were rarely, if ever, seen publicly, mostly driving down the street or pumping gas. Rita could still be seen buying groceries from time to time. Carmen could always be seen on Sunday mornings at Refuge Tabernacle, and Thelma was at Terrell's dentist office most mornings and afternoons. But the three sisters who had moved from Chicago into the mansion remained enigmas. A lot of people had heard that they were daughters of Ella Hayes, a faith healer who had once raised people off their death beds. Some heard that the oldest one had been a strip club dancer years ago, but they didn't know that the club was in Gavinville, not Chicago. Others heard that another one had married a businessman whose wealth she inherited when he died. None of the sisters had heard those rumors, but intuitively they felt what the town's people were thinking, so they purposely stayed quiet and kept a distance. They had every intension of "stirring up shit" in Gavinville, but in their own time and only after thinking about how they would do it. That all changed in the fall of 2003 when the sisters learned of the candidacy of a woman who was running to be governor of Louisiana.

Kathleen Blanco, a former State Representative and Public Service Commissioner, was the current Lieutenant Governor of the state. Her opponent was Bobby Jindal, a bright, young Republican who had formerly worked in the administration of President George W. Bush. Blanco's agenda of increasing state investment in education, including early childhood education, caught the sister's attention. They hadn't planned to dive deeply into Louisiana politics that quickly, but Blanco's political agenda excited them, not to mention the fact that she was a Democrat and a woman. They could not sit on the sidelines and let the opportunity to change the state's political landscape pass while mulling over how to twist the arms of a few local Republican politicians.

The sisters had learned much from their frays in Chicago politics, particularly the two losses suffered by Burris. They needed to move cautiously, but the choices were clear. They knew that they could not and would not support Jindal's Tea Party agenda of cutting government spending and lowering taxes. As they had done after the Harold Washington campaign and the political fallout of the insurance fraud accusation, they backed Blanco quietly, practically invisibly. Through decades of experience with Chicago and Illinois politics, the sisters had grown savvier and more politically sophisticated.

When Blanco won, they immediately turned their attention to state policymaking by hiring a lobbyist to push for cabinet appointments of individuals who were sensitive to the plight of poor people, individuals like Jeremiah Wilson, an African American native of Gavinville who had built successful careers in public service and banking. Blanco eventually appointed Wilson to be her Secretary of Labor. In appointing him, Blanco went against the choice of the Louisiana AFL-CIO, the state's largest federation of unions and one of her strongest political allies. To the sisters of Gavinville, it was a move that showed rare political courage that they had not seen in Chicago politics.

Their lobbyist worked within Blanco's inner circle of legislative strategists to push for increased investment in early childhood education and higher education in the first budget that she would propose to the State Legislature. On the afternoon of Blanco's inauguration in early January 2004, Gladys, Carmen, Antoinette, and Hattie stood on the front, third-floor balcony and waived to passersby. The passersby, waving back and honking horns as witnesses to a surprisingly rare appearance, had no idea that the quiet, reclusive old women standing pertly in their wool coats, scarves, and hats, were not nearly who they appeared to be.

Daily life at Hayes Mansion, a name the locals gave the house, quickly became routine. The sisters hired two housekeepers, both Black, female, and middle-age, who cleaned, kept the laundry, and cooked, but the sisters insisted on setting the table and serving themselves. They awoke at different times of morning but made a point to always sit together for lunch and dinner. Having their own individual suites and balconies gave them space and quietness to rest or simply sit outdoors reading, knitting, or gazing thoughtlessly at the mansion's lush gardens.

Carmen stayed the busiest, doing church business, sitting in on meetings of the Foundation, and remaining active in addressing the academic and discipline issues in local schools. Under the leadership of the newly hired director, the Foundation had begun to support programs such as tutoring, mentoring, and afterschool learning for middle school students.

The Hayes sisters were raised Baptist but started attending St. Paul when Ella left Mount Calvary in early 1947. They remained committed to their Catholic faith through all the years in Chicago. After moving back to Gavinville, they attended St. Paul regularly, often joking that the priests at St. Paul had them to thank for the church being full at the 9:30 a.m. service, since many people only went to see what the Hayes sisters were wearing. On occasion, they visited Bernard and Carmen at Refuge Tabernacle.

The first time they visited Refuge caused quite a stir among the congregation, not just by the flamboyant hats and dresses they wore. Gladys, Antoinette, and Hattie sat in the middle of one of the front rows. Rita, who had made occasional visits to Refuge, had decided to attend St. Paul with Thelma. At the sisters' ages, the sight of people raising their arms, waving hands, shouting praises, speaking in tongues, and dancing in the church aisles seemed amusing if not somewhat comical.

Before the opening Bible reading and prayer, the choir and band started the praise worship service. Within two minutes, people took to the aisles and started shouting and dancing.

"Lord have mercy," said Antoinette, speaking to Hattie without looking at her, "looks like they put a cross on top of the Oasis Lounge. There's more dancing going on in here than I ever saw on Friday night."

"Behave yourself, old woman. You're in the Lord's house," Hattie said, trying her best to whisper.

With her eyes on the women dancing in the aisles, Antoinette quickly responded. "You wouldn't know it by all that butt-shaking."

"That ain't butt-shaking. That's dancing for Jesus. These people are feeling the Holy Ghost," Hattie explained.

"If that ain't the boogaloo I don't know what is," said Gladys, who sat on the other side of Hattie and had heard Antoinette's remark.

"Puts James Brown to shame," said Antoinette, shaking her head. "Haven't seen boogaloing like that since the night we saw JB at the Blue Note."

"Girl, I'm telling *you*. Look at them," quipped Gladys.

"I can't believe y'all are talking like this in the Lord's house," said Hattie. "It's sinful."

"As good as that band is sounding, I got a mind to get out there myself," said Antoinette, not bothering to whisper. She waited a minute, then stood up at her seat and started clapping and moving from side to side. Hattie and Gladys remained sitting.

"What's that foreign language they're speaking?" asked Gladys. "Ain't Creole that's for sure."

"They're speaking in tongues," said Hattie. "That's the utterance of the Holy Ghost. That's God's spirit talking through them. Will you please remember that you're in the house of the Lord and be quiet?" Gladys looked over at Antoinette standing, clapping, and dancing, then stood up and joined in the fun. Not wanting to stand out and appear unmoved, Hattie stood and started clapping and twisting her hips.

"That's it sisters," shouted someone in the row behind them. "Let Him take you there."

"Go with the flow, sisters," someone else shouted. "Praise Him!"

Before long, the three old women in colorful, wide-brim hats had gotten the attention of the entire church, and the more eyes they felt looking on them, the harder they clapped and shook their hips.

Months later, when the church outgrew the new building and Bernard expanded the sanctuary, the sisters' hats no longer stood out in the crowd, but Carmen always knew when they had been there by the size of the offering that had been collected.

Dinners at Hayes Mansion were required attendance. At times, Thelma and Terrell would join them. Carmen and Bernard sat at the head and the others sat at their usual places, always in the same chairs. The sisters made a habit of dressing "pretty" but casual, and their hair styles always looked different from how they had been hours before. It might have been their way of stepping out on the town or entertaining guests as they had done at the many parties they hosted in Chicago, but dinner times were moments they enjoyed most, sitting around the table as if they were little girls again, talking serious and silly about whatever came to mind. Some evenings, the past simply needed to be remembered and talked about, and they sounded like the old women they were, talking as if the end of life were just around the corner.

Business was no longer a topic of conversation, but politics always came up. Dinner time was when they strategized and planned ways to effect positive change for the poor people of Gavinville and Louisiana. They had kept up with the politics of Chicago and knew that Barack Obama, the young State Senator whom they supported in1996, was in a race to become the first Black U.S. Senator of Illinois.

"It wouldn't surprise me if that young man runs for president one day," Rita remarked one evening at dinner. "He's got what it takes to excite Black people and liberals enough to get them to go vote. Folks are still talking about that speech he gave at the convention last year."

"But you can bet he'd stir up the conservatives just as much," said Hattie. "Imagine that, a Black man running America, and with a name that's African. I just hope he stays clean and sleeps in his own bed every night. They always find the skeletons."

"But that wife of his, what's her name, Michelle? I think she's got more than enough to keep his mind off of white women. And the gal is smart as a whip, smarter than him," said Antoinette.

"On top of that, she's got style," Gladys said. "Every woman wears dresses, but she makes the dress wear her."

"I heard that," said Carmen. "Reminds me of myself a few years ago."

"A few? asked Antoinette. "More like forty."

"I hear Hillary Clinton is already making moves to jump in the race," said Rita. "But she's carrying too much baggage with Bill's past to be a serious candidate. Besides, Washington and Jefferson would come up out of the tombs if this country ever elected a woman president."

"Say what you want about Bill Clinton," said Antoinette. "He was weak for women, but he was the best damn president we had since Roosevelt. At the end of the day, it's not who he slept with but who he helped to get a job to afford a bed to sleep in. And he's got soul, a Black soul at that."

"Amen for Bill," said Gladys. "One night I saw him blowing a horn and thought I was hearing John Coltrane. That man's got a whole lot of soul."

"Well." Carmen started to speak, then paused, trying to contain her own laughter. "Y'all know as well as I do. If Clinton had gone on national television and moon walked like Michael Jackson, he wouldn't have seen a second term. White folks, liberal and conservative, will put up with a little adultery and a horn, but ain't no way they would have tolerated a white president moon walking," said Carmen, laughing loudly. The other sisters rolled in laughter as well. The thought of anyone thinking of the president of the United States moon walking on national television was too much to bear.

"Girl, that's silly, but you're right. And I bet he can moon walk pretty good, fine and loose as he is." said Antoinette. "I think we should drink to that."

"I agree," said Hattie. "Uncork that wine, every bottle that's left!"

For now, the sisters were content knowing that George Bush was on his way out and the Democrats at least had a shot at taking back the White House. They also took comfort in knowing that Kathleen Blanco was running the State of Louisiana. They would pay little attention to national politics for a while and focus on ways to effect change in Gavinville and Louisiana.

On occasion, the sisters just felt the need to get away and see the big city life they had known in Chicago. They would hire a limousine to drive them to New Orleans, where they weaved slowly in and out of boutiques and antique shops in the Garden District, picking up novelties or simply browsing. They hadn't seen much of New Orleans until then, mostly passing through the airport. They had done some shopping the weekend of Carmen's wedding, but not nearly enough. They found New Orleans interesting to say the least, with its melting pot of races, nationalities, and food that they couldn't get enough of. They especially loved strolling through Jackson Square and watching the street performers, never leaving the city without stopping to dine at Dooky Chase.

That evening at dinner when they talked about Barack Obama, the sisters made plans to go to New Orleans the coming Saturday. Two days later, on August 25, 2005, they heard news reports of a strong storm that had entered the Gulf of Mexico, posing a major threat to the entire Gulf Coast. By then, Hurricane Katrina was a Category 3 hurricane spinning toward Southeast Louisiana. The next day, the storm had reached Category 5 status, and a hurricane watch was issued for Gavinville.

None of the sisters had experienced a hurricane as powerful as Katrina. They had grown accustomed to Chicago's bitter blizzards but had never been in a storm packing 175 mph winds. Gavinville, they knew was below sea level and surrounded by water, but forecasts were that the storm surge would easily top the levees and the concrete seawall bordering the downtown area. Sitting on the highest ground in town, floodwaters were the least of their worries. But forecasts of destructive force winds caused a lot more concern. The over 150-year mansion had withstood major hurricanes in the past, but Katrina was predicted to be the mother of all storms and the strongest to ever strike Southeast Louisiana. Most people in Gavinville heeded the warning and left town. Carmen and Bernard had made an evacuation center of the church and urged the sisters to go there.

"This is a killer hurricane," said Carmen. "Bernard and I are going to the church to take care of the evacuees there. Y'all should come."

"This old house can handle that storm," said Hattie.

"I don't know, Hattie," said Thelma.

"I'm a little scared," said Gladys. "I've never known a Chicago blizzard to knock down a house. Suppose there's a tornado or a tree falls on the roof?"

"Scared of what, a little high wind? We can't flood. And that roof is three floors up. I say we stay on the ground floor and ride it out."

"I agree with Hattie," said Antoinette. "This old house has survived 150 years of storms. It's probably safer here than at Refuge. I'm not leaving."

"But suppose one of us gets hurt. It's just us here. Nobody will be able to get here to help," said Thelma.

"I'm scared, too," said Rita, "but I agree with Hattie and Antoinette. I think we're safer staying right here. We stay put until this thing passes. This is my home and I ain't leaving it."

"Rita, this thing is not just some strong storm," said Bernard. "It has the strength to rip this house apart, no matter how old and well-built it is."

"I say let it come. I'm ready for whatever hell it brings," said Hattie.

"I told Bernard that y'all would say that. You old women are too hardheaded for your own good. God help you. We'll be praying for you. We'll try to get over here when everything settles down to check on you. Hopefully, we'll find you alive."

Fortunately for Gavinville, as Katrina neared the coast of Louisiana, it took a more easterly turn toward the Louisiana-Mississippi border, landing as a Category 3 hurricane with sustained winds of 130 mph. Gavinville had not suffered a direct hit, but the high wind and torrential rainfall had left Hayes Mansion and the entire town without electricity for several days. The sisters had survived their first major hurricane since moving back to Louisiana.

Boarded up within their own walls without electricity, it would be several days before the sisters heard of the levees breaching in New Orleans and the massive destruction that resulted, putting eighty percent of the city under water and leaving hundreds of thousands of residents homeless. The sisters were shocked and dumbfounded to see thousands of Black people stranded inside the New Orleans Superdome with not enough water, food, and medical supplies, and no way to get out. On Rita's recommendation, they used the Foundation to donate funds to the American Red Cross and other relief organizations. In the days and weeks that followed, they watched Governor Blanco struggle with the Bush administration to get aid to the city.

The federal government's seemingly weak and callous response to Katrina, particularly the storm's impact on the poor families of New Orleans, left the sisters feeling powerless and discouraged. They had fought a long fight in Chicago and spent a lot of money to defeat the political machines that kept poor people in slums and ghettos. In some ways, Hurricane Katrina stirred a call to activism not dissimilar to the resistance shown by Rosa Parks and the day Reverend Martin Luther King Jr. was stoned when he set foot on Chicago soil to declare war on Chicago's racist housing laws. Sitting around the lunch table while the displaced residents of New Orleans were slowly returning to see the total destruction of their homes and businesses, Carmen spoke up, but in a tone much different from days when she urged her sisters to become more active in challenging the political status quo.

"Sisters, I don't know about y'all, but I'm starting to feel old, too old to be fighting. I've seen a lot of pain and suffering in my lifetime. I've made so much money that I don't know how to spend it. God knows we've all been blessed. I have—we all have—tried to do some good, to make life better for those who haven't been as blessed as us. But after King, after all the blood that's been shed and spilled, when a storm took away everything Black folks owned and the small plot of ground they had to stand on, I never thought I'd see a day when the richest country in the world would turn its back on poor people—at a time when the government was most needed. We've been fighting a long time, but it's never been clearer to me that all the money in the world won't be enough to fix what's broken in some men's hearts. I guess what I'm saying is that maybe it's time we face the truth and just let God fight these battles."

Bernard, who had not been a part of the battles the sisters had fought in Chicago, and who typically remained a bystander to conversations they'd have about politics, made his own appeal. "So eloquently spoken, Sis. But I recall words written by David Walker and Henry Highland Garnet, men who vehemently opposed slavery and who talked about God's place in all of that. They put God at the center of it, and it was clear to them, as I know it is to all of you, that God doesn't sleep nor slumber. He's always awake and in command. He's a God of justice. But if He's up there and we're down here, how can there be justice if not through us. I'm as tired of fighting as you are, Sis. But we can't quit now. In fact, as James Baldwin would say, now is the time to step it up, to love more for sure, but to resist hatred and oppression just as much."

"It's hard to love a government that can't feel people's pain, Bernard. I'm just tired of fighting them."

"I know, Sis. We all are, but we have to find the strength to keep pushing."

"Lord knows we've pushed, and we've done some good. But how long will it take this country to start treating Black people like people, like Americans? Hell, we've done just as much to build this country as white people," said Antoinette.

"When you think about how and why we got here," said Rita, "we've done more, much more. We've had to fight and build at the same time. But I agree with Carmen. I can love and I can resist, but I can't take hate out of a man's heart. That's God's work."

"I respectfully disagree," said Bernard. "It might not happen in our lifetime, but in the end, love will conquer. That's God's promise. He needs us to keep our hands on the plow."

Chapter 12

In spite of Bernard's passionate plea that the sisters continue to fight for economic and social justice, they thought it best to retrench, at least for a while. There was little if anything they could do to help Governor Blanco in her rebuilding efforts, except to step up the Foundation's support to families and schools in New Orleans. That year, the sisters got more involved in Carmen's work to help fix failing schools. They established a new, fully staffed, non-profit organization, separate and apart from the Foundation, to advocate education reform, not solely for Gavinville schools but for the entire state of Louisiana. They secured the support of other individuals and corporations to fund the effort. Through it all, the sisters remained incognito, never appearing publicly or being the face of the advocacy work they supported. They had grown too old for that, and age was finally starting to show, not just outwardly but in how they felt waking up in the morning and climbing stairs during the day. Their minds were sharp as ever, and they still talked like women half their ages, but their bodies were growing frail and weak. They were strong enough to walk unassisted, except when they climbed the stairs, holding to the rail with one hand and leaning on a walking cane with the other. The youthful, ageless beauty that was the dominant trait of all Hayes women had begun to fade.

After Gustav, another major hurricane, made a direct hit on Gavinville in September 2008, the sisters began to question whether they could or should continue to live in and maintain the mansion or whether it might be best to move to an assisted living facility. Unfortunately, Gavinville didn't have a facility that would measure up to their standards. They couldn't imagine themselves living at St. Aloysius Nursing Home, but it was becoming increasingly difficult for them to care for themselves. They had stopped setting the table and serving themselves and spent more time in bed. Old age was bringing them closer together. As if they were an old married couple, the sisters paid more attention to each other, knowing what each needed or couldn't do alone, and were always a step away to lend a hand.

When they sat in front of the television to watch Barack Obama take the oath of office as the 44th President of the United States, Gladys, the oldest, was eighty-nine years old and Rita was eighty-five. Of all the sisters, Gladys seemed to be the strongest physically. She, more than any of the Hayes women, looked like her mama, and the older she grew the more Ella Hayes came back to life. Gladys had the darkest past, and in the years since she had left Gavinville and moved to Chicago she was the quietest and most reserved, seldom opening up to talk about her inner feelings, worries, and fears. She had always been aloof and independent, the first of them to leave home, albeit under unpleasant circumstances, the first to marry, and the first to be widowed.

When Willie died and Gladys moved to Chicago, she was only fifty-one years old, but she showed little interest in the men of Chicago. She seldom dated and had very little to say about men in general when the subject came up while the sisters were sitting around uncorking bottles of wine until midnight. At times, the other sisters talked about it among themselves. They had no answers, but they attributed it to the years Gladys spent dancing in the strip club or the bad experience that she had with Willie Frank. For those reasons, perhaps, men had become clothing she had outgrown or that had gone out of fashion, which she neatly folded and tucked away in drawers that she knew she'd never open. Why she kept them hidden instead of throwing or giving them away was the question that they had hoped she would answer without them asking.

The sister who felt most distant from Gladys was Thelma. They were five years apart. When Gladys left home, Thelma was twenty-three years old. She never really got to know her oldest sister. About the most the two had in common was marrying two men from Gavinville, but in the fourteen years that Gladys was married to Willie, she and her sister lived separate lives, Gladys living poorly in a one-bedroom shack and married to an ex-con who hadn't finished high school and Thelma married to the town's Black dentist, living in a middle-class neighborhood. They would talk as sisters do who lived in the same town, but mostly when their encounters were by chance, never inviting each other to dinner at home or to go shopping, and they seldom called just to talk as sisters.

The day of Obama's presidential inauguration, Thelma sat beside Terrell's hospital bed watching him take his last breath. They buried him four days later not far from the graves of their mother and father. Bernard would be the only husband of the Hayes sisters still living, although he, too, had health issues, having been diagnosed with prostate cancer a year earlier.

None of the other sisters had seen much of Terrell over the years and gotten to know him, largely because all of them, except Thelma, had lived in Chicago. Still, he was their baby sister's husband, and they mourned the loss of him. There was a moment immediately after Terrell's funeral when, unexpectedly, Gladys and Thelma found themselves together and alone. Thelma had gone to the second-floor balcony just to get away for a few minutes to feel her first moment alone since burying her husband. Gladys, not knowing Thelma was there, had drifted away from the others for a short walk along the porch to get a bit of fresh air.

"Hey old girl. Didn't know you were out here. It's a bit nippy," Gladys said as she rubbed her arms. "How are you feeling?"

"Fifty-two years. Fifty-two years and three children. Pretty long time. Long years, too, every one of them. We struggled to make ends meet at first, trying to pay the mortgage on that house." Thelma paused for a long time. "He was a good man, though. I'm going to miss him."

"I wish I could say that I know how you feel, but I'm happy for the good life you had."

"Yeah. We had our moments. All marriages do, but we stuck it out. First one, then two, then three babies, back-to-back, just like Mama and Daddy had us. Terrell wanted a lot more, but I put a stop to that after the third one."

There was a long silence between them, each deeply buried in her own thoughts. Thelma drifted back in time. Years ago, when Willie was in prison, she had gone to the Oasis Lounge one Saturday night, not intending to dance, but just to sit at the bar and have a couple of drinks. Jody Watkins, who had always been with Willie when they'd be at the Oasis trying to pick up women, asked her for a dance, which she graciously declined. But instead of walking away, Jody stayed standing at the bar and started rambling, talking but not looking at Thelma. She assumed that he was half-drunk and thought that if she just ignored him, he'd eventually go away. But Jody continued his senseless babble, which Thelma kept ignoring. When he said the words, "Gladys and Frankie Lee," that got her attention. Jody said that he was standing outside the Oasis Lounge the night Frankie was killed and that he saw everything that happened. Without Thelma asking, he told her.

In the nearly sixty years that passed since that night when she sat at the bar, Thelma never mentioned the conversation she had with Jody Watkins. In that moment when she and Gladys were alone on the balcony, she wanted to bring it up, but she sensed that it wasn't the right time. She had just buried her husband. Willie and Jody had long since died. "Why dig up buried bones?" she thought to herself. She didn't want to talk about death, especially the death of Frankie Lee. She had dated Frankie and was starting to fall in love with him when she found out that Gladys had slept with him after they started dating. Since that night at the bar, she had known two sides to the story, but for some reason she clung to the story Willie told. Whether Jody or Willie told the truth was not important. Even if Willie's story was a lie, Thelma felt that Gladys was still partly responsible for Frankie's death because she started the argument. But now was not the time to talk about a dead man whom she hadn't married. Still, she felt the need to get something out and let Gladys know how hurt she felt back then and how resentful she still felt that her own big sister had betrayed her.

Finally, Thelma broke the silence. "Gladys, all I'll say is that I hope you've made peace with God, because everything that's done in the dark will one day be brought to light. It's getting late, and I'm feeling tired. I think I'll let everyone know that I'll be leaving."

Thelma went into the house to grab her purse and say good-bye, leaving Gladys sitting alone, wondering what Thelma might do in the coming days and weeks, or what she might say and to whom. She would have to wait years before Thelma filled the vast empty space that the few words she spoke had created.

In the spring of 2012, Rita brought up the idea of the sisters moving. They were all starting to have health issues, nothing life threatening, but enough to cause more frequent visits to the doctor. The size and physical layout of the mansion was making it increasingly difficult for them to get around. They were spending more time in their private suites and on the ground-floor sitting rooms. Some missed lunch or dinner because they didn't feel like going down and up the stairs. They napped more frequently during the day. The mansion had become too impractical of a home for five very old women. None of the sisters were keen on the idea of moving, so they hired a full-time, live-in nurse to tend to minor health problems that didn't require a doctor's visit and to help them walk, climb stairs, and bathe.

On the afternoon of February 8, 2013, Bernard left to attend a conference in Baltimore for several days. Carmen looked forward to spending time with her sisters. Not knowing that the floor leading to the dining room had just been waxed and polished, she took her slippers off, slipped and fell. She screamed for help and the nursing assistant and housekeepers rushed to her. She was in a lot of pain and couldn't move. By the time the others got there, the nurse had called 911 for an ambulance. When the sisters arrived at the hospital, they were told that Carmen was still in the emergency room. Carmen was lying on a gurney unattended. Hattie spoke with Carmen about how she was feeling, then went to the nurse's station.

"Why is my sister still lying here? Why isn't she being cared for?"

"Ma'am, may I ask who you are?"

"I just told you that I'm her sister. Can't you hear? My name is Hattie Byrd."

"Mrs. Byrd, a doctor has examined Mrs. Hawkins. He thinks she's got a broken bone in her hip. She's stable. They'll be taking her to X-ray shortly."

"Who's the doctor? Where is he? We'd like to talk to him."

"He's seeing another patient at the moment."

"Is he the only darn doctor in this hospital? I need to talk to somebody about my sister. Right now!"

"Mrs. Byrd, if you'll just be patient. The doctor will be here soon."

Before the doctor arrived, Carmen was taken to X-ray. Her right hipbone was severely fractured. The doctor said that she would need surgery as soon as possible. He recommended an orthopedic surgeon who could be there in several hours.

Several hours passed and the surgeon had not arrived. Carmen was still lying on an emergency room bed. Hattie reached her boiling point. "Does this hospital have rooms for patients?" she asked another nurse. "When will my sister be admitted?"

"Ma'am, I'm told that we're waiting for a room on the third floor."

"Third floor! What about the first, second, and fourth? What about the fifth floor?"

"That's the surgery floor, Ma'am."

"So, there are no beds up there. You mean somebody's got to die before my sister can get a room?"

"No Ma'am, they're just getting things ready."

"Well, if it takes three hours for them to get things ready, something's wrong. I need to talk to whoever is in charge of running this damn hospital." Hattie got closer to the nurse's desk. "Listen, young lady, there's a ninety-three-year-old woman lying there in pain with a broken hip. If you don't push her up that elevator to a room, I will. And if she dies before, during, or after surgery, you'll be hearing from my lawyers, all of them."

Within minutes Carmen was taken to a room and prepped for surgery. Dr. Alfred Peterson, who happened to be Black, spoke to the family and explained that he would insert a titanium rod into Carmen's hip to replace the fractured bone. Given Carmen's relatively strong health, he was confident that she would live, but he warned that given her age, unexpected things could happen. He said that it was a slim chance that Carmen would walk again, but that he would recommend physical therapy.

After surgery, Carmen stayed in the third-floor room for a week. From there she was moved to a long-term care wing for a month before being sent to an outpatient therapy center for nearly two months. She didn't respond well to physical therapy. The doctor was right. Carmen would be unable to walk for the rest of her life. Her return to Hayes Mansion prompted another discussion about whether the sisters should move. They talked about it one evening at dinner, with Carmen seated in her usual place but in a wheelchair.

"Dr. Peterson said that I should think of moving to St. Aloysius where I can get the care of skilled nurses around the clock. Bernard and I have talked it over. We think it's a good idea."

"Sis, I don't want to hear that," said Hattie. "We can pay for all the care you need right here."

"But the doctor said . . ."

"I don't give a darn about what Peterson said," Hattie quickly remarked, cutting Carmen off. "We ain't putting you in St. Aloysius.

Nobody leaves that place alive. It's a death trap. They only send folks there to die and I know you ain't ready to see Jesus."

"Maybe the doctor is right," said Antoinette.

"Maybe he's wrong. Rita told me how poorly they took care of Mama when she was there, not changing her bed and keeping her clean. Thank God Rita got her out of there and brought her here. Nursing homes are all about making money. If they cared anything about sick people, they'd pay those assistants enough money to make a decent living. They're living as poorly as the folks they're caring for. You deserve better, Carmen."

"I agree with Hattie," said Gladys. "I remember reading about all those folks who died at a nursing home in New Orleans during Katrina. Seems like the older you get, the less the government gives a hoot about you."

"Republican government, Gladys. Get it right," said Carmen, speaking slowly in a voice barely heard. "You know that wouldn't happen under Obama. Look at what they're doing to kill his health care plan for poor people. Just plain heartless. Sometimes I wonder if they bleed."

"Well, right now I don't care who's running the government. What I care about is you, Carmen. We can get the care you need around the clock, and we can fix this place to make it easier for you to get around. In fact, we need to do that for the rest of you. As slow as Rita moves, she's just a couple of months away from a wheelchair herself. By next year this time, I'll be pushing most of y'all down the hall."

The sisters laughed but they understood the seriousness and weight of the decision. None of them, including Carmen, wanted to move. It was a question of where and how they could have the best quality of life. Money was not an issue, but this was Gavinville, not

Chicago, where there were more than enough options and opportunities for high-quality health care.

"I'd like for us to think about one other thing," said Antoinette. "We're sisters. We are the Hayes girls of Ella and Jesse. We were the Hayes sisters of Chicago, and now we're the sisters of Gavinville. We're old and broken down, some of y'all anyway, but we're still sisters. We've been through a lot together and being close has been our greatest strength. I can't imagine us not living together. At my age, I don't want to live or die in any place where my sisters ain't living and dying. We belong, together. Carmen, it wouldn't be right for you to be in a home and we not be there with you. Either we all go or we all stay."

The sisters didn't decide about moving that day, but in the weeks that followed, Antoinette's words sunk in. Several months later, they decided that Rita should sell the house. They would move and Carmen would live with them, not at a nursing home, but in an assisted living facility that they would build with a wing all to themselves. The sisters had no time to hire someone to do market research and business planning. Profit was the last thing on their minds. They would build one of the finest facilities of its kind in the South, and they would use funds of the Foundation to make it affordable for poor people who had no bank accounts and depended solely upon small Social Security checks and state Medicaid for nursing home care. They fast-tracked the project, quickly hiring consultants, an architect, and a builder. By then, Thelma had sold her home and decided to move in with her sisters. The plan was to build their wing first, with a larger, more private suite for Carmen and Bernard, and move in while the main building was being constructed. On October 3, 2014, Phase I of Hayes Place opened, and the sisters moved into their new home.

Life at Hayes Place would be comfortable and accommodating but different for the Hayes sisters. They were old and getting older, some with health problems more serious than others, but while their wing was separated from the other building by a short, awning-covered walkway—that created the appearance of separateness—the sisters no longer lived in a mansion on a hill in a secluded upper-class neighborhood. They were now part of a community where all the residents had two things in common: they were all at the stage of life when sickness and death was eminent. And with the exception of the sisters, the residents were mostly poor.

The sisters spared no expense in building Hayes Place. It had the look of an old, elegant southern home inside and out. The sisters had left some of the antique furnishings of Hayes Mansion to be sold but most of them, including the paintings, rugs, and furniture, were brought to Hayes Place. Each of the sisters had a private suite with a bedroom, bathroom, small dining room, and a spacious living room. From their living rooms, they could walk or wheel out to a private patio facing a large pond, stocked with catfish and trout and encircled by a walking path bordered by gardens that bloomed year-round. To eat, the sisters had the option of having their meals brought to them or they could go to the central dining room where the other residents ate. The sisters often joined them, especially at dinner and on weekends.

No one knows how or why the sisters became known as "the Aunties." The only nieces and nephews they had were Hattie's son and Thelma's three children, who lived out of state. When the employees spoke to them individually, they would address them by their first names, as in Ms. Gladys or Ms. Carmen, but the sisters' habits, wants, and ways of doing things were so similar that more often than not they were spoken of as a group. The name Aunties must have seemed especially appropriate to the younger workers, who wouldn't dare call them Grandma but who felt a special reverence toward the old women because they were so old. Surely, the young nursing assistants had aunts who were close, but not quite as close to them as their grandparents or great grandparents. One can only guess that their calling the sisters "the Aunties" meant that they felt personally and intimately connected. The name caught on quickly, and before long all the residents of Hayes Place, some of whom were nearly as old as the sisters, started referring to them that way. Eventually, the name left the grounds of Hayes Place and somehow made its way to the streets of Gavinville. Town residents who didn't know and had never seen the sisters but had heard about them dropped the word "sisters" and picked up "the Aunties."

Many residents of Gavinville who were around when the sisters from Chicago arrived still talked about them, even though curiosity had faded to the point that town people wouldn't drive by Hayes Place to see the Aunties standing or sitting outside the fenced-in walls of the facility. But the entire town knew, if only as a fleeting thought in the back of their minds, that there was a strange group of very old and very wealthy Black women living in Gavinville. Many had heard about their mama, and many knew of the work that the Aunties were doing through their Foundation, but to most people of Gavinville, the Aunties had become lore, often thought or talked about as history. Still, there was never a time when the Aunties' public appearances around town didn't create an almost carnival-like atmosphere, like some Saturday mornings when they'd go into the downtown shops to browse. They had long ago stopped shopping to buy, but they never stopped admiring high-quality, fashionable designs of women's clothing.

With walking canes in hand and Carmen wheeling close behind them, they'd go into the few women's stores Gavinville had, seeing mostly the same clothing they had seen the time before, but occasionally something bold, chic, and avant-garde caught their eye. On one such morning they discovered that the store owner was the granddaughter of a woman who was a seamstress who had lived in Chicago at one time and had often shopped in the Hayes stores. The woman introduced herself as Jeannette Levy.

"So, you say that your grandmother shopped in our stores?" Antoinette asked.

"Yes Ma'am. Hayes Women's Wear. She talked about it often. She'd say, 'if you couldn't get to Paris or London, you went to Hayes. That's where a woman could buy a dress that she could afford and make her feel like the richest woman in Chicago.' It was her favorite place to shop."

"Well I'll be darn. Lots of women went through that store, and we got to know many of them. In a way, they were all part of the family," said Hattie. "What's your grandmother's name?"

"Lacy Romano."

"Lacy Romano? Lacy Romano who worked at Hart?" Carmen asked with as much excitement in her voice as was showed on her sisters' faces.

"Yes Ma'am, that's her. She worked at Hart many years, until she married my grandfather when he took a job in New Orleans."

"Child, we know your grandmother! More than that, we worked with her at Hart. Ms. Lacy hired us when we moved to Chicago in 1950. Ms. Lacy. A quiet woman. Didn't talk much about anything but work. I always wondered what became of her. After we left Hart, we heard that she started dating some man."

"Probably was my grandfather, Reynard Bevin. They met when she worked at Hart."

"He worked at Hart?" asked Antoinette.

"Oh no. He wasn't working there. He worked at a hotel, and he took a job to manage a hotel in New Orleans. Before he left Chicago, he settled his divorce and married Granny Lacy. My Mama was born a year later. She met my Daddy when he was practicing law in New Orleans. After they got married, he took a job with a firm in Gavinville. I was raised right here on the Atchafalaya, eating crabs, catfish, and crawfish all my life."

"Is Ms. Lacy still in New Orleans?" Carmen asked. "Sure would be nice to see her after all these years."

"No Ma'am. She passed a few years ago."

"So sorry to hear that," said Rita. "We owe a lot to your grandmother. In fact, if it weren't for her we probably wouldn't have gone into business."

"How do you mean?"

"Well, Ms. Lacy hired us the day after we moved to Chicago, four of us. Gladys, the oldest, and Thelma, the youngest sister over there, were living in Gavinville. It's really the only job we had in Chicago working for someone else. She gave us a start until my brother-in-law James and my sister Hattie set us up in business. Your grandmother was a strong woman. She was about the same age as us but talked and handled herself like a woman much older. She sure knew how to handle those Hart supervisors who walked around in pin-stripe suits."

"My, my, my," said Antoinette. "What a small world. Who would have thought? So, how'd you get in the dress business?"

"My mama had a store in New Orleans when she met my Daddy. She sold it when they moved here, but she didn't want to get back into business, especially after I was born. I just decided a couple of years ago that I'd pick up where she left off. Took me a while to get it going but I started up two weeks ago."

"Child, I don't mean to pry, but are you Black or white?" Carmen asked. "Looks like you can pass either way, but I would guess that you've got a little of us in you."

"Yes, Ma'am my grandfather was Black."

"Lord have mercy. We had heard that the man Ms. Lacy was dating was Black, well, colored in those days. Just goes to show you. Love can be colorblind, as it should be, praise the Lord."

"Do the white women who shop here know you're Black?" Hattie asked.

"Some do, some don't. I get the feeling that it doesn't matter to most. They buy what they like seeing when they stand in that mirror."

"I always say that about a dress. If it's the right price and you like the way it looks on you, buy it. You can bet everyone else, including other women, will like it too," said Antoinette.

"Jeannette, it's been a real pleasure," said Rita, "but it's getting close to dinner. We have to get going. We'll be back. And do come visit us. We'd love to have your company."

"I certainly will. And thank y'all so much for dropping in." The sisters hadn't realized how long they had been in the store, browsing and talking with its owner. When they finally left, nearly all the shoppers and many of the downtown workers were standing outside the store waiting to see or take pictures of the Aunties of Gavinville.

It would be those kinds of surprising, unexpected encounters when chance or fate bridged the years between past and present, and perhaps portended the future, that affirmed the sisters' belief that they had done the right thing in leaving Hayes Mansion. They would see much more of Jeannette in the coming weeks and months, sharing what they had learned as dressmakers, fashion designers, and businesswomen. They didn't see it as their way of repaying Ms. Lacy for the start she gave them, but they, as much as anyone, knew how great blessings happen. One doesn't cause them to come, they just happen, and nearly always at times unexpected. In some ways, they saw Jeannette as the young women they were in 1952, stepping out on faith to start a business with the help of James and Hattie.

In sharing the story with Bernard, he said that the sisters' discovery of Jeannette was the song of the sparrow that he and Mama Ella had heard the morning their daddy was healed. He said that the song would always be with them as it has been for him, coming out of the sky, out of nowhere, to let them know that they were never alone and that they had a unique purpose to serve others.

Bernard was a quiet, soft-spoken man who was full of wisdom. All the sisters, particularly Carmen, were deeply saddened when he lost his battle with prostate cancer in June 2015. In eulogizing her husband of forty years, Carmen spoke of his special gift. "Brother Hawkins might be the last faith healer that Gavinville will know. The world has simply grown too materialistic to believe in miracles or believe that ordinary men or women could have healing hands. Bernard would often say that it's the lack of faith that keeps miracles from happening. People today can't picture God being so great and merciful. Like my mama, he knew that the gift had already been passed on to someone whose path he had crossed, perhaps a child or maybe a complete stranger, but he had no doubt that it had been passed on. That person could be any of you sitting here today, but you'll never know if you don't believe."

That would be one of the last times that Refuge Tabernacle would see Carmen. With her body growing weaker and Bernard gone, she would attend church less often. By the end of 2015, she started showing signs of dementia. Rita knew those signs. She had seen them with Charles and she knew that it would only be a matter of time before the disease made a turn for the worse.

Carmen had always been the social and political conscience of the sisters. She had the gift of oratory and could preach a sermon on social justice better than most ministers, even Bernard. She spoke from her heart and with conviction and fire that could smoke out any room filled with politicians who weren't sensitive to the plight of poor people. Dinner tables would not be the same without her sermons and calls for the political activism that was as much a trademark of the Hayes sisters as their business acumen. But the fire in Carmen was still burning, and she let it be known when they sat sipping wine after dinner one evening in late March 2016.

"Y'all know that Donald Trump is on his way to being the Republican Party candidate for President. Hillary is still fighting but I think she'll lock up the Democratic nomination this summer. Now, some things might have fallen out of my head, but I've still got my mind. And as long as I've got it, I'm going to use it to stop Trump. I'm talking about loading up and shooting everything I've got to stop him. He's dangerous for this country and dangerous for Black people."

"Is this the same Carmen who said not long ago that she was tired of fighting?" asked Hattie.

"I am, but this is Trump, not Bush."

"Sis, in your condition, don't you think it might be best if we sit this one out?' asked Rita.

"Sit it out? Granted, this will be our last one—which is another reason we can't sit it out—but the main reason is that the devil has his hand on the doorknob and is pulling on it. Trust me. If you let him in, he'll destroy the lives of millions of good, honest people in this country."

"He sure has a lot of white people pumped up. He draws big crowds with that Make America Great Again slogan," said Gladys.

"White people in this country are getting duped, especially poor whites. What he's preaching is make America white again. Keep the Muslims, Jews, Mexicans, and Africans out. Keep everybody out who's not white. And poor white folks are buying into it because he's got them thinking that they'll be better off if we weren't around. Trump is using the race card and the terrorist card to frighten poor white folks into voting against Democrats and liberals."

"Well, Sis, we can't do anything other than max out on contributions," said Hattie. "There are limits to that you know."

"I know, and as you well know, there are ways to get around that. Hell, rich white folks and big businesses have been doing it for decades. Come to think of it, we've done it ourselves."

"I think Hattie is talking about the little difference we can possibly make," said Antoinette. In Louisiana, Democrats don't stand a chance. Why should we even spend the money?"

"I can't control what happens across the state of Louisiana. White people in this state would vote for a Klansman before they'd vote for Hillary. Look what they did to Kathleen. But we can control our own house. We need to let everybody in this town know where we stand, especially Black folks."

"I agree with Hattie and Antoinette," said Thelma. "I just can't see how we can make any difference. Hell, they elected Jindal twice and all he's done is stare into the mirror and cut higher education and healthcare to the bone. The problem is that the businesspeople in Louisiana don't give a hoot about poor people. They say they do but not if it means raising taxes to help poor people. Again, what difference can we make?"

"Probably not much difference, Sis. Maybe none, but that's not the point. The point is us standing up instead of sitting down. The point is us speaking out instead of keeping our mouths shut. Standing on principle and for principle. That's the point. I honestly don't give a damn if nobody listens. What I care about is exercising my right to say where I stand on Trump."

"Do you think Hillary can beat him?' asked Hattie.

"I know she can beat him. But she won't if women like us don't stand up and be counted. And it's not just the presidential race. If the Republicans get the House and the Senate, you can kiss Obamacare goodbye, and there'll be more poor people dying."

To the sisters, especially Carmen, the thought of Donald Trump being the 45th President of the United States brought back bad memories of the presidency of Ronald Reagan. But this was a different time. The sisters weren't in business anymore. Nearly four decades had passed and they were just as much older. For what it might be worth, they decided to funnel money into political action committees to help fund attack advertisement against Trump. They put Hillary Clinton signs on the front lawn of the building, and they gave financial contributions to every Democratic candidate running for a state and local office in the state of Louisiana. It would be the last political campaign that the sisters got involved in but Carmen made sure that their voice was spoken, if not heard.

Within a year after the presidential election, Carmen's illness got considerably worse. She started wandering, leaving her suite and wheeling her way into the main building late at night. Nursing assistants kept a close eye on her, but on occasion she'd wander into other residents' rooms, not knowing where she was or how to get back to her apartment. Her sisters and the home administrator feared that she might drift off in the night, wheel out to the walking path, and accidently go into the pond. So, they padlocked her patio door and put locks on her front door that could only be opened from the outside. For all practical purposes, the sister whose voice was loudest and whose courage to stand up against racism and oppression was strongest, had been caged in.

Even as Carmen's memory got to the stage when she could barely remember who her sisters were or what names they had, the sisters took her condition in stride. There would be moments when they'd wheel her out to the dining hall to join them at dinner and they joked and laughed to keep from crying.

"Now Sis, I'm Gladys," Hattie said. "I'm the bitch of the family but the prettiest one whom all the men ran behind."

"Oh yeah, and you danced pretty good, too, if I remember."

"And I'm Antoinette," Gladys said. "I never met a man I liked, but I had lots of girlfriends."

"She's lying, Carmen," said Antoinette. "Just trying to trick you. She's Thelma. Look at her, skinny as she was fifty years ago. The only Hayes woman with no milk jugs and a butt flat as two pancakes."

"Okay, Carmen," Thelma said. "Point to the one who's got the most children."

"Well, that can't be you, because I never saw you with a man."

"No, Carmen. I'm Rita. I married Terrell and we have three kids."

"Oh, I know that y'all are just messing with me. I know who you are."

"Okay, last one, since you're so smart," Hattie said. "You were there, so I know you know this one. Which one of us once looked into the news camera and told the Mayor of Chicago to come closer and kiss you where the sun doesn't shine?"

"Now I remember that one real well. Not just that. I told him that if he looked back far enough instead of looking at the next election, he might find that he was as Black as me."

After three years of being diagnosed with dementia, Carmen's condition began to decline more rapidly. She was confined to bed most of the time, curled in a fetus position as if she were in her mama's womb. Around mid-morning, she was hoisted out of bed with a pulley to be put in the wheelchair a few hours of the day to watch television or stare blankly at the caged parakeets in the dining room. It grieved the sisters to see Carmen suffering, her vigor and the memory of her past gone completely.

Gladys took it especially hard. As the two oldest daughters, she and Carmen were closer to each other than to the other sisters. Gladys kept the memories of pigtails they wore and how they took turns holding their baby sisters like dolls. She kept the memories of them giggling at boys, and of what they said when their menstrual periods started just months apart. She still recalled when they started dating and their mama made them wear bobby socks, which they took off as soon as they left the house and slipped on pairs of nylon stockings. She wanted so badly that Carmen would remember those things.

Gladys fell into a state of deep depression over Carmen's sickness. At one point, she stopped eating and speaking, spending most of the time alone in her apartment. Concerned, Antoinette moved in with her, hoping to at least get Gladys to eat. After several days of speaking to Gladys and getting no response and Gladys not touching the covered dishes that assistants brought over, Antoinette grew frustrated and tried a different approach. One night while they sat watching television, Antoinette got up, dimmed the lights, lit two candles, and turned the television off. Immediately, Gladys spoke.

"What are you doing?"

"What do you think I'm doing? I'm setting the mood."

"Setting the mood? Mood for what? Old woman, have you lost your mind?"

"Don't play dumb. You know what I want?" At that point, Antoinette took off her robe, baring her drooping, shrunken breasts and wrinkled flesh. Then, she laughed, and Gladys laughed until she cried. Antoinette put her robe back on, and they both laughed and cried until their tears became tears of pain and sorrow, and they held each other under that dim light, as only sisters would, until the candles flickered out.

Carmen was a fighter and a strong woman, and with the support of her sisters she hung on, refusing to die when doctors had all but given up on her. She couldn't speak and she couldn't comprehend words spoken to her. Like Charles had been, she was fed through a tube in her stomach. There was nothing left of her but the breaths she took and she refused to stop breathing. She would remain in that condition for several more years.

Painfully, life went on for the sisters. They moved slower and talked less. Antoinette was starting to have kidney and heart problems, as were many of the residents in the main building. The sisters had upgraded the facility and built a small but state-of-the-art clinic as an annex to ensure access to high-quality care for the residents. The clinic was staffed with a full-time physician and licensed, skilled nurses.

As the end of the decade drew near, the sisters grew more conscious of the passing of time, counting each day a blessing. Thelma would turn ninety-five and Gladys, born in 1919, would celebrate a century. She would be the oldest person to have lived in Gavinville. Staff at Hayes Place had already started making plans for a grand celebration.

The sisters had grown closer in those six years of living together. They weren't one flesh, but they were certainly one spirit, feeling each other's joy and pain. They talked less during the day, but they honored the tradition of eating together at dinner, going to the central dining hall and sitting at the table always reserved for them. Carmen wasn't present, but they kept her chair at the table in its usual place.

For each of the sisters, there were still some unpleasant memories of past relationships among them that hung like scarves around their necks or lurked like ghosts appearing and disappearing, hovering now more frequently as they numbered their days. None of them would dare make such memories the subject of dinner conversation and certainly not in a room filled with other people. One evening, Rita thought differently. Rita and Thelma were living in Gavinville the evening when, on the fourth bottle of wine, the sisters in Chicago told each other their darkest secrets. But Rita and Thelma weren't blind to those memories that their sisters had kept hidden from everyone. For some reason that she didn't know and didn't feel that she needed to know, Rita turned to Hattie during dinner one evening, fixed her eyes on her for a few minutes, and gave one of the ghosts a voice.

"Hattie, I never told you, but I've always known that you got pregnant by Jerome Jackson and got an abortion. Not that it matters after all these years but maybe now you should know that I've known."

Hattie, Gladys, and Thelma had faces of mountain rock. Anxious to hear the next words that would come out of Rita's mouth, none of them spoke. Hattie, completely dumbfounded, searched for words to catch up with her emotions.

"Jerome and I had been dating secretly. I knew that the two of you had dated in high school. I was going to tell you that I had met him but I felt uneasy, knowing that y'all had dated for a while. So, I kept it secret. Jerome never came to the house. We'd meet at the movie theater, a restaurant, or just hang out in the park. I guess I was going to tell you eventually. The more I saw of Jerome the more I liked him. I think I was falling in love, and I think he was also. The night he said those words, he told me about you and the abortion. He felt that I should know."

"Sis, I'm so sorry. You should have told me."

"I know. But I knew that you didn't want us to know, especially Mama and Daddy. I felt that I should keep it that way."

"But Rita, all those years."

"When Jerome told me, I stopped seeing him. I just couldn't see myself falling more in love and maybe marrying him, knowing that your aborted baby would always be there, in the middle, even though no one knew but the three of us. But the hard part was carrying the burden of keeping your secret hidden all those years. It wasn't my life and my mistake, but the burden was mine. To be honest, I resented you for it. I think I still do."

"Sis, I'm so sorry. I didn't know. I saw Jerome a few times after the abortion, but we sort of avoided each other. Neither of us talked about it. We both wanted to put it as far away from the present as possible, as if it never happened. He never mentioned that y'all were dating."

"Jerome did the right thing in telling me, but sometimes I still lie in bed at night wondering how life might have turned out if I hadn't known. Don't get me wrong. I married the right man. I could never have regrets about marrying Charles. But I think that's why I married so late. It took me a long time to get over the breakup with Jerome. Seems like every time I'd meet a man, I'd look for Jerome in him, and I'd think about the secret that I wasn't supposed to know, your secret."

"Oh Rita, my heart is so full. I don't know what to say. The fact that you kept my mistake, my most regrettable, embarrassing experience, inside you all these years."

"Isn't that what sisters do who love each other? We cover and protect each other. Lord knows, I long ago stopped counting the times you picked me up when I fell down."

The other sisters didn't speak. They knew that the words that needed to be said had been. Hattie turned to get the attention of a nursing assistant and started pushing back from the table. She grabbed her cane and walked slowly over to Rita. Rita managed to pull herself up, and the two sisters covered each other in a warm embrace.

Chapter 13

Christmas was always a special time of year for the Hayes sisters when they lived in Chicago, and in the years at Hayes Place the season brought out the children and young women in them. They made the grounds and buildings of Hayes Place the most decorated residence in Gavinville, with dazzling, lighted displays, including a 50-ft. Christmas tree on the front lawn. The private road leading to the gated entrance of the main building was lined with elaborate, lighted set pieces of large bells, bulbs, Santa and his reindeer, Nutcracker soldiers, and nativity scenes. The interior had two large Christmas trees, one in the lobby and another in the dining hall. It was the only time of year that the sisters opened the private road and gate to allow townspeople and tourists to get a close-up view of Hayes Place. On those days, they were the sisters of Chicago, dressed in their finest clothing with stylish hairdos fit for the occasion.

On Fridays, they opened the main building for tours of school children and had Santa on hand to give each child a beautifully wrapped toy. The sisters beamed with as much excitement as the children and made sure that Carmen was present. Lying in a bed wheeled out to the lobby, she watched the children walk up to Santa to receive their gifts.

Christmas of 2019 would be extra special. On November 28th, they would celebrate Gladys' 100th birthday. Staff at Hayes Place had been planning a party for several weeks, but it would be private, confined to their grounds and buildings. That changed the morning of November 1st, when Jeannette Levy paid the Aunties a surprise visit to have breakfast. She had brought their favorite, a box of freshly made beignets and a jar of her homemade raspberry preserve.

"So, Ms. Gladys, how does it feel to be a century old? Never been done in Gavinville. The buzz is all over town."

"Child, I wish I had turned a hundred a few years ago when I could count to 100."

"Well, I know you're going to have a big party. I can't wait for it. What's being planned?"

"To tell you the truth, I don't know. The director and staff are planning something. A little cake and ice cream, maybe a few balloons."

"That's all? Heck, I do that for my children. You're turning 100. That's a big deal, I mean *really* big."

"Now Jeannette," said Antoinette, "don't go thinking big. Gladys will probably just end up falling asleep in a chair in the middle of the party."

"Come to think of it, Aunties, we should celebrate all of you. The rest of you will turn 100 soon. Why not make it a celebration for each of your birthdays, all at once. It would be the Aunties Birthday Celebration. A lot of people in town know the good that y'all have done. Why not let the town show appreciation? We could do it at the Municipal Auditorium."

"Auditorium?" said Thelma. I haven't been inside that place since Daddy's repast, and I saw more drunk folks than I'd ever seen at the Oasis Lounge."

"I can't imagine the mayor and council not getting behind the idea and sponsoring it."

"If it's anything we don't need for a birthday party is the mayor's money," said Hattie. "He needs to spend it where it's needed, helping to find jobs for all the unemployed Black people in this town."

"I'd be for it," said Rita, "but I wouldn't want this to turn out to be a platform for those damn Republicans to get up and make a bunch of heartless speeches. No politicians. No speeches, not one."

"I agree," said Antoinette. "This can't be a political rally. No campaigning, no signs, and no stickers. And that should apply to Democrats, too. In fact, we should keep all of them from setting a foot in the door."

"I don't think we can go that far, Ms. Antoinette. The auditorium is a public building, but it's the Aunties' party. You get to say who speaks and doesn't. I would at least let the mayor say a few words on behalf of Gavinville. He'll probably read a proclamation declaring Hayes Day or something like that. It would be a chance for the whole town to see the women who've helped to turn schools around and provide better housing and health care for poor people. Y'all have done more than any family has ever done for this town. And you've done it without expecting praises and accolades. It's past time that we show our appreciation."

The sisters supported the idea and Jeannette soon met with the director of Hayes Place to start planning the celebration. They met with the mayor, the Chamber of Commerce, and the town's Ministerial Council, comprised of the leading ministers. The sisters got personally involved in the planning, insisting that there be praying, but only two ministers: Father Antoine at St. Paul and Brother Washington, who had replaced Bernard as the pastor of Refuge Tabernacle. As a tribute to their mama and daddy, children had to be invited. There would be songs sung by children, and the children would be served first, with lots of cake and cold water on hand. The cake had to be baked by Helen's Bakery, the only Black bakery in town. They wanted only yellow balloons, not the patriotic red and blue balloons that politicians use. Lastly, the event had to be held on a Saturday afternoon, when working people had time to attend.

On the morning of the event, the staff at Hayes Place held a private, pre-celebration in the dining hall, knowing that most residents wouldn't be physically able to attend the main event. Jeannette had secretly made plans to surprise the sisters with the appearance of special guests whom they hadn't seen in a while, one whom they hadn't seen since they left Chicago. Completely in charge of every detail, Jeannette made sure that the children, nieces and nephews of the sisters entered the dining hall at the same time. Thelma's children, Joseph, age sixty-one, Michael, sixty-two, and Judy, sixty, often visited their mama and aunts, but they rarely showed up at the same time. Hattie's son Jesse, now sixty-three and still running Byrd and Hayes Enterprises, had also made frequent visits to Gavinville but hadn't been there in several months. Like Thelma's children, he never married. It would be the first time since Ella Hayes' funeral that all the sisters and their children were together at the same time.

"Well, I'll be darn," said Thelma. "Look at the sunshine coming through the clouds."

"Oh, my Lord," screamed Hattie. "Jesse?"

"My babies! What a pleasant surprise!" said Thelma as her children walked toward her.

"Now, Joseph, Michael, and Judy, I know your Mama is excited about seeing you, but y'all stop right here and give your Aunt Rita a big hug. So glad to see y'all again."

"My boy," Hattie said. "For a second I thought I saw your daddy walking. Looks like every time I see you, I see him. I'm so happy that you came."

"Wouldn't have missed it for the world, Mama. Aunt Gladys, Aunt Antoinette, Aunt Rita, Aunt Thelma, y'all looking prettier than when I last saw you."

"Hi Aunties," Thelma's children seem to say at the same time as they bent down to give each of their aunts a hug.

"Just look at the three of you," said Gladys. "So happy to see you again."

"Nephew, I don't need to ask because I see the dividend statements," said Rita, "but how's business?"

"Business is good Auntie, rolling right along. I've got a succession plan in the works to retire in a few years, but I'll stay close to it when I leave."

"I know I've said it a thousand times, Nephew," said Rita, "but thank you for staying so strong after James and Junior passed."

"And for making all of us pretty rich, too," joked Antoinette.

"And Joe, Mike, and Judy ... we're all just so proud of you, too," said Gladys. "Y'all bring a table and some chairs over here and get comfortable. I have no idea what they've got planned but they better bring some breakfast out here real soon."

When Jesse, Joseph, Michael, and Judy got settled around the table, the last special guest entered the room. Hattie hadn't seen Margie,

Junior's wife, since the day before they left Chicago sixteen years ago. She hadn't married since Junior's death and was living in Milwaukee for the past ten years. She and Hattie talked on the telephone periodically, mostly on holidays, but Margie had never been to Gavinville.

Seeing Margie walking toward them, Hattie nearly leaped out of her chair, forgetting that she couldn't walk without a cane. She would have fallen if one of the assistants hadn't rushed over to brace her. Hattie screamed "Margie" so loud that it got the attention of everyone in the dining hall. Their embrace was so long that it prompted the assistant to step in to be sure that Hattie still had the strength to stand on her feet. Tears streamed down both of their faces.

"Oh my sweet Margie. It's so good to see you. What a blessing. And you haven't changed a bit."

"Good to see you, too, Mama Hattie. I've been putting off making this trip for years. I wouldn't miss this day. And look at my aunties. So good to see all of y'all." Margie went around the table giving them each a hug, before noticing Jesse. "Oh my gosh. Jesse? Gosh, how long has it been?"

"Too long, Margie. You're looking well. I heard that you had moved to Milwaukee. How are your folks? They're still in Chicago?"

"Mom and Dad are fine. Still in Chicago. Retired of course but doing well. They got real excited when I told them about the trip. They told me to give their regards. And this must be … wait, don't tell me. When Ms. Levy said y'all would be here, I promised myself I'd get the names right. You're Aunt Thelma's, right? Judy, Joseph, and Michael. Wow. So good to see everyone."

"Margie, pull up a chair. In fact, squeeze in right here between me and your Aunt Rita."

"I heard about Uncle Bernard passing. So sorry I couldn't make the service. Mama Hattie told me that he had started a church here. How's Aunt Carmen?"

"Oh, she's taking one day at a time. We'll take you in to see her before we leave for the big bash. Speaking of which, we probably need to get whatever they've got planned for this morning started," said Gladys.

Breakfast was served and everyone chatted and laughed, talking about whatever came to the sisters' minds. The assistants brought out a very big cake with one hundred lit candles and Jeannette led the singing of "Happy Birthday" to Gladys before all the residents were served cake and punch.

The big celebration that afternoon went exactly as planned. The auditorium arena was standing room only. The ministers prayed and the children sang. The Aunties sat stiffly on the dais, watching the Mayor read his proclamation and heap praises on the Hayes Family. Everyone was served cake and ice cream. The finale was another singing of "Happy Birthday," this time to all the Aunties.

As if the declaration and celebration of Hayes Day were a death knell, the dawning of a new decade brought more health challenges for the sisters. By March 2020, Antoinette's kidneys had failed and she underwent dialysis treatment three days a week, which kept her in bed the other four days. Doctors were concerned that her frail body wouldn't endure the aftereffects of the treatments. She no longer joined her sisters for dinner. Like Carmen, she was approaching the state of being an invalid, having to be hoisted out of bed every day to sit in a wheelchair to prevent bed sores.

One evening a month later, Gladys, Hattie, Rita, and Thelma sat at dinner talking about Carmen and Antoinette. They all felt death stalking and knew that the inevitable was near. The only question unanswered was when. But the sisters took comfort in knowing how strong Carmen and Antoinette were. In watching Carmen fight for her life over the past two years, they gained strength from seeing her waking up morning after morning when doctors said she wouldn't. Antoinette, too, was a strong woman, who had already beaten the odds of a woman her age surviving kidney failure.

Gladys, typically quiet, was unusually talkative that morning, imploring her sisters to stay prayerful and keep the faith.

"I've been praying day and night for Carmen and Antoinette. It's hard seeing them in so much pain but they're with us. We've got to make every day count. Tell them we love them. They might not be able to speak but they hear us. Hayes women aren't they? That says it all. I often think about when y'all moved to Chicago. I was so proud when I heard that my sisters were in business and doing so well. Thelma, I know you stayed home, but you were keeping things together, helping Mama and Daddy. I was the one who was lost. My life was turned upside down and I didn't know it. I know I thanked you for taking me in and giving me a fresh start, but I want you to know that I love you. Carmen and Antoinette might not come through this, but they have us now and forever."

Suddenly, Gladys' speech became blurred, and she started speaking incoherently. Her body became limp, and she drooped over, sliding out of the chair unto the floor. She had suffered a severe stroke, paralyzing the left side of her body. Fortunately, there was no brain damage, and according to the doctor's prognosis, within several months she would very likely regain her ability to speak, but she, too, would permanently use a wheelchair.

Half of the sisters were now very ill. Among the staff, there was a sense of impending death, not just of Carmen and Antoinette, but for all the Aunties. Although Rita, Thelma, and Hattie were in reasonably good health, every day seemed to take a noticeable toll. Father Antoine and Brother Washington made frequent visits and the medical staff grew more attentive and vigilant, concerned for all the sisters' health. An air of gloom hung over the entire residence.

On the morning of June 10th, shortly before dawn, Hattie was awakened by a nurse bearing bad news. The nurse had gone to check on Carmen and found her gasping for breath. Her heart had failed. The medical staff did all they could to revive her.

"Ms. Hattie," sorry to wake you. I have some bad news. Ms. Carmen passed."

"Oh Jesus, my Lord, my sweet Jesus, give me strength."

"Do you want me to tell the others?" the nurse asked.

"No, no, help me to get there. I need to tell them myself."

The nurse put Hattie in a wheelchair and took her to Rita's room. Hattie went in and woke her.

"Sis, Carmen is gone."

"Oh Jesus, my sister, my sister."

The nurse helped Rita out of bed and into a wheelchair, and she and Hattie went to Thelma's room to awaken her and give her the news. By then, another nurse had joined them.

"Sis, Sis, Carmen has gone to see the Lord. She's at peace now."

"Oh no. Carmen. Carmen. God rest her soul."

The three old women were wheeled to Carmen's room. They insisted on standing, rising out of their chairs with the help of the nurses. None of them spoke or cried as they stood over Carmen's body. They had already said enough and cried many times long before that moment. Seeing Carmen's mouth open, Hattie couldn't resist saying, "That woman couldn't keep her mouth shut, even when she was dying." That would be the only words said. Gazing into Carmen's skeletal face, the sisters held hands, then released them to hold Carmen's hands. They ran their fingers across her cheeks and through her hair, then stooped to kiss her forehead before leaving the room.

"Why don't we take you back to your rooms to rest," said the nurse. "We can tell Ms. Antoinette and Ms. Gladys when they wake up."

"No, come get us," Rita said. "We need to tell them."

Two hours later, the nurse returned and brought Hattie, Rita, and Thelma to Antoinette's room. An assistant raised her bed so that she could see her sisters. Antoinette had long ago lost the ability to speak. She could hear but was unresponsive to words she heard.

"Sis, she's gone," Rita said. "Carmen is gone. We've lost her."

Antoinette closed her eyes and kept them closed. It was a shivering moment for Hattie, Rita, and Thelma, to have lost one sister and to see another one seemingly half-dead.

"She'll be okay," the nurse said. "Let her rest."

Gladys would be the last to hear of Carmen's death. She was still partly paralyzed on her left side and her face drooped slightly. The staff had taken her out of bed and sat her in a wheelchair to watch her favorite morning television show. When Hattie, Thelma, and Rita entered the room, she said, "You don't have to tell me. No one told me, but I know."

The Hayes women had felt the pain of many deaths of people they were close to, but not since Judy's death in 1943 had they lost a sister. In spite of knowing the inevitable, nothing could prepare them for that kind of grief. Nothing could ease the pain, compensate or fill the void of that kind of loss. They had been born of the same mama and daddy, grown up together as girls and young women, been separated by time and distance, and now lived together. They could handle being separated again, but not by the finality of death, when one of them would never be seen again, and certainly not a branch of the tree as big as Carmen. Time had prepared them for the loss but in the hours and days that followed, they grieved as much for the fiery voice and passion that had been silenced as for the loss of Carmen's physical presence.

Carmen's wake was scheduled to be held on the evening of June 15th, but a strong storm caused too many roof leaks at Cole Funeral Home and the wake was moved to St. Paul the next morning. The celebration mass followed. She was laid to rest a few feet from the graves of her mama and daddy. People in Gavinville, including Father Antoine, had no sense of the total person Carmen was. To them, she was simply one of the Aunties. They knew nothing of the years she spent in Chicago fighting the political machines that denied Black people decent housing. Most knew little of the stands she took against national conservative politics or her work to build a better education system for Gavinville's poor children. To many, she was Sister Carmen, wife of Brother Hawkins, who started the first holiness church in Gavinville. None of that was mentioned in her eulogy, but her sisters sat smiling that morning, with the knowledge that in her lifetime Carmen had been a true, tireless champion of social justice and equality.

Just when the sisters had begun to get back to some sense of normalcy, Antoinette's health took a turn for the worse On September 15th, three months after Carmen died, Antoinette quietly passed in her sleep, the way her daddy and mama had done. Several hours had passed before the nurses knew that she died. Another Hayes woman had to be buried. Once again, the sisters had to summon the strength to say good-bye to a sister. Antoinette was the crystal ballerina on the mantle. Born in 1921, she was the middle child, after Gladys, Judy, and Carmen and before Hattie, Rita, and Thelma. She was the one who made them laugh when they most needed laughter. She was the least noticed of the sisters when they were making their mark in the business world of Chicago, but it was largely on her advice that the sisters made decisions on design and fashion that went against the grain but always resulted in the competition following them. She was buried beside Carmen.

The surviving sisters could waste no time in turning their attention to the living. In spite of Gladys' paralysis and confinement to a wheelchair, she eventually joined her sisters for dinners. But within two months of Antoinette's death, Gladys started having periodic bouts of shortness of breath, requiring twenty-four-hour nursing supervision, and was moved to a skilled nursing unit of the clinic.

Hattie, Rita, and Thelma spent their summer days mostly indoors, sitting alone in their apartments watching television and resting in bed. Dinners were not the same without the other sisters, so they started sitting with other residents, if for no other reason than to feel connected to the outer world, the world beyond their sadness and grief. They seldom engaged in conversations with the residents, although most of them had little to say anyway. Many had mental illnesses and spoke words that made absolutely no sense to the sisters, whose minds were still very much intact.

Staff at Hayes Place was both intrigued and amused by the sisters' mental clarity. They couldn't explain it, the Aunties' bodies aging, in fact dying, and their minds so alive and quick. Thelma, in particular, struck them as being oddly perceptive, insightful, and intelligent. To them, she was somewhat of an outlier, *in* the group but not of the group. She is the only one who had not moved to Chicago and become wealthy. They could only imagine what impact she might have had if she had not chosen to stay in Gavinville. Maybe because she was younger, they thought, but Thelma also had the most youthful spirit. One minute she was at the nursing station talking about the need for better public dental health and minutes later she was outdoors cheering for both teams in a staff flag football game. She wasn't as political as her sisters, but she was clearly the most read, impressing the staff with her pragmatism and breadth of knowledge, oftentimes giving them advice on patient care.

If there was one quality of Thelma that the staff thought to be negative, it was her stubbornness. When she said "no" she meant it, and there was no convincing her otherwise, like when she refused to take medication because she just didn't like the way it felt going down her throat. Staff at Hayes Places could only reason that Thelma's uniqueness and odd idiosyncrasies were due to her being away from the other sisters for so many years. She was one of the Aunties, but, more than any of them, she displayed qualities that set her apart from the group.

As November drew nearer, staff at Hayes Place started talking about Gladys' 101st birthday. She was still prone to periods of severe shortness of breath and had been admitted to intensive care at Gavinville General Hospital. It was doubtful that she would be feeling up to any type of birthday celebration, but they were planning just in case. For several weeks, Gladys had been on and off of a respirator. Hattie, Thelma, and Rita visited her every Friday afternoon. On Friday, November 6th, Hattie and Rita didn't feel like getting out, so Thelma was taken there alone. Gladys' condition appeared to have gotten better since the week before. She was off the respirator and able to speak in a whisper.

"Hi, old girl," Thelma said, walking into the room. "Hattie and Rita couldn't make it."

"Are they okay?"

"Yeah, they're fine. Just tiredness. They're resting."

"And how are you?" Gladys asked.

"Oh, the same. Glad to see you're breathing and talking. Got a call from Judy the other day, asking how you were doing."

"How's my niece?"

"She was wondering if you were going to have a birthday party. Said they'd probably come."

"Child, I just hope I see the sun come up tomorrow. What day is it by the way?"

"Friday. You'll be 101 in a few weeks."

"My Lord. Another year."

The sisters remained silent for a while.

"Sis, this probably isn't the right time to talk about it, but then, who knows how much time any of us has left. I suppose any time is the right time when you're as old as me. Remember that night at the Oasis Lounge when Frankie Lee was killed?"

Gladys didn't think that was a question that Thelma meant to be answered, so she didn't answer. She closed her eyes and didn't respond.

"Do you remember?"

"Why'd you bring that up?" she asked with her eyes still closed.

"Because years ago, when Willie was in jail, I was at the Oasis one night and Jody Watkins said he was standing next to you and Willie when the stabbing took place, and he said he saw the whole thing. He told me a different story than what Willie said and what I read that *you* said."

"That was seventy years ago. Why talk about it now?"

"Because I'd like to know the truth. Who lied? Jody or Willie and you?"

Gladys' eyes remained closed. She didn't answer, wondering whether she should or if it would be best to just ignore Thelma and pretend to be asleep, hoping that Thelma would either change the subject or leave the room.

"Well, who?"

Thelma had long ago gotten past the resentment she had felt toward Gladys for having slept with Frankie Lee while she dated him. And she had gotten past the fact that Gladys started the argument, no matter who stabbed Frankie first. But she needed to know the truth. If, as Jody had said, Gladys cut Frankie in the jugular vein before Willie picked up the knife and cut him, then she committed murder. And she had lived her entire life lying about it. Willie had gone to jail to keep *her* out of jail. And it wasn't just that she needed to know the truth. The integrity and honor of the Hayes family was at stake. And not just the family name. The legacy of her mama was at stake, as well as all the good that the Hayes sisters had done for the people of Gavinville. Only by bringing the truth to light could the Hayes family be vindicated.

"Well, tell me. Tell me what happened that night."

Gladys opened her eyes. Looking away from Thelma, she recounted every detail of that horrifying night. Thelma listened intently, and when Gladys finished speaking she rose from the chair, grabbed her walking cane, and kissed Gladys on the forehead. "I'll see you soon," she said, walking out of the room.

For Gladys, it was a moment reminiscent of the conversation she and Thelma had the day of Terrell's funeral. She lay wondering what Thelma might do, what she might say, and to whom.

On the afternoon of December 7th, Gladys died of respiratory arrest. The last time that her sisters saw her, she was lying in a coffin at Johnson Funeral Home, a few hours before being taken to St. Paul Catholic Church.

In the days immediately after Gladys' death, Thelma kept entirely to herself. When Hattie and Rita asked her to join them at dinner, she refused without an explanation. She insisted on being alone and did not participate in discussions about the funeral arrangements. She was also uncharacteristically quiet around the staff who tended to her. Everyone was fearful that, as the youngest of the sisters, the experience of losing Gladys, Carmen, and Antoinette over such a short span of time had taken an emotional toll that Thelma might not have the strength to bear.

Chapter 14

As residents of Gavinville, the Aunties had lived a rather secluded life. Even when they got around town they paid no attention to the town's gossip. Sitting quietly in the church during Gladys' funeral service, Hattie and Rita appeared to be equally inattentive to Father Antoine's rather theatrical homily. They surely didn't know who Luther Vandross was and hadn't heard his song, and they showed no reaction to the expressions of the people seated behind them. But Thelma clung to every word and emotion. In a moment least expected, she broke the silence that had caused everyone's concern in the aftermath of Gladys' death.

"She danced alright, on every lap this side of the railroad track, and then some," Thelma said to Rita without turning her head and in a tone that was neither kind nor humorous.

"Stop it old woman. Stop it right now. This isn't the place for that," snapped Hattie.

"Well, it's true. No need for us to pretend she's some kind of saint now that she's gone."

"It wasn't our business then and it sure isn't our business now, Thelma," Rita said. "It's in the Lord's hands now. Let him deal with it. Let it be. It's time for you to let go. After all these years, you're still jealous because Frank Lee Garret got under Gladys' skirt while he got under yours. He wouldn't have married you anyway. You were too young for him. He was stringing you along like he did every other woman in Gavinville."

"Hush, both of you," Hattie leaned over and whispered. "I can hear you way over here. It's time to make peace. Hush."

"Lord have mercy," Rita said, shaking her head in disgust.

"You can 'Lord have mercy' all you want but that doesn't cover up dirt," said Thelma.

Rita grew increasingly impatient with Thelma's tirade. "Well, who the hell—pardon me Jesus. Who the hell made you the judge of everybody, Thelma Gail? How did you get to be so perfect?"

"I'm not saying I have no faults, but I'm not planning on taking a lie as big as this one six feet into the ground."

"Well, why don't you just stand up right now and tell the church your biggest lies so we don't make a mistake and close them up in the coffin when it's time to bury you? Go ahead, tell everybody. We're listening."

By then, other family members who were sitting nearby began to notice the unfriendly exchange of words between the sisters. Sharon Granger and her husband Ray walked over.

"What's the problem here, Aunties?" Sharon stooped down to ask.

None of the sisters spoke. Each sat looking straight ahead without even acknowledging Sharon's presence.

"Well, since nothing is wrong, I guess y'all can just be a little quieter if you have to talk." The noise is a little distracting. Okay?" Each of the sisters remained silent with their eyes looking straight ahead.

Thelma was still processing Rita's challenge. She knew that Rita was just trying to shut her up, and she wasn't about to back down or be outdone. Thelma bent down and picked up her cane, and with both hands on it she pulled herself up and turned to face the congregation. Her shrunken face looked old as bald cypress, but her trunk stood straight as pine. Her embroidered skull cap and white-laced collared black dress looked girly but dignified, projecting the aura of confidence that was the Hayes trait. She tapped her cane on the floor three times, each time with a pause.

"I got something to say," she said in a voice that was hardly heard by anyone except the sisters on the front row. "I got something to say." Father Antoine hadn't noticed the tall, thin woman standing to the left of the casket. "I said, I got something to say," she repeated, this time a little louder and with emphasis on "I said." Hattie and Rita looked at their younger sister with surprise and disgust, having no idea why Thelma was carrying on this way or what she was going to say.

Thelma gazed out at the faces, each one hanging on to her next breath, and she saw history. "Everybody knows my mama kept this town alive, and in more ways than one. When the moon was empty, her heart carried everybody's burden, and her hands were full of miracles. She was the only Black person with enough courage to stand up to the white man's hate, even while she was curing his sicknesses. When they stood in line a mile long to view my mama's body, they thought they had gone to see God. But God wasn't in that casket, my mama was. Nobody but her heard the thunder in her heart. Nobody heard her teeth gritting after she prayed all night or those prayer beads rattling in her aching hands. Nobody felt as much pain as she did, and nobody could heal her. Her children couldn't but she was our mama anyway. We didn't deserve her, none of us, but she healed us anyway. The only thing we can give her now is truth, the whole truth. Nobody can do that but us, and I can't think of a better place and time than right now, in the Lord's house."

Father Antoine was visibly surprised. Whatever the old woman had to say wasn't part of the program, and it surely might take a while. He looked at Sharon and other members of the family as if to tell them to politely deal with the situation. Nobody moved, partly out of respect to Thelma, but mostly out of fear that any attempt to quiet her would only make matters worse. Thelma, they knew, was the most stubborn of the Aunties.

"We all know Willie Frank went to prison for two years for manslaughter, for killing Frankie Lee Garret. But truth be told, it wasn't Willie's knife and not Willie's hand that killed Frankie Lee. Gladys killed Frankie. She cut Frankie Lee in the neck and threw the knife on the ground. Willie picked up the knife and stabbed Frankie, but he was already on the ground bleeding to death."

Thelma's sudden and unexpected revelation didn't cause an immediate reaction. This was church, a mass, the funeral of Gavinville's oldest resident, the daughter of Ella Hayes. The reaction came slowly, barely noticeable in the curious faces of those who sat absorbing the shock of what they had just heard.

Thelma continued, and the solemn, mournful atmosphere that she now commanded quickly changed. "Now, Father Antoine, don't you take another step. Don't you dare come near me. I'm speaking and I'll sit down when I'm good and ready, not a second sooner. Like I was saying, Willie didn't kill Frankie Lee. My sister Gladys did it. She killed

Frankie. I wasn't there, but Jody Watkins was and he saw the whole thing. When Jody was questioned about what happened, he lied and said his back was turned when Frankie got cut. He just didn't want to be involved. But years later, Jody told me what happened. It was 1950, December 15th, a Friday night. Jody, Willie, and Gladys were outside the backdoor at the Oasis sipping whiskey. Gladys had seen Frankie Lee kissing Clarissa Charles earlier, so when he went outdoors she confronted him about it. He and Gladys started cussing and yelling at each other, then, when Frankie turned to walk away, Gladys pulled a knife from her purse and slit the side of Frankie's neck. Blood started gushing from Frankie like water from a faucet. Gladys tossed the knife on the ground and ran. Willie picked up the knife and stabbed Frankie in the chest, but the man was already bleeding to death.

"Before Gladys died, while she could barely breathe and talk, I asked her what happened that night. In all the years after Willie died, she never talked about it. I didn't know who lied, Willie or Jody Watkins, but I knew that the only person who could truthfully answer that question was Gladys herself. And she admitted that she stabbed Frankie before Willie picked up the knife.

"Gladys never loved Willie Frank, but in his own crazy way Willie loved her. He would have done anything for that woman. She only married him because he went to jail for a killing she did. But that didn't make a wrong right, and it won't make a lie the truth.

"You buried Willie Frank a long time ago. Jody's dead. You've buried my mama and daddy. And now you're about to put Gladys in the ground. You can call me stubborn and crazy, but I'll be damned if I'll go to my grave without the truth being told. Y'all can toss my carnation into that grave. Now, can somebody please take me home?"

And with that, Thelma slowly made her way toward the exit, leaving a confounded congregation behind. No one moved. No one made a sound.

Thelma left the church. She didn't go to the interment. She wasn't present to say good-bye to her oldest sister and place a carnation on her casket before the gravediggers lowered her into the ground.

Three years later, she and Hattie buried Rita, and a year later she buried Hattie. The youngest of the Hayes sisters was now the only one living. Thelma hadn't left with her sisters when they moved to Chicago and had been apart from them for over fifty years before they moved back to Gavinville. She didn't become wealthy like her sisters, but she married a good man and lived a good life, and she had been a part of the good work that the Hayes family did to make a better life for the poor people of Southeast Louisiana. She had no regrets about the words she spoke at Gladys' funeral. Thelma loved her oldest sister as much as she loved all of them, and she felt certain that Gladys had made peace with God before taking her last breath. In her heart, Thelma felt that in speaking out that day in church she had merely brought the truth to light, and in doing so had set Gladys and the entire Hayes family free. If Ella were alive, she'd say that Thelma was the song of the sparrow that she had heard the day Jesse was healed, the song that had always been with the Hayes family, coming out of nowhere, reminding them of their special purpose in meeting the needs of people who were less fortunate than they were.

Every year after Hattie's death, one of the nursing assistants at Hayes Place took Thelma to the cemetery on All Saints Day. Thelma would step gingerly between the graves, reading headstones of people she had known, and lay one red rose on each of the tombs of her family, first her mama and daddy, then Terrell, then Judy, then Carmen,

Antoinette, Rita, and Hattie. Gladys would always be her last stop. For Gladys, she'd reach into a bouquet of pink carnations, pull one flower and place it on the headstone, then rest the remaining carnations on Gladys' tomb.

Thelma died on March 19, 2028, a day after her 104th birthday.

John Warner Smith was the Poet Laureate of Louisiana from 2019 to 2021 and is the only African American male to serve in the office in its 83-year history. Smith has published five collections of poetry, most recently *Our Shut Eyes* (MadHat Press, 2021). His novella, *For All Those Men: When the KKK Threatened to Take Control of Louisiana*, was published by UL Press in November 2022. Smith's sixth collection, *From the Flinty Rock: New & Selected Poems*, is forthcoming from MadHat Press. His memoir, *I, Too, Am Tar Baby*, will be published by Legacy Book Press in early 2025.

A Cave Canem Fellow, Smith is a 2020 Poet Laureate Fellow of the Academy of American Poets and is winner of the 2019 Linda Hodge Bromberg Literary Award. He earned his MFA at the University of New Orleans.